G. D. SMITH.
APF

MOON'S OTTERY

Also by Patricia Beer from Carcanet

Collected Poems

Moon's Ottery

PATRICIA BEER

CARCANET

First published in 1978 by Hutchinson & Co.
Published in Great Britain 1988 by
Carcanet Press Limited
208-212 Corn Exchange Buildings
Manchester M4 3BQ

British Library Cataloguing in Publication Data

Beer, Patricia
  Moon's ottery
  I. Title
  823'.914 [F]

ISBN 0-85635-789-8

The publisher acknowledges financial assistance
from the Arts Council of Great Britain

Printed in England by SRP Ltd, Exeter

FOR GEORGINA

1

'WITH my body I thee worship,' said Alice, trying out the words. She and her sister Rosalind, daughters of Farmer Mutter of Sparkhayes, were gossiping in the dairy before breakfast. The bright morning was visible only through a patch of amber horn, and the dairy, even in summer, was aggressively cold. Rosalind felt the cold very much, and hated the look, almost as much as the taste, of milk and cream; once when she was a child – she was now fifteen – she had come across a gob of phlegm in her cup of milk; whether it was the cow's phlegm or the milker's she never discovered. But the dairy, for John Mutter's sort of farming, was the most important room in the house, almost a chapel, and its dignity gave spice to gossip. It was also a place beyond the range of eavesdropping and swift sortie. True, it opened off the hall, but the door yelped as it moved and there were three breakneck steps leading down from it which needed complete, stooping attention.

On this particular morning in June 1587, the girls were discussing the wedding of William Lock and Mary How, which was to take place that day. Weddings were not so strange. The village of Moon's Ottery was small but there were sometimes five or six ceremonies a year. But this one had an unusual feature: the bride and bridegroom were both deaf and dumb. It had been the talk of the parish for weeks beforehand and had involved all kinds of special consents and ingenious practical arrangements. Alice and Rosalind were intrigued by the novelty of the affair rather than by its nobler significance, and the village as a whole regarded it much as they would have regarded a hanging or at least the arrival of the players.

'With my body I thee worship,' repeated Alice who was

7

sixteen. 'I'm longing to know how he'll mime that bit. What do you think, Rozzy?' She then made a few suggestions herself with one eye on the hall door. Rosalind was giggling heartily, for Alice had the gift of being coarse without being embarrassing, when the door yelped and Mrs Mutter, emerging from a smell of porridge and a clatter of talk, negotiated the steps, her customary upright flounce reduced to misshapen fumbling for a few useful seconds. Alice began to rearrange a pile of hard cheeses which certainly did look as if they were about to topple over.

'What's the joke then, girls? Haven't you got anything to do then, Rozzy?'

They were never left to giggle for long. This morning, however, Mrs Mutter looked as though she was thinking about something else, a most unusual expression for her.

'We were wondering,' Rosalind said, 'how William Lock would mime "With all my worldly goods I thee endow". Do you think he'll take a couple of angels out of his pouch and press them into her hand?'

'Angels,' snorted Mrs Mutter. 'Angels of Jesus, more like.' She never minded about the sense of a quip as long as she could make one somehow. ' 'Tis a good job that bit *will* be in mime because 'tis in mime 'twill stay, if you ask me. He 'adn' got a groat.'

'But, Mother, how could he possibly?' asked Alice. 'Nobody employs him.'

'I'd employ un,' said Mrs Mutter. 'And Mary. Two voices less.' She glanced shrewishly at the hall door.

'Mother, can we go to the wedding? Everybody's going.'

'Oh, Mother, please let us. It may never happen again.'

When there was something both the sisters wanted to do, Rosalind asked first and Alice second, as she was the favourite. In this way Mrs Mutter had the security of being able to refuse Rosalind and the option of yielding to Alice. They had furthermore discovered that, against all appearances, Mrs Mutter liked to be bullied and that Alice could do it. Rosalind could not, and her mother's appreciative chuckle, when Alice was daringly

8

firm, made her feel forlorn and resentful. However, on this occasion nothing worked, neither the order of their asking nor the nearly rude 'Come on now, Mother' which Alice added after a minute or two, during which time Mrs Mutter had been gazing theatrically into the depths of the milk as if she were going to spit into it herself.

'Certainly not. I'm not having people say I let my daughters go chasing round after every cheap sensation.' She started up the three steps again, pausing on each one. ' 'Tisn't decent. What's wrong with your own home? Breakfast's ready.'

That seemed to be that. They followed her. After breakfast, however, when the hall had cleared, she announced that they could go but that she would have to accompany them, to give some kind of sanction and therefore seemliness to the outing. The girls were perfectly satisfied. Her company was a small price to pay; indeed it was hardly a price to pay at all, for her comments after any event were a treat to hear, provided the listeners were not fond of the people concerned, that is, for then it could be most distressing. She came from a bitter family and had never thought of bitterness as a sin. But Alice and Rosalind had no tender feelings for William Lock and Mary How; few people had.

So the three of them prepared to set out. Mrs Mutter, who was an energetic woman and a good housekeeper, had been up long enough to get things well organized in the house. Farmer Mutter was haymaking; he and his men had gone off after breakfast with their scythes, their rakes and their pitchforks. It was early in June for the hay, but the previous year and indeed the beginning of this one had been so disastrously wet that the farmers were taking no risks, though the weather had been fine for a month and looked like remaining so. In any case John Mutter liked to get the grass while it was still tender.

Even if he had not been haymaking he would hardly have come with them. For one thing his wife would not have encouraged it; she saw herself and her daughters as a unit. For another, it would have gone seriously against his grain. By habit and conviction, work was his whole life. On Saturday

9

nights he stopped with a jolt and remained shaken till Monday morning, though in fact, as he had forty head of stock, Sunday was not such a restful day for him as to have been, necessarily, so demoralizing.

He was a prosperous farmer, a yeoman, a freeholder, with all the security and quietness of mind that that implied. Nobody could evict or threaten him; his heirs were safe. He had no son but he was certain that Alice would marry a young farmer within the next few years, in which case he would leave Spark-hayes to her and her husband. His matrimonial plans for Rosa-lind had not taken shape; she was going to be difficult.

John Mutter was well spoken of in the valley as honest and conscientious. Certain neighbours used to say – as Alice and Rosalind had heard from the farm labourers – that he had been put in with the bread and taken out with the buns, but in a competitive community nobody held that against him; on the contrary, they spoke the more warmly of his honesty and his hard work. Agriculture was booming in the whole of East Devon and particularly in the Otter Valley. Farmer Mutter may have been neither brilliant in himself nor original in his farming methods but in those days only a very idle or erratic man could fail. As it was, Sparkhayes was not only self-sufficient but could sell surplus produce at Honiton market.

His speciality was cattle, though he had some sheep as well, of course, and grew the usual crops. Not so long before it would have been sheep. There was one house in the district, three generations older than Sparkhayes – which was modern – that had been built on profits from wool. It had a short poem over the front door.

> I thank God and ever shall
> It is the sheep hath paid for all.

The first owner had no doubt genuinely entertained these sentiments; he had been a very wealthy man and it was a handsome house. But there was a tradition that the builder had helped him with the poetic technique.

Rosalind loved the verse. She had once suggested to her

father that they should copy it, substituting 'cows' for 'sheep'. Though her admiration of the couplet was sincere, the suggestion was mischievously meant. Farmer Mutter brooded over it for some time. 'It don't sound right somehow, Rozzy. "It is the cows hath paid for all." It don't sound right.' He brooded again; he had the makings of a stylist. His wife snorted and said, 'That Mr Suckbitch,' referring to the man who now owned the wool house, not to his ancestor the versifier. The Mutters thanked God for prosperity with their whole hearts but it seemed to them crude to name, and to perpetuate the name, of the earthly source of it.

Rosalind was ready first and went out into the cobbled courtyard by way of the huge oak front door. The house faced south and was set sideways on the hill that rose from the River Otter to the clearing where the warning beacon stood. As she came out into the sunshine, Obed Hosegood, her father's bailiff, was plodding up the steep courtyard from his cottage by the cowhouse. He seemed to be heading for the pigsty, which stood towards the top of the courtyard, almost opposite the front door. It was a pretty building and new, for it was only recently that the pigs had been brought in from the woods.

Obed was obviously supervising the rest of the farm while the haymaking went on. He was a man of about sixty, dignified and reticent. He had an expressionless face but missed nothing. Rosalind loved and trusted him.

'We're going to the wedding, Obed.'

'You'd be better off helping your dad. He could do with a bit of raking.'

'Oh, the wedding won't take long. I'll go out afterwards.'

'If you knows where the field is.'

'Of course I know. It's the big meadow down by the river.'

'Well done, maid. We'll make a farmer's wife out of 'ee yet. Have your dad sorted out his Fitzherbert from his Tusser?'

'His what from his *what*?'

'Do 'ee mean to say you hav'n' noticed un studying they books? I thought you might, seeing 'twas books. They'm different ways of making hay. Fitzherbert, he says flatten out all the molehills the day before cutting. Tusser, he says leave 'em, so the lambs can perch up on 'em and keep dry. Pretty.' Obed laughed, without moving a muscle.

'But Father would never be able to make up his mind.'

''Tis awkward. With him believing everything he sees in print.'

'Which do you think, Obed?'

'Fitzherbert. Lambs hav'n' got the sense.'

The latch of the front door clanked in a way that the people at the next farm said they could hear on a quiet day, and Mrs Mutter and Alice came out. It was a two-mile walk down the valley from Sparkhayes to Moon's Ottery. The lane was much drier than usual. Normally walkers had to pick their way and tack from side to side to find the dry bits, but on this particular day Mrs Mutter and her daughters could have gone three abreast if the hedges had not been so overgrown. Their valley was noted for being the wettest in East Devon, not in the sense of dingy, pelting rainfall but of bright springs and streams, sparkling in the grass, winking over the cobblestones, and lighting up rather than quenching the redness of the earth. Where other valleys concealed water, this one fairly danced with it. No man or animal ever needed to go thirsty, not even in as dry a June as this.

The pond at the first corner of the lane, it is true, was caked and cracked. They could not believe it was as dry as it looked and Alice threw a stone into it, expecting it to be eerily sucked in, but it stayed on top; the top was the bottom. Mrs Mutter, with a swashbuckling youthful air, threw a stone in too, but the same thing happened.

They were soon away from their own forty acres, which stretched eastwards down to the river and northwards back up the valley. The road to Moon's Ottery ran parallel to the river about half a mile above it and when they came to gates and gaps they saw in sunshine a long reach of the small hedged fields that were the amazement of visitors from other parts of the country, the red cattle and shining trees, fewer now than when

12

Alice and Rosalind were children but still plentiful and lovely. The foxgloves in the hedges were at their tallest and the elderflowers at their whitest. From time to time they heard voices on the other side of the hedges, occasionally voices that they did not immediately recognize. 'Who be they?' asked Alice, risking it, for the girls had been trained not to talk like that. A man went by on horseback, huge and loud and smelly in the narrow lane. They squashed themselves into the hedge with great good humour. The horse farted; they laughed; the man laughed. They did not know him either, though they recognized him as a farmer from the head of the valley. 'Who be he?' asked Rosalind. 'Rosalind,' said her mother. Soon they could hear the church bells.

They saw nobody in their own lane, as most of the inhabitants of Moon's Ottery either lived in the village itself or approached it from other directions. But when Mrs Mutter and her daughters got to the last turning the whole population seemed to be converging on the church as if to storm it. They saw every woman they knew and quite a few farmers, who, more easygoing than John Mutter, accompanied their wives and daughters. There were jolly shouts of 'What about the hay then, eh?' and carefree replies of 'Bugger the hay'. People were not wearing their best clothes, any more than they would have for a bearbaiting, but everyone looked clean and well-pressed, and, as far as country clothes permitted, brightly coloured. The atmosphere was too good humoured to be cruel but it was certainly heartless. The bells were almost painful now, in the clear air. Last time they had been rung it was to dispel a storm and they had been shouted down by the thunder. The bridal couple, wherever they were at that moment, would have been the only two for miles who could not hear them. They might have felt the vibrations.

Alice, with her black curly hair, pink cheeks and plump figure, was by far the prettiest girl on the green and would have been on most village greens in the district. She could have been May Queen any year since she was thirteen but her mother would never permit it. She got some appreciative leers from the ne'er-do-wells by the pond and a few remarks too, such as 'Yur comes Vennus', which Mrs Mutter heard but rose above on Alice's behalf. 'Poor silly gawks,' she confided to her daughters in a loud voice. Rosalind, who was thin and had straight sandy hair, expected no attention and was looking around for the only person she would have been glad to see, not very hopefully as he was neither a voluntary churchgoer nor a frequenter of raree-shows; and indeed he was not there.

Mrs Mutter, who was unpopular, did not receive many salutations and so neither did her daughters. But they were proud of her appearance. With her grey hair tucked into her wide-brimmed hat and her slight figure which had never become truly womanly, she looked young and spirited, and touchingly ready for anything. Her apron and collar were as white and smooth as petals, and though her dress was the accepted dull brown, her red underdress shone friskily through the slash. She had marked her attitude to the wedding by carrying the basket that she always took to market; it was covered with its usual clean blue cloth, though it was empty. They were awkwardly proud of her haughty bearing too. Heaven knew she had no right to it. She was the daughter of a copyholder and her sister had married a labourer. In marrying a yeoman freeholder she had stepped above her station but the airs she gave herself suggested that it was the other way round.

Though her pretensions alienated her equals and inferiors they impressed her betters. This morning Mrs Drewe, the squire's wife, who happened to be crossing the green at the most festive moment, gave her a decided bow and moved towards her as if to speak. This was only what she had earned after all her sycophancy to Mrs Drewe, though it must be added that she was working on her daughters' behalf; she wanted them to get another turn, preferably several turns, up the wheel of fortune and she understood the power of patronage, without realizing, as her daughters did, how unlikely it was to be exercised in the circumstances.

'Enjoying yourselves?' boomed Mrs Drewe.

'I was just saying to the girls, all we need is the hobby-horse.'

Mrs Mutter had gathered from the fact that Mrs Drewe was not wearing her ruff and from the direction in which she was going that the squire's wife would not be gracing the wedding, so she could afford to speak scornfully.

Mrs Drewe laughed indulgently. 'And how are the girls?'

'Very well, thank you. Rosalind's decided she wants to be a lawyer. There's no knowing what ideas these long-legged people will get into their heads, is there?'

'Well. Nowadays. With a Queen on the throne. Who knows? Who knows?' shouted Mrs Drewe with non-committal benevolence as she made for the gates of the Manor House.

Alice dropped behind. 'You'd make a marvellous lawyer, Rozzy. You look just like Mr Pollard.' Mr Pollard was an Exeter lawyer. His ancestors had made a fortune in the profession, but nobody would wish to resemble him.

'Well, I wouldn't want to wait till those ignorant turds said I looked like Veeenus.'

Alice put out her tongue, rolling it up towards the middle as she had always been able to do. Rosalind could never do more than stick her tongue straight out and let it hang, like a cat interrupted in the middle of washing, so this was a triumph in itself.

They were now nearing Mrs Clapp's cottage, which backed on to the churchyard, with a small plot of garden in the front and another at the side. There was a foul smell all round it as Mrs Clapp, who was a white witch, grew many of the herbs she needed herself. Wild arrach was one of them, the most popular remedy of all. There can have been no woman in the village who had not had recourse to it at some time, as it dealt with all ailments of the womb. It made barren women fertile, and it brought on abortions. It supported fallen wombs and cooled those that were overheated, encouraged sluggish periods and checked those that were too profuse. It was a pretty little plant to look at but it smelled like rotten fish and furthermore needed to be surrounded by large quantities of fresh dung in order to do really well.

Mrs Clapp could be seen through the crowds leaning over her

gate looking hopeful. Custom of many sorts could come from a gathering such as this. As the Mutters approached she was giving advice to a nursing mother who was on her way to church.

'And be sure to keep the dairies warm, dear.'

'Whatever good would a warm dairy be?' said Rosalind to Alice out of the corner of her mouth. The girls collected Mrs Clapp's expressions, particularly her euphemisms which not only made everything sound worse but were usually as inaccurate as this one. Mrs Clapp looked speculatively at Mrs Mutter and prophetically at the girls as they went by and raised her hand in token of meetings to come.

Moon's Ottery church was over a hundred years old even then. ' 'Tis a wool church,' Farmer Mutter had once told his daughters as he was driving them back in the cart from Rawridge, proudly pointing to the tall tower with his whip. 'Well, they've knitted it too big,' Rosalind said, and she and Alice nearly fell out of the cart with giggling. Their father looked slightly nettled but uttered nothing more than a tolerant 'Cuh'. If Mrs Mutter had been imparting the information it would have been received in something like respectful silence.

They certainly had knitted the church too big. It must always have been too large for any congregation that Moon's Ottery could muster. This morning, even with the largest turn-out since Easter Sunday, it was only three-quarters full. The Mutters went to their usual place halfway up the church. The vicar was at the altar in a state of reverent bustle. 'That Mr Hall,' said Mrs Mutter, though he was only doing his job. Indeed nobody had ever seen him doing anything else except till his glebe. Of the two his land probably gave him the greater support. His church had undergone many changes. Older inhabitants related how he had removed the brass candlesticks and the gold plate and the vestments to please one monarch, brought them back to please another – for cannily he had not sold them but distributed them among the farms – and at last let most of it go again to please a third. But his land had never altered and it had formed his peace and his stability. He did not speak of the

16

changes. They may have been the cause of his inflexible mildness. He had only once been known to flare up. It was when he preached on the text 'Cursed be he that moveth his neighbour's landmark'. His eyes went red and he breathed hard and far like a dragon.

He now went into the vestry and came back leading William Lock, very courteously, by the arm. William looked so much like a nervous animal, with his glancing eyes, pulsating nostrils and restive head movements, that Rosalind felt it would have looked more appropriate if Mr Hall had been leading him by the nose. Two young men accompanied William but, again, as two people might escort an animal, exchanging speech with each other while keeping a wary and superior eye on their charge. They reminded Rosalind of pigmen at a show; she half expected them to produce their wooden boards and steer him to his place in front of the altar.

In the event Mr Hall got him into position and then walked down the church. The young men turned round quite openly and smiled and waved at their acquaintances. William looked heavily over his shoulder once but could not pick out any one person who might be trying to communicate with him, and so seemed to see nobody. After that he stayed facing the altar, moving uneasily from foot to foot. 'Someone ought to scratch the top of his head,' whispered Alice.

Mr Hall now came up the aisle with Mary. She was wearing a variety of garments which were clearly the result of widespread charity and suggested almost every woman in the parish from Mrs Drewe down, but in spite of this and her defensively burly way of walking, she looked personable, and her usual lowering expression had lifted for the time being.

Everything went very quiet as the service began, and from then on the only noises were the intermittent grunts and moans of William and Mary themselves. Moon's Ottery congregations as a rule were chatty and wheezy, and the present hush was due not to reverence but to bated breath and to something like watchfulness in the presence of danger. Rosalind, still being reminded of animals, recalled a parade of local bulls the year

17

before when a huge red bull had broken loose and started to roam about, a potential killer. Everybody had immediately fallen from animation into a soothing stillness and let him wander around until he came of his own accord within reach of someone who caught his rope.

Mr Hall's voice barely broke the silence. He spoke of course in English. Alice and Rosalind had never heard the service in Latin. Mr Mutter who was forty-three could remember doing so in Queen Mary's reign when he was a boy, and he had a not very gripping series of anecdotes about the local rebellion caused by the first introduction of English, before her time. There had actually been a battle at Fenny Bridges, a few miles down the road, which he claimed to recall, and perhaps he really could as it would certainly have appealed to the imagination of a five-year-old boy. Fenny Bridges was in the news every year as at least two people drowned each time the Otter flooded, but there had been only the one battle. Farmer Mutter used to speak as though he regretted the Latin, though the nostalgia had to be in his tone and not in words, as his wife was openly jubilant at its passing. He could hardly have followed the Latin word for word but he could have caught the drift and in his mind it would have been tinged with his general respect for education and authority and mystery.

The first excitement came when Mr Hall asked diffidently if anyone knew of just cause or impediment why these two should not be joined together in holy matrimony. He paused and the church hummed with tension. It was at this point that at nearly every wedding for the last five years one of the Pulman brothers had got up and said, 'I do'. The brothers were two young farmers, steady well-to-do men whose only peculiarity was to object to weddings in this way. They did not do it alternately; sometimes it would be the same one three or four times running. They never exactly wanted the bride themselves; they were handsome boys who could easily have got girls of their own. Nevertheless they made some kind of distinction. When old Miss Pinn got married they did not appear; old Miss Pinn was quite a test case. At the end of five years Mr Hall had got into a routine. Those who were present the first time it happened said he was shaken then; it must have seemed to him like one more menacing innovation. But nowadays he just said pleasantly, 'Will you see me in the vestry afterwards, Mr Pulman?' Neither of them ever did. They went peacefully away with the rest of the congregation.

Rosalind, sympathizing with Mary for the first time, hoped she would not be found wanting but she was. There was a prolonged silence and then the service went on, in a puzzled anticlimax, as though a watchdog known for its vigilance had failed to bark. Rosalind was indignant that Mary, young and pleasing, should, simply because she lacked two senses, be classed with old Miss Pinn. However, Mary's behaviour did not suggest disappointment or affront. Perhaps nobody had ever communicated the story of the Pulman brothers to her – it would have been difficult, certainly – and presumably the expectant silence in church seemed to her like any other silence.

It was now time for the vows. This was what everybody had been waiting for. This was really new. And everybody's liveliest expectations were fulfilled. William and Mary moved forward like well-trained but kindly treated animals. They stopped the grunting and moaning which usually accompanied their thoughts and feelings and concentrated on the rare task, for them, of actually conveying something to someone. It is true that William's rendering of 'With this body I thee worship' fell short of Alice's mime in the dairy before breakfast but that was just as well. He simply placed his hand on Mary's bosom in a beautiful and dignified way. 'With all my worldly goods,' he represented by a gesture of giving. There *was* something reluctant about the sweep of his hands – it was not exactly a large gesture – and Mrs Mutter snorted, but quietly, for her. The star turn was William's 'Till death us do part'. He pretended to dig a grave, putting his foot well down on to an imaginary spade and heaving imaginary earth right into the face of Mr Hall, who flinched. Then he made a movement of impassioned farewell to Mary, and those who had not laughed before did

19

so now. It must have been clearly understood between the couple that she was to be the survivor as throughout this bit she stood in an attitude of pretty resignation to God's will.

'Let them that love him be as the sun when he goeth forth in his might.' Mr Hall had appeared in the pulpit and pronounced his text. 'Dearly beloved brethren. . . .' Rosalind settled down to the romantic daydreaming which she kept for sermons and the first five minutes in bed. Though the story she was telling herself was all about love and marriage it was quite unrelated to the ceremony she had just witnessed. While Mr Hall spoke of these topics in connection with the newly wedded couple she enacted them in her mind without listenng to him at all. When at one point she involuntarily came back to reality she found that Mr Hall had left William and Mary as far behind as she had.

'. . . *the sun when he goeth forth in his might,* that is, the sun in summer that blesses the earth and ripens the crops. Remember, dear brethren, what God said as he stood at the summit of Jacob's ladder, where angels were ascending and descending, feathering their flight from earth to heaven, from heaven to earth. God made a solemn promise to Jacob, that the land where he had slept that night was to be given to him and to his seed, to till and make fruitful, for ever and ever.'

Realizing that Mr Hall would be digging happily round the foot of Jacob's ladder for some time, Rosalind retired to her story, confident that instinct would let her know when the peroration was approaching – she enjoyed perorations – and it did.

'Finally, dearly beloved brethren, let us tread once more upon our own soil and meditate upon our own land which God has given to us present and to our seed. To live in England in the thirtieth year of the reign of our Sovereign Lady Queen Elizabeth is to have won a reward even before death. But a miscreant doomsday threatens our country. The hosts of the enemy, the hosts of Spain, are massing against us. Men of Moon's

Ottery, I know your vigilance. To make a whirligig of the words of Isaiah: you have turned your ploughshares and pruning hooks into swords and spears, in noble preparation to defend this kingdom and your monarch.

'But I speak also to the women and children of Moon's Ottery. *I say unto you all, Watch.* Neither the sword nor the spear is the only weapon. The tongue is the conduit of speech and can fill the cisterns of the ungodly. May there never be traitors in our midst. May Iscariot never wake from his long sleep to walk in our lanes and fields. Philip of Spain is a man of wiles and cunning. Let us recognize the foe in whatever guise we meet him, by land or by sea, in armour or in homespun, at seed-time or at harvest, by day or by night. Let us not speak him fair or treat him fair. It is not with your conscience as with the sky. A red evening prognosticates a fair day. But if the evening of your life is red, if it is dyed or discoloured with innocent blood, the morning of the next world will rise foul and lower upon you.'

'I daresay,' thought Rosalind and stopped listening again. She had meant to attend right up to the final words, but sermons in the summer of 1587 nearly always concluded on this note. It was all too predictable, and Mr Hall's gentle and tentative delivery did not set off such rousing sentiments to any advantage.

At last, however, the sermon was done, and the bride and bridegroom came down the aisle, grinning so broadly that they looked not so much deaf and dumb as mad. As the congregation stopped attending exclusively to the married couple and started noticing each other again, with returning sounds and voices, Rosalind caught sight of her mother's expression. It was one of such intense apprehension that the girl went cold and shivered convulsively. She could not understand it at all. It could not possibly have been inspired by William's mime of dying, which would have made a cat laugh.

It had certainly made everybody else laugh. The village green was echoing with happy shrieks, and family groups dispersing to their homes – quite speedily as there was work to be done –

21

could be seen pausing from time to time to dig invisible graves, throw invisible earth at each other and then double up with merriment. Mrs Mutter would in no circumstances have joined in such jokes. She believed that to laugh at God's creatures, however afflicted, was to mock their creator. But she would certainly have enjoyed herself sneering at the jokers and perhaps making remarks in a carrying aside. As it was, though she walked the two uphill miles back to the farm with her usual high-stepping briskness, she was completely silent. Rosalind had been afraid that her mother would jeer at the hand-on-bosom part which she herself had found moving but she need not have worried.

The brightness had gone out of the day or rather it had changed character. The brilliant white mist that never left the valley for long was beginning to gather over the river, and Rosalind experienced, more intensely than usual, her habitual fancy that things were going on down there in the mist, improbable things like people dancing on the bridge and men fighting duels. They came within sight of their own trees and of their own higher fields, and still there was this strange silence: no jibes, no quips, not one uncharitable remark. Alice caught Rosalind's eye; she was clearly as bewildered as her sister. She tried to provoke a discussion.

'Not much about the happy couple, was there, in the sermon?'

'I don't know,' said Rosalind, sacrificing herself. 'I wasn't listening.'

Mrs Mutter said nothing, either to the disadvantage of Mr Hall or that of her daughter.

'Anyway,' added Rosalind in her mother's manner, as if deputizing for her, 'what did it matter? William and Mary couldn't hear anything about themselves and nobody else wanted to.'

Alice started another tempting argument, this time more directly. 'Mother, I've been trying to work it out. Who told William and Mary what to mime?'

'And when to mime it?' Rosalind joined in.

'I mean how were they told? Neither of them can read, you know.'

Even this failed to draw Mrs Mutter out. In ordinary circumstances she would probably have said that it was all a put-up job and that they were no more deaf and dumb than you or me.

2

WHEN they got home dinner had already started. The big oak trestle table had been erected in the hall and the last of the dishes were being taken out of the ovens and unhooked from over the fire. The room was crowded, as Farmer Mutter's men received food and drink as part of their wages. They did well by this arrangement as Mrs Mutter was an ample provider. There was always plenty of choice, too. That is to say, there were always plenty of dishes to choose from, a rather different thing where Jane Mutter was concerned. She disapproved of card games and though she may have known the expression 'palming the cards' she never used it. But in fact it was an activity at which she excelled. The unpopular people always ended up with the unpopular dishes.

John Mutter was already sitting in his chair, the only chair in the room. It was massive, handsome affair, heavy in itself and made much heavier by the fact that Mrs Mutter stored an assortment of things from blankets to candles in the box under the seat. But Mr Mutter who was very strong in those days could lift the whole thing with ease. His daughters always remembered him as someone who could carry objects and people, literally though not metaphorically.

He had heaped his pewter plate with meat and bread and was starting on it. His wife dragged one of the stools as close to the fire as she could, eccentrically close, and sat down.

'What's up, Jane?' said Mr Mutter.

'I'm cold.'

'Cold? I'm sweating like a pig.'

'Well, I'm not. And who ever saw a pig sweat?'

This exchange followed the basic pattern of their conversation and was only slightly more skeletal and acid than usual, so that it did not seem specially significant at that moment, but there she sat as the hall completely filled up and her foes warily helped themselves to unexpected delicacies and the cider tankards banged down on the table the more heavily as they got lighter and even to those who were not watching her as attentively as her husband and daughters it all began to seem very strange indeed.

Suddenly she began to shake, so violently that everybody, even those with their heads well down into their plates, noticed and stopped eating. She was a small woman and the stool was a solid one, but its legs danced, drumming and scraping on the flagstones. Then all at once she stood up in her characteristic attitude of having come to a decision, and this was probably what she had done. She had decided to face her illness and survive if she could. She had always been a resolute woman when misfortune came, though not brave in forestalling it. Adapting herself to her own vibrations, as though she were driving a cart on a rough road, she rushed to the hall door, through the cross passage and the parlour, to the foot of the spiral staircase. Speed seemed to help her. In unnatural silence Alice and Rosalind followed, with Mr Mutter close behind them, and they saw her at the first turning, rebounding from one wall to the other, her hands held out, before she disappeared round the corner. In a sense they never saw her again.

Mr and Mrs Mutter's bedroom was at the head of the stairs. It was not the best bedroom; Alice and Rosalind had that, a beautiful spacious room with two windows, one looking south right down the valley towards Honiton, and an eastward-facing one, small but with a commanding view of the whole length of the barn, most of the farm buildings including Obed Hosegood's cottage, and the river at the bottom of the field. Mrs Mutter had sacrificed this room so that she might have more purchase on the house as a whole and complete control over the comings and goings of Alice and Rosalind who had to pass through her room to get anywhere.

By the time Mrs Mutter was in her nightclothes and lying in

the four-poster bed she was so hot that they drew back all the tapestry bedcurtains that she had recently installed and was extremely proud of, as it seemed that otherwise she might actually ignite. The heat of her body had already brought a pungent smell out of the blankets. They knew it was not the plague as her skin was clear and unmarked. There had been no epidemic of plague in the district for some years but everybody lived in dread of it and knew the symptoms, or thought they did. But it was something so strong that they felt frightened and helpless. Mr Mutter sent a man down to the village for Mrs Clapp.

The very idea brought some comfort. Mrs Clapp had been present, nobody could say assisted, at the birth of both Alice and Rosalind, and the Mutters regarded her possessively, almost like one of the family, though nearly every household in the valley had a similar claim. She was not much use when any action was required, as in midwifery, but she was well liked and people would excuse her by saying that though she was no good in an emergency she was excellent afterwards: when the patient had either died or recovered presumably. She never tried to deceive the innocent, as many witches, even the whitest, used to do, and she really understood herbs. She had remedies for everything from the snakebites which were an everyday danger to the less dramatic toothache from which most of the population suffered drearily and spasmodically throughout their lives. She had views, too. The more white witches talked in general the more the listener came to the conclusion that everything cured anything and that anything cured everything. They spoke of no plant that would not, if necessary, provoke urine, and the bloody flux could be cleared up by any plant they cared to mention. But Mrs Clapp was selective.

In about half an hour Mr Mutter and his daughters heard her stumbling and chatting her way across the cobbles and soon she came labouring up and round the stairs carrying her immense bag of remedies which had strange shapes jostling about inside it and looked alive. She was a large woman but could

26

hardly be called fat or plump as she had a hollow look about her like a scooped-out pumpkin. She greeted Alice and Rosalind very kindly and went over to the bed.

'Well, Mrs Mutter, dear. I thought something was running down the wrong gutter when I saw you this morning.' She bent over her, felt her forehead, sniffed at her breath and ran her hand mysteriously under the bedclothes. Then she straightened up and turned to Mr Mutter.

'H and P,' she announced secretively though without at all lowering her voice. Mr Mutter looked alarmed but puzzled.

'Heat and putrefaction,' supplied Rosalind who had over the years compiled a mental list of Mrs Clapp's professional abbreviations as a companion piece to her euphemisms. Mrs Clapp nodded and went to her bag of remedies which squirmed excitedly as she rooted around in it. But just then Mrs Mutter started to sweat and the white witch quickly took her hand out of the remedies, which collapsed into a slumbering half life, and went back to her patient. The three watchers, sensing some turning point, drew nearer too.

' 'Tis the cal-id-i-ty,' explained Mrs Clapp to Mr Mutter, anxious that this point should not be lost as well. 'She mustn't take anything liquid now.'

Sweating seemed an inadequate definition of what was happening to Mrs Mutter. It was more as though she was melting. She got smaller as they watched. For minutes on end she seemed to have the same contours she had always had, or so they tried to believe, but then there would come a moment, like watching a lump of ice in the sun, when they had to face the fact that there was a difference. Rosalind worried that the feather mattress would be ruined and imagined the feathers inside the ticking going straggly and drowned-looking. Mrs Mutter's pride in her new feather mattress was equal to her pride in the new tapestry curtains. Her pleasure in having more possessions than other people touched both her daughters and struck a particular chord of sympathy and loyalty in Rosalind.

The sick woman now spoke, begging for something to drink, but those present, of both generations, had been brought up

27

with the fixed precept that this was the very worst thing you could give to someone who had any kind of sweating sickness. You had to harden your heart and let them dry out. A few of the better educated people in the valley thought quite differently and recommended unlimited fluids for all fevers, but the two treatments could hardly be combined, and something had to be done. Her mother's beseeching voice broke Rosalind's nerve. She began to cry and Mr Mutter took the two girls downstairs.

The hall was now clear and empty. 'If I could afford it,' said Mr Mutter impressively, 'she should have Dr Edwards, Dr Thomas Edwards.' This celebrity was a medical practitioner who lived in Exeter. He had an immense reputation and was the regular attendant of such prestigious local families as the Courtenays. But he was out of the question for the Mutters. As Mr Mutter suggested, he came expensive, and Exeter was seventeen miles away, and in any case Dr Thomas Edwards was no doubt dancing round the Courtenays at that very moment. But the mere wish was an expression of John Mutter's concern and of his desire to do his best.

He went upstairs again and Alice and Rosalind wandered about downstairs, glancing out of the windows and picking at bits of food from the buttery; Alice used to say in later life that all she could remember about the day of her mother's death was trying to swallow a piece of marzipan. That afternoon there was disquiet over the whole farm. Obed Hosegood clumped up and down the courtyard oftener than need be and each time he turned his usual level or downward stare up to the bedroom window. The cows lowed resentfully as though it was much nearer to milking time than it actually was. Two sheep kept butting each other, round and round the front field; even when the girls could not see them they could hear the tapping of their heads. In a far field a goose kept rearing up, large as an angel and ghostly white through the yellow window. The sheepdogs, Rex and Lass, who usually slept flat out when they were not working, padded pointlessly up and down in some cage of their own making. Two rats ran across the hall floor; they were not often as bold as that.

28

Only Praise-the-Lord, sitting on the wall, looked as complacent as usual, perhaps even more so, as he thrived on the uneasiness and bad behaviour of others, though even he rearranged himself rather often. He was a black cat with yellow eyes. There were many other cats on the farm, mangy tabbies and muddy gingers, who slunk about usefully catching mice. They knew their place and Praise-the-Lord knew his. Originally he had been called Wat which suited him quite well, but one day Mr Mutter, who was in the habit of saying, 'Praise the Lord', about anything which could be viewed as at all merciful, said it once too often for Rosalind and Alice, and as soon as he was out of hearing Alice said, 'Praise the Lord', in a high sing-song voice and Wat came forward as if she had called him. So the girls surreptitiously renamed him. He was a cat who kept his beauty to the end, never going rusty or dull. Time made other black cats in the valley look like dried logs, but Praise-the-Lord gleamed like coal till his dying day.

All the afternoon floorboards creaked in the room above, unnaturally, as nobody went up there during the day as a rule. From time to time the sisters heard murmuring. Their father kept coming down to see them, but when they asked how their mother was he only said, 'Trust in the Lord.' For once he seemed to them noble and strong, almost apostolic. But after he had said it four or five times Alice whispered, 'We shall have to rename another of the cats.' Rosalind giggled. Mr Mutter heard the giggle but not the remark and turned round on his way upstairs to look at her with more anger than she had ever seen in his face before.

At last there was a thud on the floor above. Alice and Rosalind knew this sound from childhood. It was Mr Mutter going down on his knees to pray. They were terrified; they had never known him pray in daylight except in church. Then they heard Mrs Clapp's springless tread approaching the top of the staircase and soon she trundled into sight, passing the girls with her most serene expression but without a word, and on into the buttery. She returned carrying a pitcher of cider.

'But Mrs Clapp,' Alice cried, 'she mustn't drink.'

'It doesn't matter now, dear. And 'tis for wetting her lips. And your father says you'd better both come upstairs again.'

They followed her and stood beside the bed. They saw at once that their mother was dying. They had seen too many animals dying on the farm not to know the look, indescribable but instantly recognizable, like the beginning of twilight. Rosalind as a small child had stared for half a day in bewilderment at a lamb that looked normal, wondering what was wrong with it; in the evening she realized that what had been wrong with it was approaching death.

Mrs Mutter seemed to be neither asleep nor awake, neither hot nor cold. Her expression was half sharp and half dead tired. Mrs Clapp rubbed some of the cider along her lips and after a while she spoke, very wearily.

'John, tell the children. . . .'

'I will,' he said solemnly.

'You'm not getting married now, John.' And suddenly she smiled at him.

'Tell the children. . . .' She was weary again now.

'Yes, Jane, I'll tell them.'

'How do you know what to tell them?' There was something of the old edge in her voice, but then she fell silent. In the stillness they could hear the horses coming into the courtyard, stamping and blowing, bringing in a fallen branch, as Farmer Mutter had arranged at breakfast that morning. He instinctively moved to the window to check that it was the right branch but swung back immediately with a sigh. She stirred.

'Tell them. To wait for me. In the lane. To the village. Tell them. To go on. I'll catch them up.'

'Yes, Jane.'

'Away from the river. Right away from the river. If they go on. I'll catch them up. Safe.'

'Now, Mrs Mutter dear, you mustn't upset yourself. There's nothing to worry about.'

Mrs Mutter gave her a look that was both scornful and desperate but Mrs Clapp took no serious notice of looks from deathbeds.

'The girls will do as you say, dear. They'll go on towards the village and wait for you. Won't you, girls?' She winked sadly at them.

Mrs Mutter gave up for the moment but then said with a rising inflection: 'Mist?'

'Oh, don't 'ee talk like that, my dear,' pleaded John Mutter. 'But if 'tis the will of the Lord. Yes, Jane, you'll be missed.'

'No, Father. She meant "Mist".'

Obviously the word on Rosalind's lips sounded exactly the same as the one her father had said, but she and her mother understood each other in this extremity.

'That's right, Rozzy,' she said, still with a vestige of her former encouraging schoolteacher's manner. Then she lowered her voice. 'Down in the valley. Down by the river. Wicked.'

She said nothing more. Her eyes stayed shut for longer and longer periods of time. A dry pallor moved up over her face. Her breathing became louder and slower and then all of a sudden ceased. There was a moment's silence and then her cheeks puffed and her lips rippled as she released – it seemed deliberately – her last breath into the common air. Alice and Rosalind had been reared with the expression 'to give up the ghost', in connection with Jesus and other characters in the Bible, but it had always sounded formal and meaningless, sometimes a joke: Rosalind once said that she found ghosts so frightening that she would not mind giving one up. Now they saw it happen.

'She's gone,' said Mrs Clapp.

Mr Mutter kissed his daughters and said, 'Your mother's gone.'

They all stood by the cooling bed in the darkening room where she was the first person to die. The fleas began to come out of the bedclothes and a louse lumbered out of the dead woman's hair. This would have distressed her: fleas were natural but lice were dirty and she had always been particular about personal cleanliness.

The clink of the milkers returning roused them. Mrs Clapp, who was moving into her confident phase, bustled off to fetch

31

the shroud. She had known for sixteen years where to find it as Mrs Mutter had told her before Alice's birth and reminded her again before Rosalind's. The girls knew this from their mother herself who liked to impress on them the dangers she had undergone in bearing them. She presumably thought it would make them feel grateful. The shroud was beautiful and made of wool as shrouds invariably were in the valley then. The sheep may not have paid for all in every farm but they wrapped everybody up after death.

Alice and Rosalind had no wish to see their mother being laid out so they straggled after their father while he got his horse ready to ride down to the village to arrange about the passing bell. It would have been quite against his beliefs and Mrs Mutter's, particularly hers, to have got in touch with Mr Hall before, and Mr Hall, who must have seen Mrs Clapp being summoned, was not one to take any initiative. The Mutters thought – she with far more conviction than her husband - that in dying, people needed no professional intermediary between them and their God. And of course there was no question of the vicar's praying for Mrs Mutter now. She was dead, and the Mutters were not papists. In fact Farmer Mutter would not necessarily see Mr Hall even at this stage if he could find a ringer on his own. But the passing bell must unquestionably be rung. It was not only that the announcement must be made to the community – the credit of the whole family depended on it – but that the demons must be kept at bay during the momentous journey that was to come.

After Mr Mutter had ridden off, Alice and Rosalind stayed in the courtyard to wait for the bell. Naturally they knew which bell it would be. Every village in the district had a different tradition but each tradition was unvarying. Theirs was that the fifth bell, out of a peal of six, was rung for a woman. This bell was called Mizpah. Her name was taken from the Old Testament and the girls had been taught that it meant 'May the Lord watch between thee and me while we are absent from each other'. Alice and Rosalind had sometimes tried to annoy their father by maintaining that so lengthy a statement could not properly be rendered by only two syllables in any language but were rebuked on the grounds that with the Holy Ghost all things were possible. They knew Mizpah's voice well; in epidemics she seemed never to stop. It was sweet and cracked and had an unembarrassed quality about it like a madwoman singing to herself.

The evening was cool. By now it was nearly dark and the owls were beginning to hoot and swoop. There was still some light left on the opposite hills, but Alice and Rosalind stood in deepening shadow, leaning on the gate that led into the front field, while lamps and candles were being lit in the house behind them as a subdued and belated supper was being prepared, to which the haymakers would be wearily sitting down, and where no doubt Mrs Clapp was going from room to room telling everybody all about it. The mist had risen to cover the valley almost completely. Mr Mutter and his horse, in clopping downhill, had soon disappeared into it.

He must have found a ringer immediately. They had not long to wait. Mizpah started calling up the valley: six strokes for a woman; then a pause; then the woman's age. Rosalind began to count, automatically, as once a ringer had got it wrong, though he always maintained it was a trick of the wind, and the family concerned had made a great fuss. But it was not what she and Alice were really listening for. One. Two. Three. Four. Nothing was happening, and it was not that the ringer was hurrying; he was giving them plenty of time. Five. Six. Seven. Eight. The girls glanced anxiously at each other.

'There they go,' cried Alice and Rosalind at the same time, gasping with relief. Rustling came from the grass, crackling from the thatch, and even little scratching noises from between the cobbles, as the demons got up to go. They were clumsy tonight, not having had much warning. As the bell sang on and they lumbered off they banged into the hedges and against the trees. It even sounded as though one got stuck momentarily on top of the barn; the girls could hear the irritable drumming of a small hoof. But, however inelegantly, away into the distance they went, up into the hills and out of earshot. There would be no footprints next day, it was too dry, but Mrs Mutter's daughters had heard enough to satisfy them. And now through a most beautiful quietness, which the bell only intensified, the soul of the dead woman – for that was what she had thoroughly become – passed down the valley and far away.

Forty. Forty-one. Forty-two. That was all.

'Oh, Rozzy,' said Alice, with her elbows on the gate and her head in her hands. 'I feel it's all our fault.'

'I know. We never did anything but giggle.'

'And let her make our frocks.'

'We could have done something for her in a few years' time. Looked after her.'

'I don't know, Rozzy. There might have been murder done.'

'There still might.'

Alice took her sister's hand and they turned back to the house.

3

'MRS BASH reckons 'twas an imp,' said Mrs Clapp to Mrs Pook.

They were discussing the probable cause of Mrs Mutter's death, and had already gone through all the diagnoses given by the inhabitants of the valley, each opinion stupider than the one before, as might be expected from people who had not been there at the time. Rosalind, who was spinning and could not escape, was weary of it, but the idea of the imp interested her momentarily, until she realized that Mrs Clapp was using one of her professional abbreviations and meant imposthume. Of course it had not been an imposthume and Mrs Clapp did not suppose for a minute that it had. Mrs Bash was the white witch of Rawridge, and the white witch of Moon's Ottery was happy to quote such a ridiculous remark.

'I reckon 'twas they filthy feathers Jane had in her mattress,' said Martha Pook.

'' Twas the mist,' said Mrs Clapp. 'Down by the river. Your sister'd been down there the evening before.'

Rosalind was weary not only of this discussion but of all discussions, and she had had a bellyful of them since her Aunt Martha moved in, two days after the funeral. Mr Mutter arranged the funeral itself with no hesitation or requests for advice. For nearly a week he kept up the appearance of strength that had impressed his daughters on the day of their mother's death. He seemed to be sustained not only by his genuine trust in the Lord but by his conviction about what was due to his wife, of whom he had been so proud. He insisted that she should have a coffin, though this was not really necessary; many yeomen did without and indeed thought it an extravagance. Farmer

35

Mutter was not trying to show off. He simply felt that Jane deserved no less and should have no less, and he ladled as much bran into the bottom of the coffin as a duchess could have expected, so that she might lie softly.

The funeral itself was less distressing than all the discussions that followed. Rosalind always remembered the wryly beautiful things about it, such as the smell of the sprigs of rosemary that they carried to throw into the grave. It had been a good month for rosemary and its scent as they walked in the sunshine was as strong as that of the grass. She remembered Mr Hall, whose love of the earth made him a comfortable person to officiate at a burial. He made it seem like a privilege and an honour. Comfortable too was the sight of Obed Hosegood trudging stolidly along as one of the bearers. He had been greatly attached to Mrs Mutter. They used to have lively conversations in the yard in front of his cottage, that is, Mrs Mutter had been lively, shrieking with laughter and nudging him. In after days, when she was being discussed he always said, proudly and finally, 'I carried her.'

After the funeral, talk set in. The worst controversy was about the tombstone. Fortunately there was a good stonecutter at Luppitt so there was no question of having to send to London as people in some districts had to do. The arguments were about what to put on it. Name and date were not considered sufficient for a family of the Mutters' standing. Not that they had any intention of aping the gentry, with ambitious groups of angels, skulls and weepers, particularly angels which were rather suspect in those days, like saints, and had been especially so to Mrs Mutter who would have felt annoyed and uneasy at the thought of one looming over her. But there had to be some more writing. The arguments were interminable. At one point Mr Mutter produced a poem which he had adapted from a longer one that he had seen somewhere on a larger tomb.

> Farmer John Mutter's wife lieth here
> Jane Mutter was her name
> Her husband's love was so to her
> He caus'd to write the same.

36

Rosalind liked this, though the fourth line was undeniably limp. When she first heard the verse she thought it was quite unnecessary to repeat Mutter, in the second line, but then she reflected on the importance to her father of the fact that Jane had borne his name. To her mind this completely justified the repetition. Nobody consulted her about the merits of the poem but when she and Alice were alone she asked her sister what she thought about it. 'Well, it isn't lewd, that's one thing,' Alice snapped. She never cried; she talked like this instead.

In what circumstances their father's poem was finally rejected the girls never found out. They hoped nothing had happened to hurt his feelings. Aunt Martha was capable of saying anything and he was rapidly losing his assurance. The next they heard was that a text from the Bible would be best. A text entered Rosalind's mind at once.

'What do you think of this, Alice? "She was cut off out of the land of the living." Wouldn't that do? Yes, I know it says "he" but it'd be such a small alteration.'

'People would say it was blasphemous.'

'Why, who was "he"?'

'The Messiah.'

'Oh, bugger.'

What was finally chosen was 'Be ye therefore ready also'. It was Aunt Martha's suggestion, and embodied the blend of doom and unsolicited exhortation that was a large part of her character.

'Gloomy old cow,' said Alice in their bedroom that night.

'Alice. You couldn't have got away with that remark when Mother was alive. Not even you.'

'Don't be daft. If Mother was alive I wouldn't be making it, not about her tombstone. Anyway she used to say things about Aunt Martha behind her back, when she thought we weren't listening. Said she was pig-ignorant.'

'I didn't mean that. I meant about the cow.'

'Mother used to call people cows. She said Mrs Bash was one.'

'No, I mean she would have said had you ever seen a smiling cow.'

'Well, I've seen a contented cow. Anyway pigs aren't ignorant and she said that.'

Aunt Martha had moved into Sparkhayes full of sentiments about how in this life it's not what you want for yourself it's what others need and how she had always promised Jane, but in fact it suited her very well to do so. Her husband George Pook had recently died and as a farm labourer he had not been able to leave much, though Aunt Martha was very thrifty, disgustingly so, Alice and Rosalind thought, when they saw her washing the dishes with the water she had just washed the clothes in, though the fire was burning all the time.

George Pook had been a hard worker. Labourers had to be, with a twelve-hour day in summer and a ten-hour day in winter. He had worked for the same master, a farmer in Rawridge, ever since he was a boy, but had never got on really friendly terms with his employers or his fellow labourers. He did not eat with the family as the Sparkhayes men did and so could be as unsociable as he liked. In his holidays and leisure hours he kept self-righteously aloof from the other labourers who invariably hurried off to wrestle and drink on the village green. He seemed unhappy about pleasure. He was conscientious by temperament and by conviction, really earning his sixpence a day in winter and his eightpence in summer. He received a little more money at harvest time and Aunt Martha helped then too. Even so it was not much of a wage and not much of a life. The one possible consolation, that at least one third of the village lived it, meant nothing to George Pook, who stood apart.

He had died in circumstances that were superficially strange but, given one of his leading characteristics, perhaps only to be expected. He made unfortunate remarks. They may have been meant jocularly, but Alice and Rosalind doubted it, and they always gave offence.

In 1587 the inhabitants of East Devon, being less than twenty miles from the route that any Spanish invasion would have to take, were particularly on edge. For some time the prevailing spirit had been that God helps those who help themselves, and so volunteers had been manning the beacon on the hill behind Sparkhayes and drilling round the village green. They were mostly middle-aged men, and the young people teased them, but the jokes were good-humoured and almost respectful, and in any case the volunteers were upheld by the dual inspiration that their Queen and country needed them and that it made a change from wrestling.

Their Queen and country really did need them, for in the February of that year the Catholic Mary of Scotland had been beheaded by order of their own Queen. The news had taken many weeks to reach the villages of Devon but when it did most of the population realized the gravity of its implications and those who did not had had it pointed out to them. The Catholic Philip of Spain would not like it and would take rapid steps to show his displeasure. Few people felt sorry for Mary of Scotland; she had been a trouble-making bogey for too long. Rosalind felt no compassion at all for her until her own mother died and then she could not help connecting them. Mary had been about the same age as Mrs Mutter and, by all accounts, a lively attractive woman who in recent years had had little opportunity to shine. It is true that she had murdered a husband, but so might Mrs Mutter have done if he had been a different kind of husband.

But though local feeling for Queen Elizabeth was sincere, the immediate hero was Sir Francis Drake. He was a Devonian, born on the other side of the moors, at Tavistock. He was perhaps not quite so much a fellow countryman as Sir Walter Raleigh, whose home was only a few miles away – Alice and Rosalind had frequently passed Hayes Barton when Farmer Mutter had business in East Budleigh – but he was everyone's champion. He was continuously spoken of, under different appellations. Since he had been knighted, Mrs Drewe had called him Francis when speaking to the minor gentry and the superior yeomen and Sir Francis Drake to the lower orders, throwing in a few references and explanations for the benefit of the ignorant. The lower orders called him Sir Drake in the hearing of the gentry. Among themselves they referred to him simply as Er, without context or further definition, a great compliment as the only living creature on any farm to be so described was the bull. Many of the local girls had his picture and he did rather resemble a bull, with his broad shoulders and short neck, his purposeful eyes and his ears sticking up out of woolly hair, and the ribbon across his chest which made him look as if he had won a prize.

But to return to George Pook, who incidentally was not one of Sir Drake's admirers and who invariably said 'What do Er know about it?' whenever the admiral's name was mentioned: one hot day when everybody had been practising at their military assignments Robert Abbott's wife proudly showed George Pook her husband's shirt, dripping wet with his exertions.

'Sweating with fright already?' asked George Pook in his loud unmodulated voice.

This was a mistake. Robert Abbott was pompous and over-pleased with his contribution to civil defence, but his patriotism and courage were beyond question. The remark was poorly received, went the round of both villages and led to tragedy. A few days later George Pook passed Robert Abbott himself, who was on his way to some anti-Spanish manoeuvres in the village flaunting a virile blunderbuss.

'Where be going to put 'ee to then, Robert?' shouted George.

'I'll show 'ee, George Pook,' said Robert Abbott calmly, raised the gun and shot his neighbour in the leg.

He was carried home and nursed by Aunt Martha with a resentment which she allowed, or rather forced, him to see, as she could never acknowledge anyone to be ill but herself. For many years Alice and Rosalind assumed that her bad temper at the sufferings of others was a form of compassion and anxiety on their behalf but after she had been at Sparkhayes for six months they realized it was straightforward annoyance.

George Pook's wound did not heal and began to go green. Mrs Bash did everything she could. It was the beginning of May and many flowers were out which were good for this condition and could be used fresh. The plant that was locally called bluebottle was already growing in the cornfields, blue and innocent-looking, though Farmer Mutter said it took the edge off the sickles at harvest time. Mrs Bash squeezed bluebottle juice into the wound three days running but it got no better. She then tried burnet; it was not in flower yet but she had some made up as ointment from the year before. This did no good either and in desperation she tried a darnel-meal poultice.

After ten days however George Pook died. John and Jane Mutter went to the funeral and when they got back Mrs Mutter, who always over-valued her sister in public, gave a dramatic account of her deportment on this occasion.

'She never cried, girls, only the once. And that was when she saw your father. "He's an old fool," she said, "but I loves un." That's what she said when she saw your father.'

Rosalind felt it was a poor compliment and so, she could see, did Alice, but Farmer Mutter was much affected and blew his nose tempestuously.

A particularly fraught conversation that followed Mrs Mutter's death had been the question of who should now run Sparkhayes. In cold terms, the family had lost the most valuable member of the household. The obvious replacement would have been Alice if the girls had not always been treated as younger than their years so that, at sixteen, she really did seem too tender and untried. As it was, Aunt Martha's recent widowhood and the fact that she and Mrs Mutter had been genuinely close seemed to point to her. She was invited and she accepted. Again in cold terms, she was a good choice in some ways. She was a competent cook, though necessarily on less ambitious lines than her sister, and she kept her house scrubbed and orderly. Her sewing and spinning were careful and her ironing distinguished.

One of their aunt's most difficult characteristics the girls had met before, on visits to her cottage at Rawridge where they sometimes spent a few days; that was, the unsteadiness of her goodwill. When they were small children they had been greatly disconcerted by the violence of her kindness on the first day; they could not respond at all adequately. On the second day it had begun to die down and they could manage quite well. By the third or fourth day she seemed positively to dislike them,

41

which made them uncomfortable again in a different way. Now at Sparkhayes the pattern, in being drawn out and elongated, changed completely. The first day, sure enough, was loud with loving kindness, and the diminution duly set in on the second day, but on the fourth day when they were still all together, with no Farmer Mutter arriving in the cart to fetch his daughters away, her resentment settled in like a wet noon and became constant, with no unsteadiness at all beyond the occasional emotional remark about how much they all meant to each other, having been through so much together.

With Aunt Martha came her children, Nicholas aged five and Margaret aged three. Margaret was a nondescript little girl but Nicholas was an aggravation. He had been born at Sparkhayes, with Mrs Mutter presiding and Mrs Clapp in attendance. As usual Mrs Clapp had been no help at all but her very presence had been a triumph for Jane Mutter, as Aunt Martha had wished to bring Mrs Bash with her. But if Mrs Mutter was going to produce the play she was going to choose the cast, and Aunt Martha had given way. She had always been dependent on her sister. Mrs Mutter had sometimes tried to depend on her but Aunt Martha had started first and in any case was those few years younger, demonstrably poorer and temperamentally much less capable.

At first Alice and Rosalind had hated Nicholas. Their mother's two sons had died in infancy, and so on Nicholas's appearance she naturally pounced on him. He was constantly in the house, spoiled and petted by his aunt, though Alice once told Rosalind that she had just heard their mother telling him off for whining when she thought everybody was out. Mrs Mutter kept up an act that she understood him and everything pertaining to the bringing up of boys better than his own mother did.

'That dirty old thing,' said Aunt Martha in withering tones, one day when he was playing with himself.

'Martha,' enunciated Mrs Mutter, rising to heights of theatre, ' 'tis his manhood.'

Alice and Rosalind exchanged glances. The remark did not

42

square with a lot they had heard. Sparkhayes was a house where sounds carried.

'Oh, all right, Jane,' said Aunt Martha sulkily. ''Tis his manhood. Now play with your hobbyhorse, Nicholas, do.'

The girls were extremely jealous of him in the beginning. Alice retaliated by having fainting fits. Poor little boy, if he had been a poor old woman he would certainly have been burnt as a witch, with Alice collapsing every time he came to the house. Rosalind would have backed her up if she could but was no good at that sort of thing. When she tried to look ill she looked angry, and when she attempted to swoon people remembered things they had to do in another part of the house. But they both came to see that Nicholas was not a serious threat. His baby beauty of dark curls, thick glossy lips and glazed eyes soon grew coarse; his cuteness dwindled into no more than average intelligence, if that, and he had inherited his father's fatal lack of judgement about what to say to whom.

To be fair, Alice and Rosalind irritated their aunt, sometimes without trying though they did that too. In the first place they were educated, which used to annoy other people as well as Aunt Martha, as it was most unusual in a farmer's daughters. Both Mr and Mrs Mutter had always set great store on education – 'better unborn than unbred', John Mutter used to quote from something he had read – and even in their courting days, according to Jane Mutter in one of her mellowly reminiscent moods, they had had long discussions about how they would educate their sons. When their sons died they transferred their plans to their daughters, and Mr Mutter, at least, was as proud of their achievements as he would have been of a boy's. Before Rosalind was five she wrote in her copy book:

> The rose is red, the leaves are green
> God save Elizabeth our noble queen.

Alice was not as quick but she was more thoughtful and assimilated and used what she learnt better than her sister did. Rosalind was always airing her knowledge and accomplishments. Alice never did.

Their teacher was Mr Rolle, who had once been employed fulltime at St Paul's School in London. As a member of the Rolle family, which owned hundreds of acres in East Devon, he had gone to university, to Exeter College at Oxford where most men from the west matriculated. Toby Rolle owned rather less land than the rest of his family so when he left university he had applied for the post of surmaster at St Paul's and the Mercers who made the appointments had given it to him. The position required a man who was well lettered if not intellectually brilliant, and outwardly respectable if not actually godly. He had held this post for twenty years and had then fallen ill with a series of prostrating headaches. In many schools this would have been the end of him but St Paul's was still living in the afterglow of its humane founder, John Colet, who had made specific arrangements for those who fell sick in its service. Mr Rolle was awarded a pension and came back to Devon where, when his headaches allowed, he took pupils, of whom Alice and Rosalind had been two.

It would have been quite beneath him to teach reading and writing and nobody expected him to. Those in the valley who were literate had scrambled into it somehow. Alice and Rosalind had been taught to read by their mother, with a few lessons at the petty school for extra polish, and to write – a much more complicated business – by Mr Hall. Ability to read and write was a normal, even a desirable, state for the sons of well-to-do yeomen, and not too outlandish for the daughters. It was what happened after literacy that set the Mutter girls apart. Literacy and book learning were two very different things. Mrs Mutter's sons would have gone on to the grammar school at Ottery St Mary. Her daughters could not; they were sent to Mr Rolle instead.

Aunt Martha, though she frequently proclaimed that she had never had any education and never felt the lack of it – or occasionally, and in special circumstances, that it was not her fault, but her misfortune – was in fact very sore on this point, perhaps because she welcomed any deprivation, however voluntarily undergone, as yet more food for resentment. The

44

least whiff of book-learning made her lash out. Soon after her arrival Farmer Mutter bought a new goat, of great personality. Rosalind suggested it should be called Copernicus. 'Oh, for goodness sake,' spat Aunt Martha, 'have something Nicholas and Margaret can say.'

Another thing that annoyed Aunt Martha was that the girls were fully mature physically. They might not have been mature emotionally, morally or intellectually but then neither was Aunt Martha. Their periods were well established and their busts had developed, Alice's more than Rosalind's, it is true, but even Rosalind though thin was not flat. Aunt Martha chose to treat them as the infants that in certain respects they still were, but it was in the teeth of most of the evidence. To demonstrate their immaturity she made them run errands.

About three weeks after her arrival she had her usual agonizing trouble with her own periods. Alice and Rosalind were quite ready to yield her the monopoly of this respect. Throughout life she had wrung the utmost out of her womanhood. From the moment of Nicholas's conception it had been obvious that she would have the longest labour known to East Devon, and she did. She now explained to the girls at the top of her voice, sinking to a prurient, carrying whisper if Mr Mutter or any other man came into sight, that the medicine that really helped her was syrup of wild arrach.

'But I id'n' going down to Mrs Clapp for it myself. 'Tis well known, women that's fallen for a baby takes it. To pass it off, you see. And Mrs Clapp might think.'

'But, Aunt Martha, if Alice goes, or me, won't Mrs Clapp still think? Or perhaps even more?'

'Oh, no,' said Aunt Martha loftily, 'not with very little girls.'

Alice looked calmly down at her own bosom. Rosalind was furious.

'In any case, Aunt Martha, Uncle George has been. . . .'

'You wait till you'm married, Rozzy. You'll find out about these things then. Now off you go.'

Rosalind set out for the village in a rage. As she was stumping down the courtyard to the bottom gate she saw Obed Hosegood who was apparently just finishing a talk with the shepherd about tar. Like Mrs Clapp's herbs tar cured everything. It was also used to put on the geese's feet when they walked to market. The two men had been staring appraisingly into a full pot of it.

'How you'm getting on then, Rozzy?' asked Obed when the shepherd had gone. He was the only one who had actually asked the question.

'Oh, Obed, what do you suppose Mother died of? They will keep talking about it.'

'Don't know, Rozzy, don't know.'

'Mrs Clapp says it was the mist.'

'I reckon it could be. This earth here in the valley, 'tid'n' what I calls cracking earth. It don't crack, no matter how dry. So all they poisons, they got to escape somehow. And the mist draws them out.' After a pause he added 'And 'er was down there that evening.'

'So Mrs Clapp was saying. I didn't know.'

'Yes, 'er was.'

'But Obed, why? What did she go down to the river for? She never does. Did.'

'Didn' Mrs Clapp tell 'ee?'

'No, and I didn't want to ask.'

'No, 'er do go on a bit. Anyway, sounds as though 'er didn' see.'

'You tell me, Obed.'

'Well, 'er was talking to this chap.'

'What? What chap?'

'Don't know, maid. Never seed 'un before. Nor since.'

4

As it was clear that Obed could not or would not add anything, Rosalind continued on her way, thinking about what he had said and looking forward to discussing it with Alice. About half a mile down the lane she saw Mr Henry Suckbitch ahead of her, ambling towards Moon's Ottery in his usual appreciative way, contemplating the bright green landscape and stopping from time to time to make a note or do a quick sketch. He had probably not been anywhere in particular, just for a walk. He was the only man in the valley who went for walks. Rosalind knew his habits as he was friendly with her father, though some years younger.

He was a gentleman, but he inspired none of the hostility among the poorer members of the community that the Drewes, Mr Rolle and occasionally even Mr Hall did. It was plain to all that he neither mistrusted nor feared those who had no property and little money and who were therefore, according to the rest of the gentry, potential trouble-makers. Lurid stories frequently got through from other parts of the country about the insolent deeds of what Toby Rolle, with a naughty laugh, referred to as the many-headed monster, but Mr Suckbitch had a one-person-one-head attitude to life which his peers did not share, and his mild unquestioning goodwill would have remained constant even if there had been more to fear than there was. In fact in a valley where there were few masterless men, few vagrants and a great deal of wealth and charity things were relatively placid.

In spite of his general acceptability, Mr Suckbitch was something of a puzzle. In the first place there was his name. He came of a very old family and in itself it was a good name, or so Mrs Mutter, who was enthusiastic and quite reliable about good names, used frequently to tell her daughters. But Mr Suckbitch's version of it tended to embarrass people; it certainly embarrassed his relations. His was the authentic form of course. The legend – never mentioned nor apparently thought of by Mr Suckbitch himself – was that Cyrus, King of Prussia, had come across the founder of the line in a wood sucking a bitch. In modern times, however, the family, while contented with their origins, preferred to modify the name. All over East Devon there were Sokespitches, Sucpatches and Sukespices. Some cousins who lived in a tall house in Exeter had gone so far as to change it to Spicer, but this was generally considered to be a sign of weakness. There was only one Suckbitch, Mr Henry Suckbitch of Moon's Ottery.

His attitude to his own wealth set him apart too. At some point his ancestors had been sufficiently rapacious and vigorous to make a great deal of money, and some of the family, the Spicers in particular, still followed in their footsteps, but in Mr Suckbitch's case, though the money remained, the rapacity had departed and the vigour had turned into other channels. This was bound to seem odd in a striving, thriving community like the Otter valley. To be accurate, as Mr Suckbitch himself always endeavoured to be, he did occasionally buy and sell and very occasionally indeed he drove a hard bargain, which startled everybody, but then the ancestral fire would die down as he returned to his natural posture of not knowing what money was, how much he had or where he kept it.

Then there was his attitude to churchgoing which was openly and for no obvious reason reluctant. It was not that he clung to the old faith or shared its allegiances. He was assumed to be protestant and known to be patriotic. Nobody would ever have needed to ask him the famous crucial question: 'If the Pope or the King of Spain landed in England for whom would you fight?' Everyone knew he would fight for the Queen, and bravely too, even if sometimes he paused in the heat of battle to write a note.

He was not an atheist either. Some of the utterances of famous London atheists made their way down to the Otter valley from time to time. One of the most enjoyably scandalous ones was that the father of our Lord Jesus Christ was a pigeon. Mrs Mutter had surreptitiously – giving a new meaning to surreptitious – appreciated this remark, partly because at heart she was more freethinking than she ever let herself appear and partly because she always felt that God the Holy Ghost was somehow more papistical than either God the Father or God the Son, possibly owing to this very association with the Virgin Mary. But Mr Suckbitch never said anything like that. By temperament he was both reverent and superstitious, and there were far too many noble paintings of the Madonna and Child for him to speak frivolously of the Virgin Birth.

He went to church of course. The fines for non-attendance were by this time exorbitant and though he may not have known how much money he had he knew how much he paid out. In any case he would not have wished to flout society in so open and marked a way. He just grumbled.

In less important matters than religion he acted independently in situations where the rest of the community clung together. Dr Thomas Edwards was a case in point. Mr Suckbitch had enough money to send for Dr Edwards whenever he felt a twinge, but he persistently declared that Dr Edwards was a charlatan and completely unqualified. Strangely, he and Mrs Mutter had agreed on this, though their reasoning was different. 'Doctor,' Mrs Mutter had been used to say. 'He's no more a doctor than you or me.' And in fact, though her comment was based on the purest prejudice, she happened to be right. He was not. Mr Suckbitch always sent for Dr John Woolton who was highly qualified. He had nothing else against Dr Edwards. The Sokespitches, Sucpatches, Sukespices and Spicers, though they employed the doctor, despised him because he fawned on the Courtenays, who were upstarts compared with them, but Mr Suckbitch did not think like that.

'Good morning, Mr Suckbitch.' He had stopped to make a note and Rosalind had caught him up. They had not met since the day of Mrs Mutter's funeral. He swung round towards her, his face radiant with kindness. It was interesting, in view of his

49

ancestry, that he looked like a wolf-dog, a handsome wolf-dog, with a long canine muzzle and expressive intelligent eyes.

'Rosalind,' he said with a habitual slight bleat in his voice which she could not help regarding as a kind of tribute to the sheep who had paid for all. 'How are you, my dear? What a day. Beautiful but too hot. The cows are gasping.'

'But, Mr Suckbitch, it's your ruff.'

He had very good, expensive clothes but he never knew when and how to wear them. The ruff was a case in point. It was perfectly suitable for him, as a country gentleman, to have put one on but there were alternatives more appropriate to a June day.

'What about your plain turned-down collar?'

'My plain turned-down collar is badly frayed.'

'But surely Mrs Bradbeer. . . .'

'I didn't notice in time to give it to her.'

Of course it was impertinent of Rosalind to interrogate a gentleman about his clothes, but Mr Suckbitch was beaming. She had observed as a child that he rather liked impudence. It relieved him of the initiative in conversation and was a form of personal attention which he liked but was too gentle to demand in other guises.

'I'm going to Mrs Clapp's.'

'How very purposeful of you, Rosalind,' he said faintly.

'Aunt Martha is the *primum mobile.*'

They strolled along in the warm scented air. Rosalind felt very comfortable and continued showing off.

'As I came down the lane I was thinking about Copernicus.'

'Were you really?' Rosalind realized that this was no idle enquiry designed to keep the conversation going, but a plea for accuracy.

'No, I wasn't really. But I am now.'

She realized, too, that she could wait for ever for Mr Suckbitch to ask her specifically what she was, either previously or at that moment, thinking about Copernicus, so she put on her quoting voice.

' "In the centre of it all rests the sun." It's one of my favourite sayings. And the valley this morning makes me think of it. Why doesn't everybody believe it? It seems so obvious.'

'But my dear girl, you're only believing it poetically. Or rhetorically. You're not believing it scientifically. You've got to get it right. What you mean is the valley is bathed in sun. You like the look and feel of it, it affects you, and so the sun seems central to you. You're not thinking about what actually goes round what. Out there.'

He had paused to deliver this, very welcome, little lecture. They strolled on again.

'But we have to believe our senses, Mr Suckbitch, our experiences, surely. We can't wait to look through a telescope before saying anything.'

'Oh, yes, I think we can.'

'Mr Suckbitch, I want to ask you something. You know it says in the Bible that Joshua commanded the sun to stand still. Well, if it doesn't move anyway, why did he, and how could it?'

'You'd better ask Mr Hall.'

'I did. He said it was a miracle. "*Credo quia impossibile est*", he said. I told Mother and she said he ought to know about miracles, as it was a miracle he'd held his living through three reigns.'

'Dear Jane. I can hear her. But it doesn't quite meet the point.'

'No, I know. I asked Mr Rolle, too.'

'And what did Toby have to say?'

'He said that the Holy Ghost realized that the many-headed monster had to have the facts simplified for its imperfect understanding. Now, what do *you* think?'

'It's straightforward. Joshua really could lengthen the day. Making the sun stand still is just a way of putting it.' He paused impressively. 'Joshua was a magus.'

Rosalind knew where she was. Mr Suckbitch was a friend of Dr John Dee, whom he admired when hardly anybody else did and supported through fortune and misfortune. He admired him as a mathematician to the extent of using the new plus, minus and equal symbols in his own, non-mathematical, writing; he had managed to work all three into the letter of condolence he sent to Farmer Mutter. He believed John Dee to be a true magician and maintained that he used his powers benevolently and summoned angels not devils. He had had a public dispute about it with the vicar in the churchyard after morning service. He and Mr Hall were normally on the best of terms and had much in common in a society where they were superior in education to the yeomen who were also their friends. But Mr Suckbitch could not bear to have Dr Dee maligned and spoke up for him peevishly and at quite unnecessary length; rather illogically some people thought, as the lethargy and reluctance of his public worship suggested that to him a devil and an angel were all one. Mrs Mutter had been pleased to have the vicar confronted: 'That Mr Hall'; though she had added impartially: 'That Mr Suckbitch', an automatic response as in fact she got on very well with him. Rosalind now put on her hostess voice.

'Have you heard from Dr Dee, Mr Suckbitch?' At this time Dr Dee was on the Continent.

'I had a letter this morning. Poor John, he thinks that England is no place for a magus. But he intends to come back some day all the same.'

'But he was in danger here, wasn't he?'

'So are a great many people, more people than not, probably. Priests. Witches. The Queen. Courtiers. All of us if the Spaniards win. Spaniards, if they don't.' He looked into space and blinked between examples, as though he was reading from notes or mentally making them. 'Spies,' he added.

'But what about those two Spanish doctors in Exeter? They're very popular. A lot of people employ them.'

'Oh, well, they're properly qualified. That's the main thing. They studied at Salamanca. They know how to use their qualifications too. They're clever men. And sick people realize better than most of us that it's no good hallooing till you're out of the wood. It's certainly no good shouting Spaniards while you're flat on your back with sciatica.'

They had reached the end of the lane. Mrs Drewe was crossing the village green as she had been on the day of Mrs Mutter's death. Rosalind reflected that she could count on the fingers of one hand the times she had seen the village green when Mrs Drewe was not crossing it.

'Good morning, Henry,' she said in a normal conversational tone. 'There's something I wanted to discuss with you some time.' Then turning to Rosalind she shouted, 'Let me know if there's anything I can do, Rosalind,' and moved on.

'What do you suppose she had in mind, Mr Suckbitch? Raising the dead?' Rosalind said as soon as they were out of earshot.

Mr Suckbitch gave the first two notes of his guinea-fowl laugh, then thought better of it. He put his hand lightly on Rosalind's shoulder and they arrived at Mrs Clapp's gate at the same time as she did. She had been on a herb-gathering expedition and was looking as cheerful as if the plague had broken out. She carried a bunch of mixed plants, collected from the various ditches, coppices and water-meadows of the neighbourhood.

The white witch ignored Mr Suckbitch. He had unintentionally given her a fright a few evenings before by singing, which he frequently did when out walking, if not in church. Mrs Clapp had heard him on a winding footpath as she was plodding confidently home after attending the birth of a stillborn baby. She said she thought it was footpads though why footpads would be singing at their work she did not explain. Now, having once got the idea of footpads into her head, with however little foundation, it would be weeks before she could dissociate Mr Suckbitch from them. She cordially invited Rosalind to come inside. Mr Suckbitch said he would wait and Rosalind followed Mrs Clapp into the cottage, through the clematis which hung low on the porch and flicked insects into her face.

When Rosalind was a child she had spent a great deal of time in the dim redolent cluttered room that was half workshop and half parlour. Mrs Clapp seemed to like having her just sitting there while she prepared her herbs and Rosalind found it peaceful to do so. She had some wonderful recipes in which

Rosalind at that time was more interested than in her mother's cooking. One way of preparing thistle, for example, was to boil it in the urine of a healthy baby boy. Then there was darnel which had to be cooked in wine with pigeon's dung and linseed. Costmary was baked with oil and adder's tongue. Sometimes the plants were just seethed in white wine and that smelled light and wholesome, but the prevailing smell in the cottage was always that of the urine of the healthy baby boy. As a matter of fact, like all cooks and chemists, Mrs Clapp occassionally cheated. Some evenings a boy, healthy no doubt but not a baby, could be seen coming up from the petty school with a bucket.

This time Rosalind did not stay long, as Mrs Clapp always kept plentiful supplies of arrach in the form of a syrup. As she stepped out into the sunshine and fresh air Mrs Clapp called helpfully after her: 'And tell Aunt Martha, dear, to be sure to keep her little front parlour warm.'

'Well,' thought Rosalind, 'at least you do keep parlours warm.'

Mr Suckbitch was standing a few feet away and looking at her with a puzzled expression, which could not have been caused by Mrs Clapp's remark. He knew her too well.

'Mr Suckbitch,' Rosalind said when they were on the green again, 'you were looking quite startled as I came out of the house. What happened?'

'Nothing. *You* startled me for the moment, standing in front of that cosy pretty cottage with all that clematis round the porch. You looked so out of place.'

Normally such a remark would have pleased Rosalind immensely. A realistic girl at heart, she had no doubt that she was her parents' child, but to be taken for a changeling, a stolen princess, a hop out of kin, too bright and beautiful for Moon's Ottery – and by a man of the world too – would have been most gratifying had she felt in her usual spirits, but since her mother's death she had not been robust and every comment seemed an attack. Her eyes filled with tears.

Mr Suckbitch was distressed and surprised, not unreasonably.

He never considered what effect his remarks or behaviour might have and so sometimes gave unintentional offence, but thorough premeditation might well have persuaded him that this speech would cause no pain.

'Rosalind. It isn't a criticism, you know. Far from it. Far, far from it,' he repeated earnestly and with such manifest sincerity that Rosalind's confidence was quite restored.

'But Mr Suckbitch, I was born here, I live here. Where would I be *in* place?'

'I'm not sure yet. I'll think about it and let you know.' He actually made a note.

'Mr Suckbitch, what do *you* think Mother died of? Everybody says something different, but they don't really want to know. Mrs Drewe says it was an influence.'

'Well, it doesn't seem to have influenced anybody else' – they both smiled at the play on words – 'which rather goes against the theory. I can see you really do want to find out and I think it might help you. Shall I ask John Woolton for you? I'll be seeing him soon. I expect I know all the relevant facts.'

'You probably don't know that she was down by the river the evening before, in the mist. Talking to a strange man,' Rosalind added without in the least meaning to. 'Oh, yes please, do ask Dr Woolton.'

Mr Suckbitch looked attentively at her for a moment and made another note, presumably something like 'Ask J.W. about J.M.' He then said the kindest of goodbyes and set off home. The house that the sheep had paid for was called Moons and stood at a bend of the hill that wound up to the common.

That night when the girls were in their bedroom Rosalind started to tell Alice about her conversation with Mr Suckbitch.

'Oh, Rozzy, I do wish you wouldn't look like that when you talk about Mr Suckbitch.'

'Like what?'

'Oh, I don't know. Like a bright-eyed chicken. It's something about the way you hold your head.'

Rosalind went cold with fury, but she could not flounce out as the only way to flounce was through Mr Mutter's bedroom.

In any case she wanted to tell Alice the other conversation. Sulkily, she started to recount it and her sister's eager interest made her forget her rage. They indulged in speculations which had to be preposterous as in a valley like theirs the presence of a complete stranger, or rather somebody who was a stranger to everybody but their mother, was beyond the scope of reasonable explanation.

'Perhaps it was the Angel Gabriel,' said Alice at last.

'But he wouldn't have been announcing anything to Mother.'

'Perhaps he was giving her a message for Mary How. Mary Lock. She's pregnant.'

'How do you know?'

'She told me. She did this.' Alice gestured.

'She meant she'd got colic.'

'No. Then she did this.' Alice rocked an implausible baby.

'There you are. Colic. Babies are always getting it. They're known for it.'

'Listen. John and Mary are coming to work here. It was Aunt Martha's idea apparently.'

'Why should she want them to come here?'

' 'Tisn't what you wants for yourself 'tis what others need.' Alice was a startlingly good mimic. 'I promised Jane,' she added.

'She didn't.'

'No, of course she didn't. But you know Aunt Martha. She wouldn't get up in the morning unless she'd made a deathbed promise about it. As a matter of fact it'll suit her very well. She can look down on them. She thinks they're batty.'

'Mother did say something that – that morning. When everybody was making such a noise in the hall. About there being two voices less.'

'She was joking.'

'Yes, I know. But she may have said the same thing in front of Aunt Martha, and now she's choosing to take it as Holy Writ.'

'That'll be it. But wouldn't she laugh now, Rozzy? It'll be one more voice if Mary has triplets.'

'John, tell they girls not to keep you awake with their chatter and giggling.' Aunt Martha was banging on their father's door. Sounds in the background indicated that she had disturbed Nicholas and Margaret who were making the most of it.

'I was asleep,' said Mr Mutter.

Alice blew out the candle.

5

THAT summer at Sparkhayes was the most painful that Alice and Rosalind were ever to know. It was their first experience of bereavement – they had never known their dead brothers – and they had no idea what to expect, that is, Rosalind did have ideas but they turned out to be quite wrong. She had imagined, mostly on the strength of her reading, that grief was straightforward and recognizable, and on the whole dignified. 'And Sir Launcelot awoke and took his horse, and rode all that day and all night in a forest, weeping.' She found instead that it was more like restlessness and fear and anger, and that it took the form of petty anxieties and resentments.

Their father could not help. His brief heyday of fortitude changed to fretful resignation. He began to suffer from palpitations and pains in the chest and he tried to transfer his dependence on his wife to his daughters. As July and August went by he looked more and more to them for company and emotional support. The first they were prepared to give him, though they would rather have been on their own. They rode with him in the cart when he went on business trips, sometimes as far as Exeter, but these were not childish jaunts any more. The girls had become, overnight, responsible equals, soon to be superiors if Mr Mutter had his way. Emotional support they could not give him, especially as they realized they would get nothing in return but fond and blind reliance, but they did pity him and they did truly try to be kind. Day after day they saw him building up a myth of their ability to cope with the world and particularly with men. Not that he minimized the dangers that awaited nubile women; if anything he exaggerated them, but he liked to think of his daughters as experienced women where romantic approaches were concerned, able to discriminate, able to look after themselves. If either of them made some brash remark to this effect, even such a silly commonplace as 'I know men', he treasured it and repeated it, though it clearly sprang from crass ignorance. Heaven knew where and how they were supposed to have acquired their expertise. Nothing could have been further from the truth. From the day of his wife's death he never gave his daughters a word of advice, not even when they specifically asked him, which they did at first, till they saw how useless it was.

He got into the habit of surveying them with melancholy affection while quoting a text from the Bible: 'A threefold cord is not easily broken.' They were quite used to hearing practical statements from the Bible, about domestic or agricultural matters, being invested with deep spiritual relevance, but this became unbearable. In their bedroom conversations Alice and Rosalind suggested to each other various uses of threefold cords which had nothing to do with family affection, but even bedroom conversations were not safe any more. Mr Mutter would come into their room and just stand about sucking his teeth while they thought up some way of, as it seemed to them, tactfully getting rid of him.

He had always got on quite well with Aunt Martha, regarding her as a necessary adjunct of his beloved Jane, but now that Jane was not there for them both to lean on their relationship deteriorated fast. He became afraid of her increasing shrewishness. He disliked Nicholas, too; perhaps he had suffered from his wife's infatuation as much as his daughters had. 'Poor spoiled child,' he kept saying to them, and he seemed to think it would do Nicholas good to go into the army, but as Nicholas was only five it was rather a long-term suggestion.

Aunt Martha was not equal to her new situation. She appreciated the fact of her improved position in society, and intermittently gave herself airs about it, but did not know how to deal with those who worked at Sparkhayes, indoors and outdoors, as Mrs Mutter had done. Jane Mutter had not been born to command but she had learnt, fast probably, and had become an excellent mistress of a household, lively, amusing and confident, and, in spite of her bracing remarks, essentially considerate. Aunt Martha veered from clownish familiarity to what she would have called haughtiness but what everybody else would have called plain bad manners.

It did not matter too much as she had little real authority and Devonians love to have a foe, but in fact she alienated everybody, including Praise-the-Lord. He was cleverer than anybody in his mode of retaliation. Whenever he saw her coming he feigned intense alarm, threw up his paws, bushed up his tail and fled. He was a highly theatrical cat. This infuriated Aunt Martha and indeed was most unjust, as although she had no sympathy with him she would not have ill-treated him.

It never crossed the minds of Alice and Rosalind that Aunt Martha could have been grieving. In later life it crossed their minds but they never really believed it. In the weeks that followed their mother's death, they suffered, naturally, when they came across her things lying about – the half-sewn dress, the unfinished knitting – and these glimpses ended in tears, but to see her possessions being handled disrespectfully by Aunt Martha made them rage with an anger that frightened them. Rosalind could not bear, in particular, her aunt's rough and ready treatment of a preserving pan which Mrs Mutter had been proud of and which was a beautiful object. Once Aunt Martha had even let Nicholas piss into it. It was raining and he had been whining about going outside.

The arrival of William and Mary Lock to join the household created a diversion. They were given the room on the ground floor beyond the parlour. It was a kind of store room but quite big. They would be the only two of Farmer Mutter's employees, except old Joan, to live in. All his labourers had property of their own and however small their cottages and pieces of land they considered themselves and were considered by everybody else to be thoroughly free men, which accounted for much of the tranquillity of work at Sparkhayes.

In different ways the newcomers were a success from the first. Mary was to replace old Joan; at least she was not actually a replacement as Joan would stay on, having been there since before Mr Mutter's marriage. She had not been up to the work for years. Day after day she sat in the chimney corner. She had been there on the day that Mrs Mutter had been taken ill, though she had not reacted to the event at all. It was impossible to tell whether she enjoyed life or not. The lines on her face all turned up which made her look unreasonably happy, but as Rosalind sometimes reflected, the fish that were brought up from the Otter often looked as though they were grinning. But happy or sad, everyone treated her kindly, there being no call to do otherwise, and close by the fire she would sit till her dying day.

'It's a pity the English don't believe in funeral pyres,' said Alice to Rosalind, 'then when the right moment came they could just tip her on.'

'I say,' said Mr Rolle jauntily to the girls on another occasion, 'I'd like Phil Sidney to see old Joan. She'd really prove his point.'

'Which point, Mr Rolle?' asked Alice with polite indifference.

'That poets can tempt children from play and old people from the chimney corner,' said Rosalind.

Mr Rolle, who seldom welcomed the right answer from anybody and never from girls whom he did not consider pretty, looked rather put out.

The idea had been that Mary was to work indoors, but Obed suggested that she might try her hand at milking, and offered to teach her. It was an inspiration. She was led out, sulky and frightened, early one morning to Button, the most docile cow on the farm. Alice and Rosalind stood quietly in attendance and the lesson began. Within a week the helplessness with which she first laid her cheek against the cow's flank had changed to the relaxation of competence and sympathy, and she used to come back across the yard carrying her pails with a deportment worthy of the Three Wise Men.

William's transformation was equally striking though it came about in a different way. His wedding and all the entertainment it had provided, as well as the fact that he was now employed at Sparkhayes, had made him of some account in the community, and it occurred to the defence volunteers during one of their sessions at the inn after an evening's drilling that William could be enlisted to help man the beacon. If he could not speak or hear he could see perfectly well and, with practice, would no doubt become as handy with the tinder-box in a high wind as anybody else. Moreover the beacon was nearer to Sparkhayes than to any other farm. There were only two difficulties. The first was to get his new employer's consent, but Farmer Mutter agreed at once. The second was to explain to William what was required of him. Two of the men from Buckhayes, Zachary Gollop and Joseph Priddy, took this task upon themselves.

The next evening Mr Hall who was working in his garden heard raucous laughter coming from the village pond and hurried out, spade still in hand, fearful that William, whom he had noticed earlier approaching the green, was being baited. He met quite a different scene: Zachary Gollop and Joseph Priddy were propelling resolute-looking bits of branch along the water, pausing at intervals to mime approaching danger and the consequent lighting of a warning beacon. Their intentions were perfectly serious but they could not help clowning, and the laughter, which turned out to be entirely jovial, was being directed at them and not at William, who had risen from his hunkers, a position from which he had been used to begin any encounter, and was watching with pardonable mystification but apparent enjoyment.

Mr Suckbitch approached the group. In recent weeks he had come down the hill and into the village far oftener than had been his custom and seemed to have a keener eye than usual for who was about. On this occasion he hesitated, communed with himself as though making a vital mathematical calculation, then entered the inn and returned escorting a tray with tankards of ale on it.

'Noah,' he said, catching sight of Mr Hall leaning on his spade in the background. All except William grinned into their ale. It was considered uncouth to laugh openly at a parson, but Noah was felt to be an amusing name and indeed it was inappropriate to Mr Hall in several ways, though it did suit his ability to keep afloat in killing waters. Zachary and Joseph explained their plan to the two gentlemen, who both looked benevolently at William.

'Are you sure he's understood?' asked the vicar.

'I know,' said Mr Suckbitch, 'I'll mention it to Rosalind Mutter.' There were more grins into the ale which he did not appear to notice; he was jotting down something. 'She and Alice can make sure. We don't want,' he added in an undertone to his friend, 'William setting fire to things whenever he sees Zachary and Joseph, or a stretch of water, or a few twigs.'

'Come into the house, Henry. I'd like your opinion about some malmsey that arrived this morning.'

The two unmarried men moved off together, one looking like a celibate, the other like a bachelor, and turned into the vicarage.

Alice and Rosalind took considerable pains to make sure that William understood, and soon he could be seen doing long turns of duty up at the beacon, staring devotedly to the south-west at the hill where the fire would spring up that he was to send on its way across the country. In his increasingly brief absences from the beacon he worked on the farm and here too he came into his own for men working in different fields need as many gestures as though they were dumb and their fellow labourers deaf.

So the Locks settled in, and only one problem remained: some of their personal habits. William was discovered pissing into the chimney. It is true he was using the side opposite to old Joan's feet but the practice was pronounced by all to be unhealthy and Obed taught him better ways while the girls undertook the re-education of Mary, introducing her to the privy that stood over the stream behind the house. Here again she learnt quickly. 'She's taking to it like a duck to water,' Alice remarked to Rosalind.

August wore on. The sun was still hot but autumn was in the air.

'Here comes your swain, Rozzy,' called Alice to her sister one morning. Rosalind was out in the kitchen making a spinach tart from a recipe given her by Mrs Bradbeer, Mr Suckbitch's house-keeper, who had been encouraging the girl in her cooking for some time past, having noticed both her interest and her potential talent. Mrs Mutter had been pleased by these attentions for Mrs Bradbeer had belonged to some of the best households in England, including Lord Burghley's, before widowhood and a longing for her native country had brought her to Moon's Ottery. From Mrs Bradbeer Rosalind had learnt the vital lesson that when confronted with a new recipe you double the ingredients, halve the number of people it is supposed to satisfy and that makes it just about right. Unfortunately she was still at the stage of occasionally doubling the flavouring as well, and whereas this particular recipe diffidently suggested a dash of rosewater she had lavishly poured in a ladleful, so that the ground floor of the farmhouse was redolent of high June and not even Aunt Martha's wintry glare – for she was jealous of Mrs Bradbeer and thought spinach tarts were affected – could dispel the heady whiffs.

The atmosphere was at its most fraught when Obed came clumping through the cross passage from the front courtyard to the small one at the back. 'Summer is icumen in,' he suddenly sang as he passed the hall door. Everybody jumped. No one had ever heard Obed sing before and the effect was not soothing in general, though Rosalind, appreciating his grasp of the situation and his wish to give support, giggled gratefully.

Alice repeated her remark and as the tart was now ready for the oven Rosalind came into the hall and glanced out of the window in time to see the tall broad-shouldered figure of Mr Suckbitch appearing and reappearing in the gaps of the hedge that bordered their front field. Rosalind scowled at Alice. Aunt Martha scowled at Rosalind.

'Now, Alice, don't be putting they silly ideas into Rozzy's head. She'm only a little girl. 'Tis me Mr Suckbitch'll be coming to see more like.'

Mr Suckbitch disappeared behind the cowshed on his way to the lower entrance to the farm. At this moment another figure rounded the corner into the lane. It looked like one of the

Pulman brothers and he seemed to be holding something behind his back.

'Here comes *your* swain, Alice,' said Rosalind.

'Now, Rozzy, don't tease your sister. They Pulman brothers've got a fine farm. We all have our little ways. Alice could do worse.'

'Well,' said Rosalind as Aunt Martha bridled her way into the passage, 'I suppose they won't declare their own impediments. Which one is it? If you can tell the difference.'

'As a matter of fact,' said Alice without looking out again, 'it's *Dick* Pulman.'

So it was. Dick Pulman was of course a Pulman brother, but he was never so called. He was the elder brother of the impediment-declarers. He was twenty-two and the owner of Sweethayes, a farm adjacent to theirs, which they had inherited from their father. He had been left his by an uncle and was making a great success of it.

'Why ever doesn't he do something about those two loonies?'

'Well, he's very worried,' said Alice with a proprietorial air.

'Does Aunt Martha really think you'd marry one of the loonies?'

'Oh, do stop calling them loonies. Yes, I expect so.'

Rosalind went on glancing. Dick Pulman reappeared, making for Obed Hosegood's cottage on the door of which he knocked. This was not surprising. Obed was friend and adviser to many of the young farmers in the valley. His agricultural lore was impressive and he was generous in praising the crops and cattle of others when they rivalled his and Farmer Mutter's. By this time Mr Suckbitch was crossing the cobbles to the front door.

'Good morning, Mrs Pook. Is Rosalind at home?'

'Yes.' Aunt Martha's tone was so rude that she might just as well have said, 'Where d'you suppose 'er'd be at this time of day, you great gawk?' In fact Mr Suckbitch answered as if she had said precisely that.

'I thought perhaps she might have gone down to Mrs Clapp's.'

There was a tingling silence while Aunt Martha wrung as

many kinds of offence as she could out of this remark. Even Mr Suckbitch noticed something was wrong.

'What a beautiful smell,' he commented with peaceful intent.

He was not a chatty man and it was unlikely that he would be led on to speeches about Mrs Bradbeer and spinach tarts but Rosalind could bear it no longer and came out of the hall.

'Good morning, Rosalind. I came to ask you a favour. I need your advice.'

Aunt Martha, wordlessly exclaiming, 'Favour! Advice!' went back into the hall and the air cleared.

'Shall we go for a walk, Mr Suckbitch?' Rosalind suggested dashingly.

They went up to the top gate and into the footpath that led up to Beacon Hill where against the sky the competently stacked pile of wood was standing ready with its protective cover neatly pegged down, and beside it William Lock. He was slewed to the south-west like a steady weathercock, but they guessed he could see them out of the corner of his eye and waved. Without changing direction he replied heartily with both arms, either because he was in exuberant mood or in recognition of the fact that there were two of them.

> 'Too soon he climbed into the flaming car
> Whose want of skill did set the earth on fire.'

Mr Suckbitch had by now as much confidence as anyone that William would set fire to the right thing when the time came. The gloom of the quotation, as Rosalind realized, was indicative of his own feelings at the moment.

'I do pray,' she said, 'that when the Spanish fleet arrives, it'll be William up at the beacon.'

'That's too easy, Rosalind. Is William ever not up at the beacon? Couldn't you pray that the Armada doesn't sail at all?'

'You think it will?'

'I'm convinced it will. Not this year perhaps.'

They clambered on. Praise-the-Lord, to whom going for a walk was as much a novelty as it was for Rosalind, stalked beside them, smooth, impersonal and relentless.

'Praise-the-Lord looks as though he's escorting traitors to the Tower.'

'Farther than the Tower,' said Mr Suckbitch. 'He's all in black.'

The walk did not last long. They sat down on a warm bank above Sparkhayes while the birds shouted and the flies grumbled. Praise-the-Lord changed his act and rolled over on his back and chewed his tail in the character of an engaging kitten. Rosalind humoured him, but he soon collapsed in the stretched-out sleep that he kept for the hottest days of the year.

'Oh, dear,' moaned Mr Suckbitch.

'My Lord, alas, what means your woeful tale?' Rosalind was in her element. She had an idea that the original said 'Madam' but she felt that some adaptation was justifiable.

'It's Mrs Drewe,' replied Mr Suckbitch inadequately. 'She wants me to get up a pageant for Accession Day.'

The Queen had been on the throne for twenty-nine years but the heart had by no means gone out of the celebration. Rosalind remembered it from early childhood as a festival to be placed beside Christmas Day and Easter Sunday, exciting and radiant.

'Oh, we haven't had a pageant for years. Last time it was bell-ringing and the usual holiday things. Hurling. Dancing.'

'And an endless sermon.'

'Sermons can't be too long for me. When Mr Hall turns over the hourglass it means another stretch of time to myself. But I do listen to the texts. Last year it was "The meek shall inherit the earth". Not very appropriate to Queen Elizabeth.'

'But extremely appropriate to Mr Hall. That's probably the best way to compose a sermon.'

'Mrs Drewe was in London for Accession Day last year. She went to the Tilts. She's never stopped talking about it. Them. The expression that came over her Majesty's face when, oh I can't remember, something or other.'

'Well, now she feels her place is in Moon's Ottery. Perhaps she wants to take our minds off the invasion.'

'Bread and circuses. She doesn't seem prepared to organize it. Them.'

'She's paying for the bread and circuses, Rosalind. The Drewes made their money honestly, and they're generous with it.'

'Oh, yes,' said Rosalind perfunctorily, 'the poor.' She was longing to get on to the subject of the pageant but Mr Suckbitch had not finished his corrective lecture.

'I know they keep going up to London.'

'And Bristol. They went to Bristol for the Progress.'

'But they bring back ideas.'

'More than they take anyway. Honestly, Mr Suckbitch, I'm not running them down. And I do want to hear about the pageant, but I don't see the difficulty. You've seen pageants and plays, really good ones. You've seen *Gorboduc*.' Rosalind spoke reverently.

'I've seen *Gorboduc* seven times.' Mr Suckbitch sounded resentful. 'It was so successful they included it in the court repertory and now every time I go up there I happen to coincide with it.'

He brooded for a while and then suddenly broke out.

'O heavens send down the flames of your revenge.
Destroy I say with flash of wreakful fire
The traitor son and then the wretched sire.'

Mr Suckbitch's spirits were rising. As he declaimed he raised his hand in a gesture appropriate to one urging heaven to send down vengeful flames. It was a grand gesture and William up at the beacon saw it and responded, with one arm this time. Mr Suckbitch reorganized his sternly invoking fingers into a waggle of friendly greeting. Rosalind laughed.

'One of the difficulties,' Mr Suckbitch continued, his spirits temporarily sinking again, 'is lack of material. Mrs Drewe thinks a pageant simply about the Queen would be rather strained and I must say I agree with her. And we can't have poor Sir Philip Sidney's funeral again. She thinks some local history. But nothing has ever happened in Moon's Ottery.'

There they sat, Rosalind thinking of Mr Suckbitch's last words. Suddenly she turned to him and put her hand on his arm. His sleeve seemed to be empty. She had noticed from childhood that sometimes he had arms in his sleeves, sometimes not. It did not depend on his goodwill but on how stalwart he was feeling. The prospect of the pageant had reduced him utterly.

'Mr Suckbitch, we'll make a virtue of necessity. We'll take the theme "Moon's Ottery was spared". You see. The Black Death. Mr Courtenay's blockade of Exeter. The Vikings. They all passed us by.'

'By a fairly wide margin in the case of the Vikings.' But he was already looking more hopeful.

'Oh, no, they went up the Severn.'

'And what about the Romans? And the Normans? I spoke too soon. They didn't pass us by. What about the name of this village?'

'Oh, we can say that we were spared any evil they might have inflicted. The historians,' said Rosalind happily, 'agree that the Romans saved us from barbarism. Anyway,' she added practically, 'we'll be able to find enough incidents to make up a pageant somehow.'

'Rosalind. You've saved the situation. Now. Will you help me write the words?'

'Poetry?'

'Certainly poetry.'

'Indeed I will. One thing, it's not till November.'

They parted, both in better spirits than when they had met. As Rosalind was entering the farm again she saw Dick Pulman still talking to Obed. It had been as long a consultation as theirs but was obviously coming to a close so she joined them. She now saw what Dick had been holding behind his back, a magnificent clothful of cherries, finer than any they grew at Sparkhayes. He held them out, blushing and blinking.

'Rozzy. I wonder if you'd mind giving these to Alice. I thought she'd like them.'

'Can't you give them to Alice yourself, Dick? She's in the house.'

The words could have been kind but her tone was not.

'Well, I thought. I mean. I'm sorry.'

Dick Pulman was a good-looking, good-humoured young man. His expression began to affect Rosalind and when she looked down at the cherries they disarmed her completely. They were paradisal: large, beautiful and innocent.

'Yes, of course I will, Dick, they're lovely. I'll take them to Alice right away. They're the most beautiful cherries I've seen this year. I'm sure she'll like them. They're lovely.'

'So they be,' agreed Obed heartily. 'We'm past summer here. Except in the kitchen.'

Dick missed the allusion, but took himself happily off, tripping over a cobblestone.

'There was no call to take the lad up sharp like that, Rozzy.'

'I'm not a go-between, Obed.'

'Silly little maid. Such airs and graces.' He paused, then without seeming to move his head glanced up at the grassy bank. 'Alice can have a friend as well as you, can't her?'

'Dear, tactful Obed,' thought Rosalind. He was astute enough to have caught the atmosphere of her conversation with Mr Suckbitch even from afar and she was sure he knew as well as she did that there was a world of difference between that discussion and the bashful presentation of a bunch of cherries; by a third party moreover.

6

THAT was the last sunny day for weeks. The weather broke and the light faded. There was mud everywhere. Obed laid cinder paths across the courtyard to the outbuildings, and Alice and Rosalind put down rushes in the cross passage. The harvest was one of the poorest anybody could remember. The grass died back sooner than usual and people started looking forward to the Michaelmas goose at least half a month before they normally did.

Now that the brightness had gone out of the season, Rosalind felt that her mother had really left Sparkhayes. The girl had always been particularly susceptible to grey weather: the days when the candles were lit earlier than usual and indeed should never have been extinguished. This autumn she started going for walks alone, seemingly in search of her mother, for she always took the road that led down to the river. It was quite easy to keep these walks from Aunt Martha. Rosalind's technique was to make a great show of carrying buttermilk from the dairy across the courtyard to the pigsty, which involved leaving the house dressed for outdoors, and then slip away, hoping her aunt would assume she was engaged somewhere else on some other chore.

One grey morning when the rain had stopped for a while and the air was mellow and disturbing she returned to Sparkhayes to find her sister making candles.

'Alice, do I look ill?'

'Dreadful,' said Alice, not even looking up from the candles. 'All white.'

The heartlessness of this overwhelmed Rosalind with fury and self-pity. If she had been all white it would have been serious. She might have been going to die. And Alice had not even bothered to look. Rosalind's silence at length made her sister raise her head.

'Rozzy, you're all red. Have you hurt yourself? Sit down.'

'I've just seen the Pulman brothers.'

'What do you mean?' Alice sat down herself.

'Down by the river. They were kissing and embracing and – and –'

'All right.'

'But isn't there a law against it? What would happen to them?'

'Well, worse than to Robert Abbott.'

'They're in terrible danger.' Rosalind burst into sobs.

'If you don't shut up, we'll have Aunt Martha out here. Then there'll be two more people in terrible danger. Listen, Rozzy. Nobody in the valley's going to tell on them. A lot of people haven't even twigged. They think all the carry-on at weddings is just daftness. Look at Aunt Martha, going on about their little ways.'

'*I* used to think they were just being daft.'

'Yes, but Rozzy, you do see things when they're under your nose.'

'You knew.'

'Dick told me. At least he didn't exactly tell me. Now look, love, why don't you get on with your pageant. The dinner's well under way. I can say you helped me with the candles. Look, I'll make you a new pen.'

Basking in Alice's kindness, Rosalind watched her sister make her a new pen, which she did not really need. Leaving the candles, Alice found the penknife – usually the most difficult part of the process – chose a strong clean goose quill from their store and deftly scraped and cut it. Rosalind went off to write her pageant, feeling better though still overwrought.

The trouble had started the night before. Just as the family were going up to bed. Rosalind had heard Praise-the-Lord yelling in such a horrifying way that she thought he must be caught in a trap or that a fox was tearing him apart. She rushed out. It was brilliant moonlight and there he was sitting on the wall by the pigsty comfortably giving a full-blooded imitation of a damned soul, with not a snare or an enemy in sight. She might have known. He stopped when he saw her, poured himself off the wall and curled round her ankles in his impersonation of man's most affectionate friend. Then he went indoors.

She walked to the gate and leaned on it. The sheep were in the front field and were due to be for the next few days. They were supposed not to hear the church bells from the same field twice running: an unnecessarily poetic warning against overgrazing, Mr Suckbitch, who could afford to be down to earth about sheep, used to say. There seemed to be more of them than usual tonight, a great sea of rounded and pulsating bodies in the moonlight, and there was a sound of munching and tearing like waves on shingle. All of a sudden Rosalind was filled with terror and wanted to scream at them, 'You're going to die. You're going to die. Perhaps you're going to die tomorrow.' She imagined them leaving their sweet field of contentment for the last time and going to the noisy horrors of slaughter. She had no reason to suppose this would be so, though the time for autumn killing was drawing near. She did not know her father's immediate plans for them. And she was ashamed that she felt no relief when they were all there next day.

Working at the pageant was indeed a great help. She had first suggested the theme 'Moon's Ottery was spared' in a facile way. Mr Suckbitch had appealed to her to provide a solution to an undeniable problem and she had been determined to say something, however ill-considered, but now she was becoming seriously involved. Indeed she was dreaming about it. She and Mr Suckbitch had frequent consultations.

'If you don't mind, Rosalind, I think it would be best if you kept in the background.'

'Oh, why?'

'Haven't you suffered enough already from being educated?'

'Oh, I see what you mean. The boys on the village green shouting after us when we went to our lessons, you mean. I didn't know you knew about that. But it was all right for Alice.

They just called "Vennus". Nobody minds being teased about their beautiful figure.'

'In any case I imagine it wasn't only a tribute to her physique. It was probably supposed to be a rich piece of satire on schooling and culture in general, which makes it less personal. But what about yourself?'

'Well, I'm thin, you see.'

'So, didn't they shout anything?'

'Oh, yes, they shouted something. "Squitter-book", they shouted.'

Mr Suckbitch brooded over this and then said mildly, 'Well, we don't want that to happen again, do we?'

'No. I'm too set in my ways now.'

Mr Suckbitch grinned. 'It should be quite easy for you to stay out of sight if you want to. Most of the actors and the audience will think the words wrote themselves by magic anyway. And I'm going to let the funny men make up their own parts.'

'That's usually done in London, isn't it? And do a lot of them want to be funny?'

'A great many. Either humorous Romans or humorous Vikings. Nobody seems to think the Normans were amusing.'

'Mr Rolle will make up his own words, won't he?'

'Oh, yes. I asked him about it yesterday. He'd like to be the Prologue.'

'Typical. First, and all by himself.'

'Rosalind. You don't do him justice.'

'He's never taught you, Mr Suckbitch.'

'You always were a hasting, even as a little girl.' Mr Suckbitch looked at her indulgently. There was no question in the Otter valley of calling people more able or less gifted, as the case might be. You were either a hasting or a harding. You soon found out which and made your plans accordingly. Nobody was too sensitive about it.

'And he never got his degree. *You* did.'

'Not much merit in that, my dear. You know me better. When I put my hand to the plough I don't turn back.'

'But the Bible says that's virtuous behaviour.'

'Yes, but it's not always intelligent. In any case Toby Rolle *can* keep his hand to the plough sometimes. Don't you remember how he mounted that campaign to coerce the waywardens into rebuilding the bridge on the Honiton road?'

'So he did. That's true. And his headaches disappeared completely. But he despises women.' Rosalind was suddenly voicing the resentment of years. 'You must have heard what he's always saying about Mrs Rolle and their marriage. "Nobody else would have stood it." He says it proudly.'

'You make too much of it, Rosalind. I imagine Beatrice Rolle married Toby with her eyes open, and they're still open. She's a wise and spirited woman. I admit he underrates her. But if she doesn't mind – and she doesn't, she just laughs – why should you?'

'No, I suppose not. But he's been suggesting that Mother's illness should have been looked into more closely in case it was infectious. Do you honestly think he would have done that if she'd been a man?'

Mr Suckbitch considered this carefully. 'No,' he said at last, 'no, I'm afraid you're right. I don't think he would.'

'Well, all I hope is there won't be anything about birds in the Prologue. He somehow makes them sound as though they had four legs.'

Rosalind did not feel free to tell Mr Suckbitch about the time outside Mr Rolle's house when Alice had suddenly said, 'Mr Rolle gets his tits mixed up,' timing the remark perfectly so that Rosalind was beginning to giggle just as the door opened.

There was nothing arbitrary about the casting of the play. The village would not have stood for it. Those who wanted to take part were asked what they would like to be. It said a great deal for life in the valley that on the whole everybody wanted to be himself with no fantasies or unfulfilled wishes clouding the issue. Everybody wanted to be herself, too, for women were going to be allowed to appear. Mrs Drewe had stated that it would be perfectly proper. The performance was to be held in the Manor barn and would therefore be private.

Mrs Clapp and Mrs Bash, the latter co-opted from Rawridge

for the occasion, decided to be the nurses in charge of the lazar-house to which victims of the plague, which had struck some less fortunate village than Moon's Ottery, were to be carried. There was some friction about which of them was to be first in command and this was not easy to resolve in a community that believed as firmly in natural order as they disbelieved in any unwarranted assumption of power. What was needed was an authoritative example from history or literature of equality between two commanders but none presented itself to anybody at first.

'God the Father and God the Son on the Holy Ghost's day off,' suggested Alice to Rosalind.

'Castor and Pollux,' suggested Rosalind to Mr Suckbitch, who blinked up at the sky. 'Or Romulus and Remus,' she added more wholeheartedly. 'You should be the one to mention them. Your name, you know. Your ancestor.'

'Dear Rosalind, you surely don't believe that nonsense, either about Romulus and Remus or the first Mr Suckbitch.'

'Why ever not?'

'Does it really seem to you possible that a child brought up by a wolf or a wolf-dog could grow up normal? He wouldn't be able to speak, let alone found a great city. Or make money.'

Mrs Drewe solved the problem. She explained to the warring witches, who were rapidly turning from white to black in the bitterness of the controversy, that it was like the triumvirate that ruled Rome after one of them had been assassinated. This did it. The analogy had just the right prestige and weight, which was supported by Mrs Clapp's simple pleasure at the very idea of assassination and Mrs Bash's simple relief at having to imitate one of the two who were not assassinated.

Mr Suckbitch asked Rosalind to find out what Dick Pulman and his brothers wanted to be so with pointed courtesy she consulted her sister. Alice hesitated.

'Dick Pulman could be a courtier,' said Rosalind. 'Craving a boon. Then he could practise going down on one knee.'

'I think perhaps Brutus,' said Alice, soaring beautifully above the innuendo.

76

'And what about the Pulman brothers?'

The girls were feeling much more buoyant about them since their recent discussion. Rosalind, moreover, had been at some pains to discover, by means of very devious conversations with Mr Hall, that the archdeacons' court which dealt with sexual offences, and was therefore most unfairly known as the Bawdy Court, had not condemned anybody for years for either homosexuality or incest. She spent some time trying to decide whether that made it half as likely or twice as likely that an incestuous homosexual would be punished, but gave it up in the end, resolving to consult Mr Suckbitch as soon as she could think of some analogy of a more mentionable nature. Meanwhile she was comforted, and was reminded of the local hunt which had not caught anything for nine years. The apparatus of destruction was present but there was a reassuring lack of victims. She was also reminded of Mr Hall's views about hell. He considered it essential to believe in the existence of hell but unnecessary to suppose that there was anybody in it.

'I know,' said Rosalind. 'The Princes in the Tower. Moon's Ottery was spared from the Plantagenets. We've got to work in a tribute to the Tudors anyway. Then they can cuddle up in bed together.'

'Don't be daft. The princes were young boys.'

'Well, the brothers can sort of double up their legs.'

'I met Mrs Drewe on the village green,' said Alice shortly after this. 'Do you know what she wants us to be?'

'What?'

'Queen Elizabeth and Mary of Scotland. Queen Elizabeth on one side signing the warrant and Mary on the other being executed. Moon's Ottery was spared, you know. From a Popish ruler.'

'And from an adulteress.'

'From another adulteress. Don't forget Mrs Bust.' Mrs Bust was the widow of a former churchwarden.

'What's she going to be?'

'The Whore of Babylon in the final tableau. Cringing at Mrs Drewe's feet while truth triumphs.'

77

'She isn't.'

'No, she isn't. At least not that I know of.'

'Well, anyway she'd have her penitential white sheet ready.'

'It's worn out.'

Few people could remember the exact number of times since the death of her husband that Mrs Bust had been condemned to stand in church between the first and second lesson in her white sheet holding her white wand, and many said she should have started even sooner.

Rosalind began to reflect on Mrs Drewe's plans for her and Alice and the more she reflected the uneasier she became. Both were fine dramatic parts but which was to be which? This was an orator's question and she knew the answer. Mary of Scotland was a beauty. Queen Elizabeth, in spite of loyal pretence, was not. So Alice would be Mary. On first thoughts this was the most painful part of it. Rosalind in spite of considerable areas of self-confidence had never become resigned to being the less pretty of the two. She still went hot with rage whenever she recalled Mr Rolle's saying to a friend, well within earshot, when first the girls became his pupils: '*Alice* Mutter. Oh yes, that's the pretty one.'

Even more painful thoughts followed however. The fact that Mary was the villain would not matter in the least. A pretty woman, brutally done to death, would, unless the presentation was completely unconvincing, win all sympathy away from the upright signer of the warrant. There would be no trouble for Alice there. But then Rosalind thought of herself condemning Alice to death. She was always dreaming of being beheaded herself. Most people in her day dreamed of being burned alive but the other death was her dread. Too often in nightmares she had knelt blindfold and stretched out groping hands for the block. Invariably they were met and guided by the kindly hands of her destroyers but this did not lessen the cold terror. She could not condemn Alice to such a situation. She shuddered with superstitious fright.

'Which is to be which?' she asked.

'You're to be Queen Elizabeth,' said Alice with a spurious note of congratulation in her voice.

'Why?' Rosalind asked savagely.

'Oh, I suppose because she's got a red nose.'

'All right. I'll do it.'

7

'Summer farewell, whose flowers we long did wear,
And hail, November, with your branches bare.
Darkness at noon, rough seas and couchant birds
Shall never move us to lamenting words
For in the welkin, lo, a lightsome Star
Doth shine where'er Her loyal subjects are.'

THE crowded barn was hushed for Toby Rolle, the Prologue.
He looked exotic as he stood on the low stage in the flickering
light, declaiming and pointing up at the shadowy rafters. A
handsome man, he was in the habit of saying humorously that
he looked like an Indian: a bold remark, the Indians of the New
World being so curious and so despised, but as long as Mr Rolle
was showing off to an appreciative audience his confidence was
boundless. Mr Suckbitch who had really seen an Indian,
brought back from across the sea by a sailor and put on show
in London, said that in fact there was a strong resemblance,
though he added that the Indian was one of the most melancholy sights he had ever seen which Toby Rolle was not.
Certainly tonight in his gaudiest clothes, his outlandish face
emerging from his finest ruff, he looked triumphant. The
audience was clearly with him and he continued with increased
panache.

'And in this fair and pleasant vale I ween
Bright buds of fealty do spring up green.
The tide of Otter laves the feet of those
Who nightly watch to guard their Queen's repose.
The walls of Isca greet us from afar.
Who in these fields prepare ourselves for war.'

80

This sentiment was very well received. Congratulatory glances were exchanged among the local defenders and the feet the Otter had laved, only too abundantly in recent weeks, stamped on the straw. The fact that Exeter was unanimously regarded as a whoreson gurt city, and that its citizens were suspected of double-dealing and malpractice of every kind, melted away in the warmth of Toby Rolle's rhetoric.

> 'What can the ugsome might of Spain contrive
> Gainst those who for their God and homes do strive?
> Wanhope be gone. A valiant lustiness
> Has kept this valley in all healthfulness
> A thousand years and more, in wind and rain
> In broil and calm, and shall do so again.
> Long may our Sovereign Lady rule in peace
> To see the fruits of this fair land increase.
> From plagues and serpents and from bloody wars
> From quakes in daylight and from midnight jars
> From men of wrath whose tyrant swords are bared
> May She and may Moon's Ottery be spared.'

Mr Rolle bowed low with the correct flourish and floated down the steps on a wave of popularity. He disappeared into the bustling semi-darkness behind the stage where Vikings would be adjusting their horned helmets and Romans winding the thongs round their ankles. The applause turned into expectant chatter. At this point there was to have been a Dumb Show, enacted by William and Mary Lock. In assigning these parts, the villagers had had no malicious or satirical intention whatever. It was a practical matter. Every play started with a dumb show and Moon's Ottery had two dumb inhabitants, so it was a simple question of supply and demand. The mimic talents of the couple had been so well displayed in church on their wedding day that a religious scene suggested itself, namely, the Annunciation, an event that had spared Moon's Ottery from hell. The fact that Mary was heavily pregnant was no difficulty. She incurred no moral censure though it was now obvious that she must have been pregnant at the time of her marriage. Betrothal was taken very seriously and though couples who had anticipated the sacramental union of marriage occasionally found themselves up before the Bawdy Court their penance was light. In the case of the Locks their deafness excused them in yet another way, so that with people reflecting, simultaneously, that they knew no better and that it was probably the best thing they could have done, their exoneration was complete.

Considerations of realism were no trouble either. Certainly a woman who was eight months gone would hardly in real life receive with holy surprise and joy the news that she was about to conceive, but then – for the Nativity had been another suggestion – neither would she be bending over the manger-cradle of a newborn baby. The audience would feel that as the birth of a child was the point, a woman who was at any stage of pregnancy was very satisfactorily cast, in the same way that a bare stump of wood was an adequate representation of a tree in full leaf with birds singing in the branches and lovers' names incised on the bole.

But now the Dumb Show was to come at the end, as a grand, elevating finale. The reason for this was the active kindness of the Pulman brothers who had offered to take over from William up at the beacon immediately after their own performance so that he could watch the rest of the pageant before participating himself. The brothers had decided to be the dragon, front legs and back legs, in the statutory St George scene. It is true that not only Moon's Ottery but every village in the kingdom had been delivered from the dragon, but not all blessings can be exclusive, and the incident could hardly be left out. With the help of some of the matrons in the village the brothers had constructed a magnificent dragon, with a row of sails along its back, a winter-forest of teeth and a bloody-minded expression. Rosalind had seen it earlier that day on her way down to the manor barn to help with the preparations. The brothers were sitting in it, sideways, the right buttock of each hitched on to the bench outside the inn, so that the alignment of the monster was only slightly out of true. Dick Pulman was pushing tankards of ale up to them under its spiky flank.

Dick had been asked to be St George, and he would certainly

have looked the part, in a youthful, pure, heroic way, but, as Alice remarked to Rosalind with great meaning, *he* wouldn't be seen condemning his relatives to death in public. So Dick retired to the original suggestion of Brutus, and Mr Suckbitch asked Mr Hall to take the role.

'But, Henry, I'm not saintly.'

'My dear Noah, who in the village is? In any case George, whoever he was, wasn't a saint when he killed the dragon. You know as well as I do he couldn't have been canonized till after death, and it was probably because of an edifying old age and a few miracles, not for killing a wretched dragon. *Post hoc sed non propter hoc.*'

'I'm not young. I'm not handsome. I'm not warlike.'

'I've no doubt dragon-killers come in all ages, faces and temperaments. Couldn't you imagine the dragon was rooting up the vegetables in your garden?'

'Yes,' said Mr Hall after a pause, 'I think I could.'

'Rosalind will write you some fierce words, and you've been trained in the proper gestures, like the rest of us.'

So it was decided, with only one later modification. The next day Rosalind took Praise-the-Lord down to the church to catch mice. He was much in demand for this service. He seldom caught anything at Sparkhayes, leaving that office to his inferiors, and the girls, contrary to good farming tradition, used to feed him, but when he was carried down to the village in a market basket, looking arrogantly over the edge, and ceremoniously given the run of the church, his prowess was astonishing. On this occasion Mr Hall came in at the end of the massacre and, having thanked Rosalind and complimented Praise-the-Lord, suddenly said:

'Could the dragon answer back?'

Rosalind, with her head full of cat and mice, had to think quickly.

'Of course he could. You mean abuse St George? Cheek him?'

'Not exactly. No. Put his own point of view, as it were.'

'Does a dragon have a point of view?'

'I think so.'

'I'll certainly do my best then. I like the idea.'

So Rosalind had gone home – Praise-the-Lord now comatose and heavy as a tombstone in the basket – to change St George's monologue into a duologue. For once she blessed Mr Rolle. He had certainly given her a good knowledge of English poetry. When she and Alice had first gone to him for lessons, they had started in the conventional way on accidence, but either they were not good at learning it or Mr Rolle was not good at teaching it. Mrs Mutter assumed the former and kept having highly charged and envious talks with them about the grief caused to God, and in this case to herself as well, by people who wasted their opportunities. Alice and Rosalind thought the latter. However, it had all turned out for the best. As it happened Mr Rolle was far more enthusiastic about English literature than about the Latin language, and, the girls suspected, far better informed. He had had no opportunity at St Paul's to impart his knowledge and his admiration, so his country pupils got the full benefit of it, and benefit it really was. Day after day he spoke to Alice and Rosalind of the poets he had met, the manuscripts he had handled and the literary taverns he had frequented. He read to them, he quoted from memory, he showed them copies he had made from manuscripts and sometimes lent them works which had gone into print. They would have got none of this at the grammar school at Ottery St Mary. They would have been wrestling with Tully, Caesar and Livy instead of dallying with Sir Thomas Wyatt, Sir Philip Sidney, the Earl of Surrey and George Gascoigne.

Rosalind felt she had made a good job of the duologue, but as she sat in the barn that evening she was full of the cares rather than the triumphs of authorship, although St George and the vocal half of the dragon had been flattering about their scripts. She was to change into her Queen Elizabeth costume later, while the Romans and the Vikings were being humorous and the Normans solemn, but she had already taken the step of pinning up her front hair into tight curls and dyeing them bright red with cochineal. As the rest of her hair, which was to go under the head-dress, was as straight and sandy as usual, she felt she had better keep out of sight and had tucked herself well back into the shadows between two posts. Her face, which was always rather sad in repose, had settled into melancholy.

There was clearly going to be a considerable interval before the appearance of the dragon. The men who were to herald its approach with fireworks had wanted to hear the Prologue and had only just gone behind the stage to get their equipment ready. Mr Suckbitch, who had been leaning against a post, keeping an eye on things, stepped over to Rosalind.

'Wanhope, be gone.'

She looked up and smiled brilliantly.

'Oh, Mr Suckbitch, it almost is. In quarter of an hour it may completely be. We've started well, haven't we? Mr Rolle was very good, wasn't he?'

'Yes indeed. Toby Rolle always rises to the occasion. In fact he seldom descends from it.'

Mrs Drewe here claimed his attention, which gave Rosalind opportunity to observe Mr Drewe. He was a tall, pale, thin man who was hardly ever seen outside the Manor grounds. Tonight, in his own barn, he was making every effort to be agreeable and was seeming to find it no great strain to talk to Alice. She was blushing and looking prettily shocked.

'What on earth was our liege lord saying to you, Alice?' asked Rosalind as soon as he had moved off.

'Oh, he was telling me that riddle where the answer is the eye, only you're supposed to think it's something else.'

'You surely don't mean:

> A vessel I have
> That is shaped like a pear?'

'That's the one.

> Moist in the middle
> Surrounded with hair
> And often it happens
> That water flows there.'

Alice recited this rhyme with the face of an angel.

'But, Alice, you've known that riddle for years. Why were you looking shocked?'

'Oh, well, he seemed to expect it,' said Alice kindly. 'And looking shocked when you aren't is much easier than not looking it when you are.'

The first firework landed on the stage followed by dozens more. One or two went into the audience, causing delighted screams and shoving and exaggerated drawing up of skirts. As the explosions died away and the billowing smoke calmed down into a fine autumnal mist, the dragon made his entrance, splendid and stalwart – so unlike Mr Drewe whom he passed on his way to the stage – and looking as though he owned the barn. Everyone roared approval, everyone that is except Nicholas Pook who decided to be terrified and was dragged out yelling by Aunt Martha whose murderous expression was far worse than the monster's. The dragon mounted the stage and took up an argumentative stance ready for the debate that was to come. Mr Hall as St George now entered, with a slightly firmer tread than usual, and was greeted with less rapture but considerable good humour. The duologue began.

Mr Suckbitch had had trouble rehearsing Mr Hall. He made him practise stamping resolutely up and down his garden path, with a fair degree of success, but more was needed and Mr Hall had no more to give.

'Couldn't you gnash your teeth, Noah?'

'No, I couldn't, I'm afraid. I'll stamp but I won't gnash.'

'Mr Hall says he'll stamp but he won't gnash,' reported Mr Suckbitch to Rosalind. 'And even his stamping is like most people's tiptoeing.'

Rosalind thought hard. 'All right, then I'll alter his words. I'll reconcile them in the end. It'll be just as well, anyway, because if he won't gnash he probably won't slay. Is it all right to tamper with history?'

'It isn't history, my dear. You tamper as much as you want to. I'm most grateful. Won't it mean a lot of work?'

'Oh no, I'll just do a different last verse. It'll sound a bit patched on but perhaps the surprise will sort of tide people over.'

So it was decided, and there the protagonists stood, reciting Rosalind's words.

'Foh, stand off, worm. The hour has come
For you to yield this place.
Your scorching breath is troublesome
That reeks upon my face.
No lion, dog, monkey or crow
Can bar, with any right,
The way that virtue has to go
And I am virtue's knight.'

'Then learn, Sir Knight, this is my earth.
My dam in days of old
Bequeathed it to me at my birth
And it is mine to hold.
I care not for your warlike state.
Your threats to make me go
Are idle toys. Let parrots prate
Of what they do not know.'

'All beast, you have a beastly mind
That cannot be reformed.
Those who make ashes of mankind
Shall be to dust transformed.
How is't you do not see the dark
That presses on the sun?
You had this land to vex and cark
But now your reign is done.'

'Your chiding words, Sir Knight, forsake.
You are too credulous
In speaking of my deed you make
A mountain of a mouse.
I do no greater wrong than you.
As far as I can see
You do not come to bring virtùe
You come to murder me.'

'Then, dragon, let us not be wroth
That weigh in malice even.
Eternal time shall slay us both
And throw us up to heaven.
If we should combat, what's the gain?
For one would part in sorrow
Today, so let us both remain
And we'll be wise tomorrow.'

Rosalind had been right in thinking that the reconciliation of the two characters might be even more acceptable than the slaying of the dragon. They left the stage to roars of applause, St George's hand placed with pastoral concern on the monster's neck and the dragon loping amiably along whisking his tail in a gesture of cordiality which happened to catch Mr Drewe across the shins. In the shadows Alice hugged her sister with pride. Mr Suckbitch's eyes were shining through the gloom. 'I had quite a lump in my throat in the last verse.'

Zachary Gollop now took the stage. There was a pleasurable stir that could not be explained by his appearance – he looked his normal tough jovial self – or by the nature of his act which was clearly going to be straightforward recitation with no drums, guns, fireworks or serpents. But everybody, with the almost certain exception of Mr and Mrs Drewe, knew what was coming and was greatly looking forward to it.

When Rosalind had first mentioned Mr Courtenay's blockade of Exeter as a possible example of Moon's Ottery's preservation, she was alluding to a current situation which certainly had not affected the village directly but which had caused a great deal of local resentment and even an intermittent feeling of solidarity with the citizens of Exeter. The Mr Courtenay in question had an estate at Topsham, a little village on the east bank of the Exe, a few miles south of the city. The constant sight of prosperous vessels coming into the estuary and passing his house on their way to the capital, not only laden with valuable produce but also manned by potential spenders, worked on him to such an extent that one day he threw enough stones and rubble into the river north of his house to block the passage completely. From then on the produce and the spenders landed at Topsham, to his great enrichment. He was ordered to remove the blockade but refused to do so.

This subject showed every sign of providing one of the most popular scenes in the entertainment, but when the Drewes heard of it they forbade its inclusion on the grounds that it would give offence to a neighbouring, and now influential, landowner and friend. The Drewes were paying and the scene was dropped. But that was not the end of the matter. Zachary Gollop, after discussion with his friends, had come forward with the offer of an innocent-seeming contribution to the evening: a poem composed by himself and bearing the refrain 'Then shall Moon's Ottery conquerèd be'. The lines leading up to this burden were to describe ludicrous impossibilities of every kind. With great cunning Zachary explained to Mrs Drewe that he was afraid she might find parts of it perhaps a little too free. Mrs Drewe assumed he meant bawdy and graciously replied that this did not matter too much on an occasion like the present. At the Tilts and the Progress even Her Majesty had smiled at certain indelicacies. Zachary put on an expression of relief and gratitude and went home to write his poem. Now he stood on the stage in his everyday brown clothes, the picture of an honest, independent but respectful, working man.

'When the Pope shall wear curls on the top of his head
When the hunchback of Bosworth lies straight in his bed
When the princes he murdered shall sing merrily
Then shall Moon's Ottery conquerèd be.

'When gallant Sir Francis no longer wins praise
When the sun does not follow him round with its rays
When he quakes at the sight of the wind-shaken sea
Then shall Moon's Ottery conquerèd be.

'When the lame get there first and the blind eat no flies.
When the weepers on tombstones have tears in their eyes
When the Bishop of Exeter falls on his knee
Then shall Moon's Ottery conquerèd be.'

The allusion to the Bishop – who was not in favour with the Drewes so it was perfectly safe – brought the subject matter nearer home. Zachary marked the change by moving to the front of the stage and the audience guessed that this personal local vein was to continue for a while. It did.

'When Spaniards are humble and Dutchmen hate butter
When the lads on the green do not whistle and Mutter
When parsons Hall cabbages out of the sea
Then shall Moon's Ottery conquerèd be.

'When the poor summon Edwards and rich men get Clapp
When the babe shall Suckbitch and the dog shall suck pap
When the barber at Honiton charges no fee
Then shall Moon's Ottery conquerèd be.'

The flow of Zachary's recitation was punctuated by delighted shrieks at each reference. There were seven more such verses, in the course of which he succeeded in introducing the names of all the families in the district and of most of the single personalities, such as Mrs Bradbeer, as well. Mrs Drewe was seen to be smiling broadmindedly and Mr Drewe guffawed unaffectedly at some of the jokes. Then, after a significant pause, Zachary stepped forward again and sat on the edge of the stage dangling his legs.

'When gentlemen covet no rich merchandise
Nor seek to rob others of custom and prize
By throwing muck heaps in the estuary
Then shall Moon's Ottery conquerèd be.

'When the tall ships can pass to their lawful resort
And the poor can find labour and pence at the port
And the citizens follow their true destiny
Then shall Moon's Ottery conquerèd be.'

Most people present knew that Zachary gave not a rap for the poor of Exeter or of anywhere else, experienced little sympathy with the problems of wealthy merchants and had no feelings for the principle of free speech as such but was simply annoyed at Mrs Drewe's embargo. This knowledge did not in the least affect the reception of these fine sentiments or inhibit Zachary in his recital of them. As he let himself down on to the floor of the barn and walked off, wild cheers broke out, which after some minutes died down into excited speculations as to what the Drewes would do. They had stopped smiling broad-mindedly and guffawing, at the first line of the offending verses, but seemed to be taking no further steps. There could, however, be reprisals later. Zachary's motives might be less than noble, but it had been a brave thing to do.

'Did you know what was coming, Mr Suckbitch?'

'Officially, no, Rosalind. Did you?'

'Officially, no, too. Will they do anything to Zachary?'

'Be more wary of him in future, I expect, that's all. They've been afraid of him for some time. He's a leader.'

'But there's nothing definite he really wants to lead people up to or away from, is there?'

'That makes him more dangerous, not less. He can't be met. He might come round any corner.'

Mr Rolle went past them. 'Splendid stuff, splendid,' he cried enthusiastically. 'That's the man for me. When the Gollop Rising breaks out you know where to find me.'

'And what would the Rising be rising *about*, Toby?' asked Mr Suckbitch querulously.

'That's entirely up to Zachary. We must trust him,' said Mr Rolle with a madcap smile and walked on.

People were now lugging mattresses and palliasses on to the stage and thumping them down. The nearby lanterns were moved away so that the platform was in darkness as the Black Death victims crept on in their nightshirts and lay down. Mrs Clapp and Mrs Bash, in joint command, entered side by side carrying candles with an air that, as Mr Suckbitch whispered to Rosalind, recalled the Old Faith. The sick began to moan and roll about, and the white witches moved among them with comforting murmurs. Joseph Priddy, lying near the front of the stage, overdid the rolling about and Mrs Clapp's murmur rose to a more normal pitch.

'Now, Joseph Priddy, you don't want the whole barn to see your hey nonny no, do you?'

The remark was clearly audible to Rosalind and Mr Suckbitch but, they hoped, exchanging glances, no further away. The man on the next palliasse to Joseph gave a shriek of laughter but this might perhaps be interpreted as delirium: a bold stroke of imaginative acting. Joseph Priddy pulled the blanket over his hey nonny no and fell into a realistic coma.

When the scene was ended and the lights had been brought back, there was a great deal of moving about. William arrived from the beacon, bringing cold air in with him; the Pulman brothers had set off to relieve him as soon as they had got out of their dragon skin. Aunt Martha dragged Nicholas in again, to test his nerves against the Romans, Vikings and Normans. Alice, Rosalind, Mrs Rolle and Mrs Bradbeer went behind the stage to change. As they entered what Mrs Drewe called the tiring-room – some old blankets from Buckhayes casually rigged up on poles and smelling of urine which was certainly not a healthy baby boy's – a river of Romans flowed out from the opposite side of the stage, some in armour clamped over short frilly skirts, others in togas clutched anxiously to their stomachs. Dick Pulman, handsomely bare-legged as Brutus, was distinguished by a crested helmet and a red cloak draped over his breastplate.

As the women got ready they could follow well enough what was happening on the stage. After considerable stamping, shuffling and clanking, there was a comparative hush and the voice of Dick Pulman rang out boldly:

'Here I stay and here I rest
Until this place be called Totnès.'

From beyond the stage came roars of laughter. Everyone knew this time-honoured verse but opinions as to its merits were divided. The gentry tended to regard it with respect or at least lack of comment. The more free-thinking of the rest of the population found it hysterically funny that Brutus should have written a poem in English immediately on his arrival and felt that his selection of the name Totnes was arbitrary to the point of high comedy.

Feet moved forward and another voice declared satirically:

'Here I stay nor move I on
Until this place be called Honitòn.'

'Well,' said Mrs Bradbeer, 'at any rate we needn't hurry. This will go on for at least half an hour. Do you want any help with your ruff, Rozzy?'

She was right. Nearly all the towns and villages in East Devon, and even some in West Dorset, had a verse each: Dunkeswell, Broadhembury, Sidmouth, Budleigh, Ottery St Mary, Axminster, Luppitt, Awliscombe, Stockland. The necessary ingenuity of most of the rhymes drew groans as well as cheers from the audience.

Still the Romans had not finished. They now started on a free-for-all of jokes and puns based on local place-names.

'Have you heard about the legionary who took his wenches to Moridunum?' came a voice which the listeners could not identify. They all knew of course that Moridunum was the British name for Seaton and meant exactly the same.

'No, what about the legionary who took his wenches to Moridunum?' said another unidentified voice.

'The Moridunum the lustier he felt.'

'Oh, really,' said Mrs Bradbeer and then laughed heartily.

The jokes went on and on.

'Oh, God,' said Mrs Bradbeer. 'They'll be on that stage as long as the Roman occupation itself.'

'Three hundred and sixty-seven years,' said Rosalind.

'Well, Philip Sidney would have been pleased,' said Mrs Rolle. 'That's one thing. He always used to say there was a ludicrous discrepancy in English plays between the actual length of the performance and the time it was supposed to represent. He was very funny about it.'

'That's no comfort to me, Beatrice,' replied Mrs Bradbeer amiably. 'We shall all smell of Buckhayes piss for the next fortnight.'

'We're so nearly ready, Mrs Bradbeer,' suggested Alice, 'we could just step outside the tiring-room, ha ha, and watch the Vikings and the Normans.' So they all did.

The Vikings, whose turn it finally was, were less verbal than the Romans. Fists raised high above their horned helmets they rushed out from behind the stage hallooing and showing their lower teeth, seized a maiden each from the audience and rushed out of the door at the end of the barn into the night. Not all the maidens had been warned so some of the screams were genuine.

The Normans were different again. The only person who had offered to be one was the blacksmith, a man of sober and steady character who had no wish to appear lecherous or amusing. He had prepared a boring informative dialogue about the Dooms-day Book which he and his apprentice were now delivering. After the Vikings it was being greatly appreciated by those few of the audience who did not find rape and pillage funny. Farmer Mutter was one of them. He was nodding gratefully as one improving fact followed another.

It was now time for the execution of Mary, Queen of Scots. As the four women characters climbed through a slit in the tiring-room they met the male members of the supporting cast, Mr Drewe and Obed Hosegood, waiting behind the stage, accompanied by Mr Suckbitch. The presence of Obed was a triumph. He had counted on spending the evening drinking a great deal of cider and sitting with his friends at the back of the barn. Alice, however, upset his plans. When it became known that she was to be Mary, offers to be the executioner poured in. Apart from the black glamour of the part, the applicants coveted it for other reasons. Those whom Alice had snubbed or sweetly ignored in the past few years felt it to be a gesture of revenge. Others who still had hope, or perhaps more charity, were inspired by the simple wish to be as near her as even an axe-length. Alice rejected them all.

'I wouldn't trust any of those silly shits not actually to cut my head off. Obed or nobody,' she said to Rosalind who, fully appreciating her sister's point of view, went straight down to his cottage to plead with him. He was touched by the confidence the girls placed in him and was soon persuaded.

'You look splendid, Rosalind,' said Mr Suckbitch. 'Those jewels. That ruff.'

'Mrs Bradbeer showed me how to starch and crimp it, and she lent me the jewels Lady Burghley gave her.' She glanced down her dress. 'I don't look very majestic, though.'

'Nonsense, my dear. The Queen has a very light figure. The Earl of Leicester used to be able to lift her high off the floor in the dance.'

Feeling light rather than thin, Rosalind stepped up on to the stage, attended by Mrs Bradbeer as gentlewoman-in-waiting, a part she had applied for as being not too demanding. Behind them came Mr Drewe, as a grave experienced courtier whose place it was to give solid advice. Rosalind took her seat at a small table and Mrs Bradbeer stood beside her. Mr Drewe fell back condescendingly, not before his Queen but before a yeoman's daughter, with the air of some deity who abnegates his powers for one day of the year. Rosalind, looking up at Mrs Bradbeer in the well-rehearsed pose of someone in a dilemma seeking counsel and support, saw the lady-in-waiting's comely face distorted in an effort not to laugh. A woman who had been in the household of Lord Burghley was not impressed by a country squire. Hoping that in some way this expression might be received as yet another piece of imaginative acting, Rosalind turned to Mr Drewe.

> 'My Lord, whose grave advice and faithful aid
> Have long upheld my honour and my realm
> And brought me to this age from greener years
> Guiding so great estate with great renown,
> Now must I use, as ne'er I used before,
> Your truth and wisdom in my governance.
> Then do not counsel me so cruelly
> To shed the blood of her I cousin call,
> Who helpless lies in prison at my will.
> Bid me not hateful slaughter to perform
> Without all cause, against all course of kind.'

95

Mr Drewe shook his head dolefully, then stepped forward
and laid a paper before her in a marked manner.

'My gracious lady and my sovereign dear,
Not without cause do I thus counsel you.
This heathen Mary lives to work you woe.
No helpless prisoner she, but strives and plots
To shake with garboils your well-ordered state.
And she has friends enough who bear her love
Who steal about by night with poisonous craft
To lift her treacherously into your place.'

'Then must she be confined with triple guard
Her parasites be taken to the Tower.
I will not have her blood upon my hands.
Tear up this warrant. I will none of it.
Let her be watched I say but not be killed.'

'Think, madam, think of this our native land.
Divided claimants make divided hearts.
One single rule with no pretenders by
Is what preserves the country and the prince.
There is no other way.'
                              'Dear madam, sign,'

urged Mrs Bradbeer comfortably.

'You cannot stay the lewd rebellious hands'

(Mr Drewe was putting real feeling into his words)

'Of those who call Mary of Scotland queen
Without consigning her to deepest death.
This side of death she will not abdicate.'

'I cannot prosper in the sight of God
By murdering those who have what I would have
Or who might take it from me by assault.'

'It is not what you have but what you hold
In trust for all the subjects of this land
That you must cherish at all other cost.

Your reign in quiet shall the longer last,
Your people shall the longer dwell in peace
When this fair peril is removed from hence.
You that have ruled us, noble sovereign,
For public weal and not for private joy
Do not deliver us to wars again.'

Queen Elizabeth was silent for a while in a posture of cruel indecision and the audience was tensely silent too. Mr Drewe was a gargoyle of anguish. Mrs Bradbeer looked as worried as she could.

'Then I will sign, and may God pardon me,' suddenly declared the Queen and signed.

'God will reward you for your princely care,' promised Mr Drewe, whipping the warrant away.

The audience bellowed, clapped and whistled their approval. Farmer Mutter, beaming, gave a strangled shout.

The warrant-signing episode had taken place on the right-hand side of the stage. Its three protagonists now turned sideways to the audience and gazed at the other side where the execution was to be. During the applause someone had quickly placed a block on a shallow pile of straw, and now Obed with his axe came heavily up the steps, terrifying in black clothes and mask, and took up his place, as sinister and wooden as the block itself. The gasps of appreciative fright which his appearance evoked changed into quite different gasps as Alice came forward, as beautiful as Helen of Troy, her hair piled high and her dress tucked down to expose her neck. Beside her trotted Turk, a mean little dog belonging to Mrs Rolle, of no recognizable breed and looking more like a bad-tempered heraldic emblem. It was common knowledge that Mary of Scotland had been accompanied to her execution by her lap dog who had crouched under her skirts as she lay headless, and everybody felt this was too good to leave out. The difficulty was to find a suitable animal. Rex and Lass, the Sparkhayes dogs, were workers like all the others in the valley and much too muddy and rangy to be the pet of a queen, apart from which when they were not working – the only thing they enjoyed doing – they

97

slept and would certainly have slept through a bloodbath of executions. So Mrs Rolle had lent Turk, who now ran round the block several times sniffing it, to encouraging suggestions from the audience, but before he could lift his leg his mistress, as gentlewoman-in-waiting, caught him and gave him an order to sit at the back of the stage, which he morosely obeyed.

Mrs Rolle had asked to be gentlewoman-in-waiting to Mary not because, like Mrs Bradbeer, she felt that such a part would be effortless but because, on the contrary, she felt she could put a great deal of effort into it. Now having settled Turk, she began to wring her hands. It was a fine performance. Out of the corner of her eye Rosalind could see Mr Rolle muttering something to Mr Suckbitch that was obviously expressive of acute embarrassment, after which he put his hands over his face. Nobody else, however, thought Mrs Rolle was over-acting. Hand-wringing was an accepted gesture, the occasion called for it, Mrs Rolle wrung her hands superbly, and the audience enjoyed it. She knew when to stop too and soon retired to the back of the stage beside Turk where she stood with hands clasped and still.

Everyone's attention was now focused on Mary as she knelt gracefully down behind the block. Rosalind had decided that dumb show would be best for this whole sequence. She felt that after the worldly political talk about the warrant, silence would be dignified, and that without comment the execution would seem like an inescapable projection of an evil discussion: the horrible result of a horrible decision. Mary prayed for a while. Mrs Rolle, face working with woe, bandaged the queen's eyes and helped her lay her head on the block. She then spread out her arms in a well-researched gesture of immensity as Obed, whose motionless presence on the stage had been powerfully felt throughout, slowly raised the axe and held it poised.

In the dead silence of that moment, the door at the back of the barn burst open, knocking over some of the bystanders and banging noisily against the wall, and one of the Pulman brothers ran in shouting something which he was too out-of-breath to make plain. Everybody in the audience jumped up and turned round. On the stage, Obed justified the confidence placed in him. Slowly and steadily he lowered the axe on to the straw by his feet. Alice pulled off her bandage and sat back on her heels. Turk yapped piercingly.

Apart from the din and shock of the interruption it was startling to see one of the Pulman brothers by himself. Rosalind's heart had been pounding as the execution scene moved to a climax and the sudden crashing-open of the door had made her scream, but she was still able to think that he looked like someone bitten in half lengthwise by a shark. He was now surrounded by a vociferously inquiring crowd. He bent double to draw his breath and his shouts became words.

'The beacon. Danger. My brother. Come.'

He ran out again, followed first by Dick and then by William who had immediately understood that harm was threatened to his beacon. Zachary Gollop, Joseph Priddy and all the other able-bodied men pushed towards the door. Lanterns bobbed, dust rose from the straw as it was kicked aside and a few lurking rats sped away. The actors jumped off the stage and caught up with the others, Alice and Rosalind hitching up their skirts and turning from monarchs into country girls as they ran. At last the only ones left in the barn were the very old, the heavily pregnant, Mr and Mrs Drewe and Turk, whose hurrying days, if he had ever had any, were over; and the road that led up to the beacon and then on to the Somerset border was full of running people.

At the first corner Mr Rolle sat down in the hedge. 'I've got a bone in my leg,' he said comically. Mrs Rolle took no notice but jogged along with Mrs Bradbeer. Mr Rolle's action was not that of a coward. If there were enemies about a straggler would be in the greatest danger.

'He can't bear,' panted Rosalind, 'to run with the herd.'

'Especially,' puffed Mr Suckbitch, 'uphill.'

The road was rising steeply now. The moon was high and bright, and even Sweethayes, the farthest farm up the valley, showed up white and clear. The dogs at Buckhayes started barking and all the way along others joined in. Mr Suckbitch and the girls began to draw ahead of the rest, though Dick, his brother and William were still well in the lead. Mr Suckbitch ran with his knees bent and his feet flat, but with considerable speed and staying power. Rosalind threw out her thin arms as she sped along, which gave her the outline of a starfish. Alice moved strongly, though she had to keep putting her hands on her bosom to stop it swinging.

As they came in sight of the great cluster of trees that marked Beacon Hill, they could hear Rex and Lass crossly coming to life. 'Good dogs,' shouted Rosalind hopefully as they turned off the road into the stony lane that led finally up to the beacon. Dick and his brother and William were now up on the skyline and running across the flat space above the trees to where the beacon stood. Mr Suckbitch and the girls put on a spurt and arrived at the top in time to see the Pulman brother who had been left on guard standing in front of the beacon, his arms stretched out protectively. It was a courageous stance. For at least ten minutes he must have heard the approach of pounding feet and excited voices, and the growing chorus of barking dogs, and perhaps seen the swaying light of the lanterns. Only when his brothers came into sight could he have known that this was rescue and not attack.

Dick stopped short in relief at seeing him standing there uninjured. His other brother ran forward and clasped his outstretched hand. Alice and Rosalind exchanged apprehensive glances at what seemed to them too revealing a gesture, but they had no need to worry, for William, to whom no gesture was more complicated than a straightforward expression of immediate feelings, hurried up and took his other hand. And there in cordon the three of them stood. Moon's Ottery was spared.

Other people were now coming up and the story of what had happened began to be passed round and round. Soon after their arrival at the beacon the brothers had gone into the bushes to relieve themselves, the moonlight being so bright that this retirement seemed necessary. Just as they were returning to their post they heard what sounded like the scraping of a tinder-box and as they sprang forward they saw a man bending down as though to light the bottom branches of the beacon. They shouted and tried to seize him but he escaped, racing over the rough grassland at a speed they could not match and disappearing over the edge and down into the trees, where they heard him crashing into the distance.

Nobody present underestimated the danger that had been averted. Fire was the speediest means of communication but likewise the least flexible. Once the warning flames had shot up there was no way of recalling the message or following it up by another, no way to prevent the defenders of England from springing to arms. True, they could ultimately be told to lay down their arms again, but the vital alarm system would be discredited, perhaps for ever.

By the time the chattering groups had discussed all this, there was no question of returning to the barn to finish the pageant, for it had in fact finished, dramatically, in the most appropriate place. Even the later comers had by now arrived: Mr Hall whose first thought had been the safety of the church, and Mrs Clapp who, accompanied by Mrs Bash, had stopped by at her cottage to pick up her bag of remedies, a sensible step, though, as Alice remarked to Rosalind, she had taken so long about it that anyone who was bleeding would have bled to death, or even turned gangrenous, by the time she got there. The very last two were Mrs Bradbeer and Mrs Rolle who, like unaggressive animals that had forgotten they were supposed to be fighting, had fallen into a peaceful amble.

But although the pageant was over, there was need for some closing act. It was a mild night for November, and Zachary Gollop organised a dance. One of the musicians had caught up his rebeck as he ran out of the barn and under Zachary's direction he now struck up a country dance. In minutes the set had formed and everybody was skipping in the moonlight. Dick and Alice were siding and turning single, Dick's face full of affectionate pride as he turned his head from beautiful Alice to his brave brothers. Like Janus, Rosalind thought as she set to Mr Suckbitch who was padding about as sure-footed and dignified as a bear.

101

Finally came the grand chain, and away went Alice and Rosalind, weaving in and out, taking hands and dropping them. In the circumstances it was a very long chain and for a time they were almost out of their partners' sight but at last Mr Suckbitch saw Rosalind coming back to him, arms flying and cochinealed curls working loose. 'Moon's Ottery was spared,' he said with his most lupine grin when she reached him. He put out his hands and, though it was only a country round, he lifted her as high in the dance as ever the Earl of Leicester had lifted Queen Elizabeth.

8

DECEMBER was as bad a month as anyone could remember. On some days the wind raged down and across the valley with a boom that made William and Mary laugh as much as they did during thunderstorms. Other days were still but cruelly cold. The frost thawed first on the Sparkhayes side of the valley, but even so the icicles that formed on the thatch and looked like grotesquely prolonged straws did not melt until just before darkness came round again, and the roof did not begin to steam until the sun was low in the sky. The only flourishing plant seemed to be old-man's-beard which was prolific that year, but so prolific that it looked like dirty snow and did not brighten the landscape at all. The only colourful patches in the scene were by the gates in the corners of the fields where the earth was churned up and bright brown.

Farmer Mutter was mostly busy in the barn, which he always put in order at the beginning of winter, regarding it as too important a task to be delegated. He arranged the chaff in neat piles and sorted out the different kinds of straw. The horses had to be fed throughout the winter months, and the straw had to be eked out for as long as possible. They would not go back to it once they had tasted hay.

The pageant had its repercussions in Sparkhayes, as no doubt in every other house in the valley. Aunt Martha gave Nicholas a severe whipping for having been afraid of the dragon and letting her down in front of the village. She whipped him, Rosalind felt, *at* herself and Alice, who if they had not been involved in the pageant and consorting with the gentry whom Aunt Martha resented so bitterly, could have been deputed to take him out of the barn or even take him home.

Farmer Mutter had been cheered by the part his daughters had played. He confided to them that ever since Richard Tarleton had appeared on the London stage he had wished to see him, but that now he felt he could enjoy good acting at home and would not have appreciated any performance more than the execution of Mary. The girls were gratified by his admiration, though Rosalind thought Tarleton was an odd choice, famous as he had become in the past few years for dancing jigs and playing funny peasants in russet coats. She felt that Alleyn and Burbage, whose names had also come into the news, would have made better comparisons when such a lofty scene as hers was being discussed, but she realized that her father knew none of the details of Tarleton's work and simply considered that the very name was the best-sounding and therefore the most complimentary of the three. 'How proud your mother would have been,' he concluded.

The village had admired the girls, too, and indeed they had become altogether more popular since their mother's death, and not only because people were sorry for them. Born to the security of being the daughters of a prosperous farmer, they put on none of Jane Mutter's airs and graces. They were known to be good and skilful workers. Alice knitted beautifully and made excellent soap while Rosalind's cooking was becoming quite a theme for gossip. Their education was by now forgiven them. It was safely in the past and at least they did not ape courtly accomplishments; they did not play the lute or the virginals or dance the volta or sing. The fact that Dick Pulman appeared to be courting Alice gave her prestige in the eyes of the community and that a gentleman like Mr Suckbitch should be taking an interest – a very different thing – in Rosalind improved her standing too.

She continued going to Mrs Bradbeer for cookery lessons. When she was in Lord Burghley's household Mrs Bradbeer had more than once heard foreign guests say of English food in general, 'God sends meat, the Devil cooks it', and was determined that the remark should never be made about her own table or that of any girl who turned to her for advice.

Aunt Martha, though she continued to express her preference for good plain English food and her detestation of messed-up fal-lals, found Rosalind so industrious and eager in the kitchen that she handed more and more of the cooking over to her and treated her visits to Moons with nothing worse than silent scorn.

One day very soon after the pageant Rosalind, wrapped up to the eyes against the bitter wind, was climbing the hill that led up to Moons, worrying about sorrel sauce. She had tried it the day before, to serve with boiled chicken. Though she had taken it off the fire at what seemed to her the exact moment, as described by Mrs Bradbeer, it had lost colour and turned into an unappetizing brown that defied description, or rather, thought Rosalind, who under the influence of Mr Suckbitch was constantly trying to be more accurate, only too readily invited description. She had attempted to correct it with gooseberry juice and spinach water – hints from Mrs Bradbeer, part of whose optimism it was always to keep the worst firmly in mind – but the result had looked even more unpleasant.

As she came within sight of Moons she at once noticed Mr Suckbitch's small dilapidated coach standing in front of the house. She realized he must be preparing to go to London. When he visited Exeter or Taunton or even Bristol he always went on horseback. The next moment she saw Mr Suckbitch himself, also wrapped up to the eyes, standing on top of the mount which was a feature of the garden that stretched out behind the house and which had a commanding view over the mile-distant village. He was the only person in the valley to have a mount. Indeed he was the only person to have a garden in the accepted sense of the word. The Drewes concentrated on their wavy acres of parkland and had only a few perfunctory flower beds as a kind of draggled fringe round part of the house. Mr Hall's devotion was exclusively to the kindly fruits of the earth in their season, among which he did not include ornamental shrubs or inedible flowers.

Everybody, high or low, had some kind of an orchard and a plot for vegetables and herbs, but only Mr Suckbitch had a formally arranged garden with clipped box hedges and shrubs set out in geometrical patterns and interlacing designs; only he had long straight alleys covered over by vines and creepers. Only Mr Suckbitch had a fountain. It had not worked for years and he worried a great deal about it, but there it was. One thing he refused to go in for was the fashionable topiary, saying pedantically that God made peacocks and God made the box plant but he had not intended the latter to be confused with the former. When Mr Suckbitch invoked the mind of God it meant that he had thoroughly made up his own.

He now waved to Rosalind and immediately turned his back on her in order to descend the corkscrew path that spiralled round the mount. Each time he reappeared he waved again. After four revolutions he reached the ground and soon came round the side of the house towards her.

'Come in, my dear. This wind.'

They passed the coach which smelled musty even in the cold air.

'You're going to London. Is it business or pleasure?' Rosalind tried to sound worldly rather than inquisitive.

'Both. But some pain, too.'

'Pain?'

'Yes. I have to have a tooth seen to. I don't trust the barber at Honiton to get to the root of the matter.' They both laughed.

'And the pleasure? Oh, I see, you mean you're going to stay over Christmas? Oh, dear.'

'Oh yes. I can't resist the opportunity. There'll be too many things that I simply wouldn't be able to do in the country.'

'What sort of things?'

'Well, I know for certain that Tallis is doing a new motet. And there's sure to be a new play on Twelfth Night.'

'Not *Gorboduc*, anyway. Not on Twelfth Night.'

'No, indeed. Wedding bells and people dressed up pretending to be other people.'

'It sounds lovely. Oh, dear.'

'Now what shall I bring you back?'

'Something to wear, please. Something not too, well, you know, not too expensive.'

'A necklace?'

'Oh, *yes.*'

'A year ago it would have been a book.' He sounded rather sad.

Next day word went round that he had been seen driving off towards the London road. Rosalind followed him on his journey with her thoughts. At least he could not be going into worse weather than he was leaving behind. A freezing mist that was as thick as fog descended over the whole valley. As it moved across the trees they turned black; if it cleared for a moment they became lighter than the black sky.

But before Mr Suckbitch could have got anywhere near London, perhaps before he was across Salisbury Plain, Rosalind sank into a state of depression which allowed her to have no thoughts outside herself.

Night after night she had such bad dreams that she was afraid to go to sleep, and woke every morning sick and shaken. Apart from anxieties and terrors of every sort, there was one dream in particular which recurred: she and Alice had, by means of something they had done – it was never clear what – driven their mother out of the house and for a time it stood empty except for themselves. Then, in the dream, one evening as darkness was falling Rosalind heard a strange sound coming up from the river and very steadily, with no alteration of pace whatever, getting nearer. It sounded like something, perhaps a chain, being dragged along the road. Inexorably it approached the bottom gate and came up the courtyard, over the cobbles towards the front door. She went down to open it and there stood a woman with bright-red eyes burning like coals, and hot breath. Rosalind could not see the rest of her but in the same way she knew it was a woman she knew that what had been dragged along the ground was a hard scaly tail. One night, walking in her sleep, she really did go down and open the door and woke up with cold air and fine rain playing on her. Farmer Mutter, who had been roused by the squeal of the latch, came downstairs but by that time she had recovered sufficiently to pretend she had heard a fox trying to get at the hens.

By day she bravely attempted to learn something from the dream. The obvious interpretation was that the newcomer was Aunt Martha, arrived to take over from her mother, but she knew this was not the right meaning, and the only result of such a line of explanation was that she began to doubt whether her aunt was really as monstrous as she had up to then believed.

The twelve days of Christmas were drawing near. The Mutters had never made very much of the feast beyond having a particularly good dinner on Christmas Day itself. They certainly had no aspirations to motets and plays, and they did not even go in for the mumming and misrule which many local families did. But they had been used to decorating the house with ivy, holly, bay and any other greenery they could gather. Jane Mutter had always been very active and high-spirited during the Christmas Eve decorations. Rosalind had a vivid memory of her mother standing on a stool in the hall, her neat ankles much in evidence, reaching up to a beam and singing in her raucous soprano:

'Oh, the holly and the ivy
Have fallen down *again*.'

Her daughters had shrieked with admiring laughter. Her husband had lifted her off the stool and kissed her.

This year Dick Pulman brought Alice a beautiful bunch of mistletoe. She hung it up in the cross passage and it was much admired by everybody except Aunt Martha.

'She'd rather it'd been from one of the loonies,' said Rosalind, though for some months past, and particularly since the episode of the bonfire, she had been careful to pronounce the word as though it was a silly quotation.

Farmer Mutter realized the significance of the gift, and in general he was pleased at the idea of Dick's courtship of Alice. It exactly fitted in with his plan of eventually leaving his farm to Alice and her husband. Dick was such a steady, good young man and such an excellent farmer that Sparkhayes and Sweethayes together would be a noble empire. But he felt that he still had the first emotional claim on his daughters. He insisted on kissing them both ceremoniously under the mistletoe. The year before he had just given them an informal Christmas Day kiss when he happened to meet them.

Christmas dinner at Sparkhayes usually started with the flourish of graces recited by Alice and Rosalind, and John Mutter wished to continue a custom which had given Jane such pleasure. Alice began.

> 'O Lord our God we yield thee praise
> For this thy gracious store
> Praying that we may have the grace
> To keep thy laws and lore
> And when this life shall flit away
> Grant us to live with thee for aye.'

Alice sat down and Rosalind stood up.

'I'm hungry,' whined Nicholas.

Rosalind, speaking as slowly as she possibly could without actually provoking comment, started her grace.

> 'O Lord, which giv'st thy creatures for our food
> Herbs, beasts, birds, fish and other gifts of thine,
> Bless these thy gifts that they may do us good
> And we may live, to praise thy name divine
> And when the time is come this life to end
> Vouchsafe our souls to heaven may ascend.'

Finally Farmer Mutter prayed. He had a decided taste for extempore prayer and was good at it in the sense that he never hesitated or dried up. Unfortunately his technique was largely informative. On one occasion which the girls had never forgotten, when the subject of the prayer was repentance and forgiveness, he advised the Almighty that the great writer Malory had movingly portrayed a remorseful queen and a king who pardoned her.

'Do you think God'll get down to reading *Morte d'Arthur* after this?' Rosalind asked Alice in their room that night.

'If he does it'll be more than Father ever has. Actually reading it, that is.'

On this Christmas Day, Farmer Mutter from the depths of his sorrow and loss, which had been stirred by the allusions in the graces to life flitting away and souls ascending to heaven, told God at considerable length about his wife's death and, as he rather complacently expressed it, the empty chair in their house. At last after much circumlocution, many tags from the Bible, and a final reference to the empty chair, he got to 'in the name of Jesus Christ our Lord, Amen,' and all bowed heads and lowered eyelids were raised again.

'Mother always used to sit on a stool,' said Rosalind.

'Rozzy,' stormed Aunt Martha, 'how could you talk to your poor father like that?' Nicholas smirked.

'Leave the maid alone, Martha,' said John Mutter, defying his sister-in-law for the only time in his life. 'She understood her mother.'

For the whole of the first course Rosalind sat in a torment of self-reproach at her own heartlessness, but then she noticed that her father was beginning to look more cheerful than she had seen him for some time. Reflecting on this, it occurred to her that her appalling remark was so exactly what her mother might have made in similar circumstances that her father was feeling that his wife had not wholly gone from them. The meal ended quite pleasantly.

When Epiphany was over, the January days left nothing to hope for except a distant spring. The first calves were born. Farmer Mutter, like most of the farmers in the valley, always arranged that some should be born at the beginning of the year, on the principle that if they experienced cold weather in the earliest stages of their lives they would better face the following winter. But they were a pathetic sight, and Rosalind was by no means comforted by this theory that adversity in youth was a good preparation for later and worse horrors. She was feeling even more wretched than she had before Christmas.

The weather was by no means as wet as it had been in December and she was able to resume her walks down to the river. One day started with such bright sun that the shadow of the house was cast on the back field with startling blackness and the chimneys towered right up towards the top hedge. Rosalind worked hard all the morning stocking up the larder but after dinner the impetus left her completely and when the hall was cleared and everyone had gone off to the outdoor tasks which the weather had suddenly made possible, she went out to the buttery and drained one of the larger cider jugs. Half an hour later, the ever-watchful Obed saw her making her way unsteadily down to the river, realized something was wrong, guessed what, and immediately set out in pursuit.

It would take him a good ten minutes to catch her up but for most of the way he could see her in the distance, now leaning over the rail of the bridge. Her attitude suggested to his discerning eyes that she was gazing solemnly rather than distractedly into the water and he did not hurry. He was right. Rosalind was in fact concentrating hard on stopping her head from spinning and her stomach from heaving.

The road beyond her swung sharply round to the left before it started climbing again, so that anyone approaching the bridge from that direction would have been within a few yards of it before coming in sight. The river was running quietly that afternoon and as Rosalind leaned there, her abnormally quick hearing unaffected by her giddiness and nausea, she caught above the noise of the water the sound of footsteps just round the corner, that is, not footsteps, for they neither advanced nor receded, but the rustle of someone moving from foot to foot. She took this in with no curiosity or fright, feeling too ill to experience either. Fright indeed was hardly called for, in broad daylight in a peaceful neighbourhood, but curiosity at the presence of a watcher in this unfrequented place certainly was.

Yet Rosalind stayed where she was without even glancing round, until, after a few minutes, during which the watcher might have been deliberating and coming to a decision, she heard the footsteps again, and this time they could really be so described, for they were moving, and moving towards her. She turned her head sharply, but the nausea, that she had been warding off by keeping still, overcame her, and leaning low over the rail of the bridge she was noisily sick into the water. When she had recovered she heard a new sound, one that she recognized, the plod of Obed's boots as he came round the last bend of the hill from Sparkhayes. He found her lachrymosely watching the contents of her stomach swirling round in the eddy before being carried on down the river.

'Come on now, Rozzy.'

'Oh, Obed,' she sobbed, 'I don't get on well without her. And I can't find her.'

'You've found the cider jug seemingly. Come on, maid. I'll help 'ee home. I knows 'tis hard.'

'Alice doesn't find it hard. She doesn't cry.'

'Alice grieves, I reckon. 'Tidn' for us to judge what others feels. Come on now, maid, 'fore I turns into one of they 'tinerant preachers.'

Itinerant preachers, a group of whom were sent to visit the valley from time to time, were the object of Obed's profound contempt. Mr Hall's spiritual counsel he respected and occasionally followed, but those who delivered rousing sermons and then moved on seemed to him like boys who knocked on people's doors and ran away.

'Obed, there's someone round the corner.' Instead of brushing the idea aside, Obed immediately went to look.

'No,' he said returning to her. 'Nobody there now.'

'I'm staying here, Obed.'

'You'm coming home if I have to fetch the dung-cart and push 'ee up the hill.'

'Oh, all right.'

She took his arm and they struggled up the road, Rosalind lurching and dragging her feet at first but getting soberer as they went along and more alive to the realities of the situation.

'Where's Aunt Martha?'

'Gone down to the village.'

'Where's Father?'

'He've decided to start sowing the oats. Reckons the moon's right. I'll tell Alice to say you'm ill. Not too ill, else somebody'll send for Mrs Clapp, and 'er may be useless but 'er idn' daft.'

'But Alice can't say I'm ill. It's not true.'

'You bin seeing too much of a chap who believes in what they calls the letter of the law.'

'I don't know who you're referring to,' said Rosalind with tipsy hauteur.

'No, no. Course not. But I can think of a way that 'ud please un. You knows how he likes words that means two things at the same time?'

'Yes.' Rosalind was sufficiently interested to drop her pretence.

'Well, do 'ee remember what Mrs Clapp says when young maids goes all hysterical and screeches and kicks up about nothing much?'

Rosalind could recall several of Mrs Clapp's descriptions of this condition but not one that she felt she could repeat.

' 'Er says they got the mother,' said Obed triumphantly.

'So she does. That's right.' They had reached the house by now and Rosalind was much more herself. 'So you think . . .'

'Us'll say 'tis the mother that's troubling 'ee. See?' Though Obed's face remained as expressionless as ever he was glowing with delight at what was certainly his first attempt at wit. Rosalind took his rock-hard hands.

'Obed, I really think you're a guardian angel.'

'Do 'ee reckon? Now don't 'ee start again.' Rosalind's eyes had filled with tears. 'You get straight up to bed, maid, and I'll go and find Alice.'

The episode passed without further comment. A few days later Alice came in with the news that she had seen Mr Suckbitch driving through the village and up towards Moons.

'He was looking very cheerful,' she said, with a kindly glance at Rosalind, but Aunt Martha monopolized the remark.

'Well, in London he can get *that* whenever he wants it. 'Tis probably what he goes there for.'

'Why?' asked Rosalind. 'What's wrong with Mrs Bust?'

'Rozzy. Don't talk so vulgar.'

'You raised the subject, Aunt Martha.'

'I was talking to Alice. *Alice*'ll soon be a married woman most like.'

9

FOR whatever reason, Mr Suckbitch certainly was looking well, though his expression when he saw Rosalind suggested that he thought she was not. He had walked up to Sparkhayes in the late afternoon of the day after his return from London. It was already dark and he found a peaceful scene in the hall. Farmer Mutter was sitting by the fire making new forks and rakes from the wood that had been drying in a corner since Michaelmas. Alice was doing accounts and Rosalind was bringing her recipe book up to date. Mary had just led old Joan off to bed. Aunt Martha was in her room making the most of a bout of toothache, and Nicholas and Margaret were with her. She had spent the day querulously debating whether she should try Mrs Bash's remedy – the root of prickly asparagus boiled in wine and then held in the mouth – or Mrs Clapp's, which was to put water-pepper seeds in the hollow tooth itself. In the end, as far as the girls knew, she had tried neither. From time to time they could hear her in the distance shouting at the children.

Farmer Mutter gave his friend a cordial welcome. Alice fetched him some cider and Rosalind a seed cake from a batch she had baked earlier in the day. For a while they all spoke of London, so remote, so brightly lit, Mr Suckbitch giving them the news and details that he knew would interest them. Then there came a knock at the front door. Alice, excusing herself to Mr Suckbitch, went out and did not come back. They all knew it must have been Dick, they were all pleased that it should be, and so nobody commented.

Farmer Mutter began to nod. He had had a hard day hedging and ditching. There had been no frost for twenty-four hours and it had been an opportunity he could not let slip. Mr

Suckbitch and Rosalind sympathetically lowered their voices, and before Mr Suckbitch had got through a deliberately soporific résumé of the sermon he had heard at Paul's Cross on the Feast of Stephen, his friend was soundly asleep.

Mr Suckbitch looked down at Praise-the-Lord who, while his kindred, the hard-working mousers, were presumably keeping as warm as they could in sheds or barns, was lying in front of the fire, his front legs affectedly crossed as though he was posing for a sculptor.

'The silent night that brings the quiet paws,' punned Mr Suckbitch.

Rosalind laughed, but then said with some concern 'Oh, Mr Suckbitch, it couldn't have been *Gorboduc*. Not *again*.'

'No, it wasn't. I suspect *Gorboduc* has had its day. There's a new young man. Christopher Marlowe.'

'Oh, I know. He's the one who made the remark you told us about: that Jesus Christ's father was a bird. It made Mother laugh.' Rosalind's voice quavered and Mr Suckbitch looked at her attentively. 'But what sort of plays does he write? What's new about him?'

'He's written a play about Tamburlaine the Great, who had a lust for land and power and killed a great many people.'

'That doesn't sound so very different from *Gorboduc*.'

'No, put like that, I suppose it doesn't. But there are far more corpses and they met their death in more ingenious ways. And they talk a great deal more before they die. And they talk much, much better. I think perhaps that's the real difference.'

Rosalind still looked doubtful.

'At any rate, *he*'s convinced he's completely different. He starts by being very rude about existing plays.'

'I'll tell Mr Rolle about him.'

'I'm quite sure you will. Now don't tease poor old Toby, there's a good girl. Or giggle when he calls him Kit, as he certainly will. May I give you your present now?'

'Oh yes, please.'

He handed her a packet. Inside was a piece of red silk in which was wrapped a necklace of pearls. As they lay in the bright

116

material on Rosalind's homespun lap in the sparsely furnished room, they looked like beautiful visitants from another world. Rosalind went pink and burst into tears. Mr Suckbitch looked concerned again. He knew she was crying with pleasure but it was not typical of her. When something delighted her as much as these pearls obviously had, she usually smiled brilliantly and exclaimed.

'Do try them on, Rosalind,' he said when she had recovered and thanked him.

Rosalind dried her face carefully so that no splodges should spoil the effect, turned back her collar and put on the pearls.

'You'll have to tell me what they look like. My looking-glass is upstairs and if I go up to get it Aunt Martha'll come popping out.'

'Beautiful. Truly lovely. It's strange, Rosalind, you've just answered a question that I once made a note of, that day last summer when you asked me where you would look in place. Do you remember?'

'Yes, I do. It was the time you made a note to ask your doctor about Mother's illness.'

An odd expression crossed Mr Suckbitch's face. 'I did ask him, but all he said was "We just don't know". More honest than helpful.'

Rosalind swallowed hard. 'How have I answered your other question?'

'You look just like the Empress Theodora.'

This sounded splendid, but as Rosalind did not know whether the empress was alive or dead, or in which part of the world she was to be seen, or indeed anything about her at all, she could think of no way of finding out more without revealing her ignorance. Fortunately Mr Suckbitch was going on to give one of his short lectures in any case.

'I saw her on a mosaic wall at San Vitale in Ravenna. She's a sixth-century Byzantine empress and she's offering gifts at the consecration of the church. She's wearing a headdress with strings of white jewels – they must be pearls, I think – hanging down from it and lying across her neck and shoulders. You've always reminded me of someone and the pearls have made me realize who it is. Of course, she's older than you; she looks about thirty.'

'What colour is her hair?'

'It's completely hidden under the headdress.'

'Is she – I mean. . . .'

'Yes, very, if you mean handsome. Her eyes are big like yours and have hooded lids. She looks rather sad about the mouth as you do sometimes, but I think her smile would have been as pretty as yours. Of course she couldn't be smiling.'

'Naturally you can't expect any sort of animation from a mosaic,' said Rosalind who had never seen one in her life.

Mr Suckbitch grinned at her affectionately. 'Yes, you can. The poses have to be rigid and courtly, but as you walk along and the sun moves – the earth, I mean – you get a play of light which is a kind of animation.'

John Mutter stirred in his sleep.

'John's going to wake up in a minute. Listen. Mrs Bradbeer and I want you to play cards with us.'

'I don't know how to.'

'We'll teach you. We have a game of Primero or Trump nearly every day. We've got so used to each other's style of play that we need a third. Will you?'

'I'd love to. How shall I explain to Aunt Martha?'

'There'll be no need to. You don't really have cookery *lessons* any more, do you? You just write down the recipes.'

'Yes.' Rosalind handed him her book where just before his arrival she had inscribed: 'To roast a calf's head with a pudding in it. My Lady Pomeroy. Mrs Bradbeer's way.'

'Well, it wouldn't take long to jot that down and then we could play cards.'

John Mutter now woke up and asked about the news from Spain.

The news from Spain was what the whole village wanted to hear, and Mr Suckbitch was appealed to wherever he went. What he had to relate was not comforting. Reports were reaching London daily that the Spanish fleet was mobilizing at

118

Lisbon and few Londoners had any doubt at all that it was against England that it would be sailing. An equally cheerless fact was that the English fleet was not mobilizing, at Greenwich or anywhere else. Her Majesty was still hoping, apparently, that war might be averted and saw no reason to pay out good money for keeping her ships manned and provisioned until this hope had been altogether dashed.

This much Mr Suckbitch was bound to say, in the interests of truth, but after some heart-searching, he decided not to reveal that in the capital there were many shrewd and well-informed men who considered it far from certain that England could resist the coming invasion. In East Devon such doubts were easy to conceal. In the first place there were few Catholics in the district. Had there been they might well have been expected to betray their nationality in favour of their religion, and join the Spaniards when they arrived, but in fact there were no Catholic families nearer than Chideock and Lulworth to the east, and than Chudleigh to the west. The handful of Spanish doctors practising in Exeter were regarded perhaps rightly as men of healing, not of war. In fact, adherence to the old faith was not held against anybody by the inhabitants of Moon's Ottery. Mr Hall was not the man to whip up Protestant fervour in his parishioners, nor, had he done so, would he have been supported by such members of the gentry as Mr Rolle, Mr Suckbitch or even the Drewes. The yeomen, too, were tolerant of Catholics. Even Jane Mutter had been known to speak well of them, though in general her assumptions of broadmindedness had always had something sinister about them. Her daughters had maintained that she was capable of saying 'Well, 'tis a personal matter you know', about a witch's spiritual allegiance even as she bustled about helping to collect wood.

The only person who might have undermined local confidence about the defeat of the Armada was Sir Walter Raleigh, now Lord Warden of the Stannaries, who had expressed the opinion that when the Spaniards landed half the population of England would support them, but he was known to be eccentric and suspected of being an atheist. In any case, his words would have carried no weight at all compared with those of Sir Francis Drake. Maddening though it must have been for Drake to be kept in Plymouth all these months, farting into the wind, as he said himself, his presence was good for his fellow countrymen. He frequently came up to Exeter, and many patrons of the Ship Inn, near the Cathedral close, were able to quote what Er had said on the subject of the invasion. Both in and out of his cups, Er had no doubts whatever about the outcome, and such faith was infinitely heartening, especially as his own life and honour were so directly at stake.

All the same, as the days lengthened, fear grew. Winter had kept everybody safe. There had been scares and false alarms, it is true. One day the inhabitants of a fishing village on the south coast heard that foreign sails had been sighted. It was never determined who had started the rumour. There was talk of a stranger who spread the news and then disappeared; there was also talk of a citizen who made a stupid mistake, when drunk probably, and then put about a story of a mischievous stranger who afterwards disappeared. Whatever the source of the panic, however, they all ran inland in the teeth of a deadly blizzard, but got short shrift from the towns where they took refuge, their disgruntled hosts saying that they ought to be sent on to Bedlam where, it was well known, the inmates were always seeing soldiers with snow on their helmets.

But now spring was coming. Farmer Mutter walked heavily over his ploughland every day in expectation of the moment when it would stop squeaking under his tread and be dry enough for him to sow his peas and beans in silence. And when spring came, so almost certainly would the Armada. The six months' respite would soon be over.

Nobody forgot the attempt on the beacon. It had been endlessly discussed afterwards and there was no doubt whatever that all the inhabitants of Moon's Ottery could be accounted for on the night of the pageant. Even those Vikings who had stayed outside the barn longer than dramatic effect required had returned before the vital period of time. It must have been the work of an enemy and a stranger. Opinion as to his tactics was divided. Some thought he was clever to choose a time when everybody was known to be in the barn. Others felt it would have been cleverer to make the attempt on some evening when a great many people could have fallen under suspicion.

It was with a mixture of pride and resentment that the villagers received the news from Exeter that a similar attack had been made a few nights later on the beacon on the Haldon Hills, the one that preceded Moon's Ottery's in the chain. The watchers had been as quick and resolute as the Pulman brothers, and no harm was done, but it was disquieting.

It was unfortunate that the prophecies and predictions for 1588 were so horrifying. It was over a hundred years – and the news had had time to get round and round again – since Regiomontanus had stated categorically that in this very year, even if land and sea did not suffer complete collapse, as was most likely, whole kingdoms would be devastated and cries of grief would rise up from all over the world. More recently, Melancthon had specified the year as one in which the seventh seal would be opened and the last judgement take place, events which, though of a more spiritual nature, would be sure to involve painful upheaval.

The more sophisticated scoffed at these doleful forecasts, pointing out that none of the seers had committed himself as to which kingdoms would be devastated or, in describing how at the opening of the seventh seal the angel was to throw the fire-bearing censer down to earth, had indicated where it would land. Unluckily, however, the prognostications were given credibility by the fact that all the almanacs included among their more spectacular utterances news of exceptionally bad weather, and January and February had indeed been unusually bleak and tempestuous.

Mr Hall, for professional reasons, felt he had to find out what was being said at court. Loth as he was to preach sermons on topical subjects, he would have at least to refer to the invasion and he preferred to give the official view rather than anything more fanciful or revolutionary.

121

'Does Her Majesty pay any attention to these prophecies, Henry?'

'Do you, Noah?'

'I have to. "The stars in their courses fought against Sisera", you know.'

'So you're doubly bound to. The Bible and the stars. I shouldn't imagine the Queen is overawed by what the *Revelation* says. You need more than blood-curdling yells and a few earthquakes to scare princes. But I think she believes in astrology. She asked John Dee to cast her horoscope, you remember, though admittedly that was some time ago.'

'While he was still looking at the stars and not listening to – angels.' Mr Hall had been going to say 'devils' but remembered Mr Suckbitch's views just in time and felt that with so much strife abroad he deserved a little peace at home.

'And I do know that she's arranged to have more than one refutation published, which looks like paying attention.'

Although the Queen appeared to be doing little else in the way of preparing for the invasion, her subjects could be more straightforward. The trained bands exercised and manoeuvred more energetically than ever and their captains went to even greater lengths to get them proper equipment. The militiamen of Moon's Ottery and Rawridge were no longer the subject of jokes, however good-natured, but the object of admiration, and a spirit was growing among them that their training not only made a change from wrestling on the village green but had become the only way in which they might live to wrestle or have a green to wrestle on.

There was growing, too, a more national spirit. The previous year, when the scope of their activities had been explained to them by no less a person than the Lord Lieutenant himself, the common reaction had been the one expressed incredulously by Joseph Priddy in the tavern afterwards: 'Us don't have to defend they buggers up Churchinford, do us?' The prevailing mood had now become a vestigial feeling of responsibility towards even they buggers up London.

Some of the community considered themselves too free and

ranging to drill and march, and these the authorities wisely allowed to use their initiative in whatever way seemed to them best, as long as it had some bearing on the work of defence. One of these wild spirits, it need hardly be said, was Mr Rolle. The approach of danger had stimulated him even more than had his battle with the waywardens about the bridge over the Honiton road a few years before. He was a changed man. His headaches disappeared again; he took on more tutorial work and improved his professional standing. He had always held the necessary teaching licence which had been granted him by the Bishop of London, but as the natives of the Otter valley might not have appreciated the full weight of this qualification he also got testimonials from Mr Hall and Mr Suckbitch, to show to parents. Mr Hall's was a network of agricultural metaphor: Mr Rolle's pupils would be well rooted and grounded; they would be cultivated; they would flourish; their labours would bear fruit. Mr Suckbitch's was laconic and mathematical: plus Mr Rolle's tuition and minus personal indolence and recalcitrance any pupil's progress would equal a triumph.

In the matter of local defence, Mr Rolle had a plan which he put up to the Lord Lieutenant with enough enthusiasm for it to be ratified. His notion was that should the Spaniards land in the south-west they would move east along the road that led through Honiton to the Somerset border and so on to the capital. He proposed to stop them in their tracks at the very bridge that he had coerced the waywardens into repairing. He got hold of a small cannon and there he sat, full in the path of the enemy, through all the hours of daylight, visited with food and drink by his wife. She was usually accompanied by Turk who often collapsed moodily by the cannon and refused to go back with his mistress. There was a striking likeness between the gun and the dog as they sat there on their haunches, cross and plump, side by side.

The days lengthened and the spring came. The life of the farms went on. Farmer Mutter and his men were out early and late spreading dung, pruning out the pigs, picking up stones and sowing the last of the crops. The women of Sparkhayes prepared the vegetable garden and the herb garden and then started making cheese. In the pastures, the sheep were nearly ready for washing and shearing. Some of them had little enough wool but a few were getting quite luxuriant and as they stood with their tails to the sun they looked as round and light and shining as the dandelion clocks in the grass beside them.

Of the wars across the Channel, of the comings and goings of generals, and the rise and fall of kings, only confused and out of date rumours got down to the Otter valley, but one day a precise piece of news arrived: the Marquis of Santa Cruz was dead. His had been one of the two names on everybody's lips that winter, the other being that of the Duke of Parma, or, in the local version, Pamra. It had been surmised for some time that Santa Cruz would be leading the great fleet that was to sail from Lisbon and that Pamra would be bringing the army across from the Low Countries, on barges probably. Now the more ferocious of these two bogeymen was dead. There was considerable relief. The prowess of Santa Cruz at the battle of Lepanto had become a terrifying legend. Pamra, though his name was easier to frighten children with, had less real power to alarm. He was said to be a highly competent commander – far better, it was hinted, than the Earl of Leicester – but the great fear was of what was to come by sea. The activity of the trained bands was essential and sincerely believed to be so, but most people felt, by tradition and instinct rather than reason, that the real issue would be faced at sea; and there, instead of the none too brilliant Earl of Leicester, they could look to Lord Howard of Effingham, whom they respected, to John Hawkins, whom they trusted, and of course to Er, whom they adored. So the death of Santa Cruz built up an already existing confidence, even before it was known who his successor was to be. When the Duke of Medina Sidonia was finally named – by Mr Suckbitch, who had had a letter from London – confidence increased still further. Mr Suckbitch described him as a mild and scholarly man, in spite of his high birth modest and courteous in all his dealings. This sounded promising.

124

The time of waiting dragged on and every day the atmosphere grew more tense. People lost their tempers and the dogs never stopped barking. Drake had nearly reached explosion point. He could only approve of the way the western squadron was being kept ready and had nothing but praise for William Hawkins who was having the galleons scraped, tallowed and careened and arranging for the men to be well fed ashore, but what Er said in the Ship about the peace discussions between England and Spain still being carried on at Bourbourg could be repeated only in the coarsest company.

In the middle of April the Lord Lieutenant of Devon decided that in his county May Day celebrations should go forward as though it were a normal year. Some relaxation of the strain was clearly necessary, and if the Armada had not yet set sail it could hardly arrive till after the festival. So in Moon's Ottery the preparations began. Alice was to be Queen of the May. It was her first chance, as Mrs Mutter had been so set against the idea. It was also probably her last. The village had now completely made up its mind about her and Dick Pulman. Dick was a man of good feeling and would not suggest a betrothal until after the anniversary of her mother's death. Then – and nobody mentioned the Spanish invasion – there would be a wedding in the autumn and a christening the following summer.

Rosalind was shocked that Alice, in becoming May Queen, was going so exactly against their mother's wishes, but at the same time she admired her sister's strength of mind and argued for her in the face of Aunt Martha's mutterings of, 'How 'twould have grieved Jane', more than Alice argued for herself. Farmer Mutter was gratified and once caught himself saying 'How pleased your mother would have been', before he remembered that she would not.

Rosalind, though dreading the approach of June, was feeling better. The card games at Moons had helped her. She found the beautiful house soothing in itself and loved the cushions and the paintings, the silver and the handsome furniture, the like of which she saw nowhere else. There was even a birdcage, though never with an occupant; Mr Suckbitch disapproved of imprisoning birds, though he liked the cage for the charming object that it was.

She kept her pearls at Moons. She had expressed her anxiety to Mr Suckbitch.

'I'm so afraid Aunt Martha will find them.'

'Why, what would she do?'

'I had a brooch, and she let Nicholas and Margaret play with it and they broke it. And then she told me, in that triumphant way she has, that she'd asked Father for his permission to lend it to them.'

'And had he given his permission?'

'Oh yes, I expect so. She'd counted on that. Can you imagine him refusing?'

'I'll ask Mrs Bradbeer to look after them for you. She's got a jewel casket.'

So this was arranged and several times a week Rosalind sat at cards in the room with the leopard tapestry wearing her necklace over her country dress. Her relationship with Mrs Bradbeer was a source of satisfaction to them both. Mrs Bradbeer's daughter had died in childhood and Rosalind felt that, as she herself was motherless, they were rather like a sheep and a lamb, both bereft, that a clever shepherd had persuaded to take to each other, a relationship that was quiet and realistic. She also reflected sometimes as she saw Mr Suckbitch and Mrs Bradbeer together that it was strange the village should be so right in never suggesting any emotional involvement between them, though age, temperament, and, with only a slight inequality, station, would have made a liaison or even a marriage quite suitable. It was as though Mrs Bradbeer, pretty and womanly as she was, stood on some neutral ground. She had loved her husband dearly and he was dead. She had loved her children and still mourned for them, but she was not looking for consolation.

May Day was cool but dry, and oddly quiet without the bells, which, except for the passing bell, were being kept for warning and could not yet be used for rejoicing, so the Lord Lieutenant had decreed with a reassuring emphasis on the 'yet'. Rosalind went down to the crowning of her beautiful Alice, or rather Dick's beautiful Alice now, as she thought forlornly though she was fond of Dick. Afterwards she went back to Sparkhayes, glad to be out of the festivities for a while. There was work to be done. She had left Aunt Martha on the green telling Mrs Clapp all about her piles, a subject she normally kept for mealtimes, and had overheard part of Mrs Clapp's advice: 'Be sure to keep the little back yard clean and tidy.' At Sparkhayes, even if there was work, there was peace. Mary had not been robust since the birth of her handsome, loud-mouthed, sharp-eared son before Christmas and had to keep sitting down to rest in the chimney corner that old Joan had left for ever in the bitter winds of March. But she was getting stronger and did what she could and on the whole they passed a pleasant morning.

In the afternoon, Rosalind returned, though without any enthusiasm, to the village. She felt staid and ungirlish and out of things. For the first time for years she had not gone into the woods with the young people the evening before to get flowers and branches. Mr Suckbitch, she knew, would not be present at any of the events. He had stated that he had things to do at his desk. What they were Rosalind was not sure, but that he was not doing them she was certain. She was just working herself into a thoroughly bad temper when fortunately she saw Mrs Bradbeer sitting under a tree.

'You do look comfortable, Mrs Bradbeer.'

'My love, you surely don't expect me to run about playing Prisoners' Base.'

'No. I'm not going to either.' Rosalind sat down beside her. 'What a beautiful ring. I haven't seen it before.'

'No, I haven't been able to wear it before because of my chilblains. It's a present from Lord Burghley. Mr Suckbitch brought it back after Christmas.'

'I didn't know he'd seen Lord Burghley.'

'Oh, yes, he usually does. This time he dined with him and Sir Francis Walsingham.'

'Mr Suckbitch never wears rings, does he?'

'No. He says they make him feel trapped.'

'Well, I wouldn't mind being *imprisoned* in rings as beautiful as that.'

Their conversation died peacefully down and they sat there in amiable isolation as the revels went on around them. At one point a row broke out among the wrestlers. Unexpectedly a Cornishman was visiting the village and had been invited to join them, but took exception on moral grounds to the fact that while he was wearing thin-soled shoes as was customary in his country, the Devonians had put on heavy shoes, the better to kick their opponents' shins. Zachary Gollop resolved the situation by offering to lend him a spare pair of his own shoes. The Cornishman immediately dropped his argument about the unsportsmanlike nature of the equipment, accepted the shoes, and began to give as good as he got, to everyone's satisfaction.

It began to get cold and the women pulled their shawls about them. It began to get dark. Cressets were lit and suspended from the tavern, bringing a weird green glow out of the trees.

Hundreds of miles away the Spanish ships had already begun to leave harbour.

10

LOOKING back on it all, the following winter, Rosalind wondered a great deal about the nature of ignorance. On that May Day a dreaded event which was bound to have far-reaching consequences for everybody had taken its first step nearer, and nobody had been conscious of the fact. There were no portents and no premonitions. The might of Spain was on the seas, as one of the more flowery of the dispatches put it, and there were the objects of its violence dancing round the maypole, not bravely but ignorantly. She was tempted to conclude that reality consisted not of what you had imagined but of what you had not. Then she remembered the expression of terror on her mother's face in church at the Lock wedding and realized that her mother had known what was coming to her. So perhaps foreknowledge was a private not a public matter. Certainly she had seen no such fear on anybody's face when the Armada – which they all knew was coming to them sooner or later, like death – manoeuvred its way out of Lisbon harbour and turned towards England.

That it really was approaching was not announced in Moon's Ottery for some weeks. The villagers heard soon enough that Lord Howard had arrived in Plymouth and that Drake had been appointed Vice-Admiral and that the entire fleet was on the alert; news travelled fast across the county. In this case, however, it did not seem to mean anything specific. Spring was nearly over. What was going to happen must happen in the next three months, so all this activity could be merely common-sense preparation. There was a little half-hearted gossip to the effect that Drake should have commanded the whole fleet, but as he *was* the whole fleet in the minds of his fellow countrymen, and, indeed, it was said, in the minds of the Spaniards, too, there was little warmth in the discussion. Drake never mentioned the subject in the Ship but confined himself to cursing that he had not been allowed to scotch the Armada before it ever left home.

Definite news came first at the end of June. One of Walsingham's spies, stationed at Corunna, reported that the Spanish fleet had put in there on its way north. He spoke of victualling troubles, fever epidemics and tempestuous weather, but made it clear that not for one moment did he suppose that the Armada would not proceed as planned, and against England. He enumerated and described the ships: galleons, galleasses, armed merchantmen, craft for dispatch-carrying and reconnaissance, hulks, freighters and supply ships: a hundred and thirty vessels altogether.

It could not be long now. (Drake usually traversed the Bay of Biscay in under a week.) Midsummer was past and the days were drawing in. The cuckoo had left, the hay had been made and carted, the harvest was ripening quickly. The anniversary of Mrs Mutter's death had come and gone; to Rosalind's surprise it had seemed a day like any other, yet she felt better for its passing. A baby, the first of six conceived on the night of Accession Day, was born and pronounced by the village wags to be the spitting image of Mr Drewe who had been so un-precedentedly lively on that occasion, and in fact there was a resemblance of expression as Mr Drewe always looked as though he was experiencing discomfort in some part of his digestive tract.

One Saturday towards the end of July, Rosalind stepped into the courtyard and noticed that the wind had changed. It was blowing from the west.

Neither she nor Alice could settle to their work. In the early evening they went outside and leaned over the wall, looking down the valley as they had done on the night of their mother's death. It was a peaceful evening with the wind blowing pleasantly and a subdued but clear light bringing out the colour of the golden fields.

'I can hear church bells,' said Rosalind suddenly, clutching Alice's arm.

'Ow. Don't do that,' said Alice, but she listened carefully. Her hearing was less keen than that of her sister who could catch sounds almost as soon as Praise-the-Lord. Rosalind waited with the impatience of those gifted with superior faculties until a gust of wind brought to Alice as well as herself the notes of a faint insistent peal.

'Oh, I can hear them now. Not ours, though.'

'No, farther down the valley. Monkton, I think.'

'We must go up and warn William. We're the nearest.'

They set off up the little path towards the beacon, their hearts pounding so much that they could not run as fast as usual. Rosalind felt she was trying to run in a nightmare. At one point, just before the final ascent, they had to pause.

'How on earth,' gasped Alice, 'can we mime bell-ringing? He may never have seen it done. It might look like chopping wood or anything.'

'It doesn't matter about the bells. He doesn't depend on them. Obviously. He has to wait for the beacon at Haldon. We'll point at that and look sort of urgent.'

They set off again. As they stumbled up the last bend of the stony path and into the clearing they saw at once there was no need to point at anything or to look urgent. William was staring steadily at the line of hills that sheltered Exeter, seventeen miles away. He saw the girls out of the corner of his eye but did not budge. They stood beside him and stared too.

The Haldon Hills were blue-grey in the evening light with a crisp edge against the sky. They were flat and wide on top so there was no natural peak at which to gaze, and Rosalind saw at least twenty fires starting up and disappearing again before anything really happened. When it did it was unmistakable: a little curl of smoke wriggling up out of the ground. Then came the first spurt of fire, shooting out sideways, and then another flame stuck a tongue out in the opposite direction, so that they got a clear impression of the shape of the bonfire they could not see.

William waited no longer. He swung round, his eyes full of tears, at the thought, no doubt, of his own usefulness and the importance of his beacon. He knelt down with his back to the wind and opened his tinder box. With steady hands he struck a spark, lit the tinder and pushed it through a gap above the bottom logs. Smoke started to eddy about inside, feeling its way through the carefully-constructed flues and vents and at last into the outside air. Fire followed with a crack that turned into a roar as the flames streamed upward and eastward, towards the Blackdown Hills of Somerset.

And now the bells of Moon's Ottery tumbled into their peal. They had been silent since the day of William's wedding. As he had not heard them then and could not now, he did not turn towards them like Alice and Rosalind but kept staring at his beacon, though he stepped back several paces from the heat. Sweat had replaced the tears on his face. The relentless one-two-three-four-five-six beat through the air; the ringers were not risking any fancy changes on a night like this. Mizpah's cracked voice could be heard, but contained by those of her saner sisters. It was difficult to recall how she had sounded alone, as a passing bell.

The girls knew the valley must be springing to life, though what with the fire and the bells they could hear nothing: neither shouts nor bugles nor horses' hooves nor the barking of dogs. But in the fading light they could see below them three men riding down the valley, the first alone, on a grey cob, followed by two others, riding abreast on bay rouncies: Dick Pulman and his brothers off to the wars.

Everyone, they realized, including the militiamen, would be converging on the village, and in fact only Obed came up to the beacon. He stumped into the clearing as stolidly as if he had come to gather a bit of kindling and looked with unwinking approval first at the fire and then at William.

' 'Er's a proper beauty,' he said and patted William on the shoulder.

They had all forgotten about the beacon on Haldon. It had served its turn. It was not a fire to roast an ox on or dance around. They now gazed past their own, which was still blazing away, towards the Blackdown Hills. The watcher there, whoever he might be, was not as quick as William, which is what the village would have expected from they buggers up Somerset, but at last his flames too streamed up into the sky.

'Dunkery next,' said Obed.

The great beacon on Dunkery, far out of sight, was the giant of the chain. The responsibility of Moon's Ottery was over. Rosalind looked at their own fire. Nobody in the district had been brought up, officially, on notions of hell fire – Mr Hall consistently refused to invoke it as a deterrent – but the great blaze was vivid with thoughts of destruction and punishment and pain nevertheless. The wind was tearing red and yellow flames off it and throwing them away into darkness. Then, almost imperceptibly, it began to die down. It too had served its turn.

'Be you maids coming down to the village?' asked Obed. 'I'll go with 'ee.'

'I'd like to,' said Alice.

'I think I'll go home,' said Rosalind.

So Obed, Alice and William went down to the crowded, clamorous, flaring village, and Rosalind walked clumsily down the path towards Sparkhayes. She felt depressed rather than afraid and kept asking herself why she had refused to go to the village, and liked none of the answers. The moon, in its first quarter, was rising, and the wind was still blowing from the west. The bells rang on and on.

At home she found Mary at the front door. Rosalind took her hand, touched her wedding ring and smiled and nodded vigorously to show that William was well and doing his duty. Mary seemed reassured and they went indoors together. Aunt Martha was in the hall, mopping her forehead and neck emotionally.

' 'Twill kill me, the agony of it. After all, 'tis somebody's boys.' She seemed to be including the Spaniards.

Not wishing to dispute either of these statements Rosalind went up to bed, for it was now almost time, but she could not sleep. Alice came home and snuggled down rather complacently. In the east room Nicholas had a querulous nightmare. Next door Farmer Mutter snored. The bells at last stopped ringing, and Sparkhayes creaked its way into the night.

Sunday was a terrible day. It would be Sunday, thought Rosalind, when nobody could work to take their minds off what was advancing up the Channel. The militiamen were fully occupied of course and the church congregation consisted almost entirely of women. Rosalind nudged Alice satirically at the response, 'There is none other that fighteth for ùs but only thou O God.' Mr Hall, attempting to rise to the occasion, preached on the text, 'How are the mighty fallen', but was handicapped by the fact that they had not yet, and, in his experience, tended not to. In the afternoon rumours arrived of a battle off Eddystone. The wind rose towards evening, bringing squally gusts of rain.

Rosalind was first down the next morning though everybody got up with more alacrity than usual. As she was crossing the passage a knock came at the front door. It was Mr Suckbitch, looking like a stranger in the early light. She could see Mab, his black courser, tethered in the yard.

'Rosalind, I have to go down to Sidmouth. Would you like to come? I've put a pillion on Mab. We might see the Armada going past.'

'Oh, yes, please, Mr Suckbitch.'

'There's no danger.'

'Oh, how do you know? I mean, I'd come in any case. But how do you *know* there's no danger?'

'They have orders to go up the Channel to Calais without stopping.'

Too eager to get ready to ask him how he knew that, Rosalind hurried off to get her cloak. At the foot of the stairs she bumped into Aunt Martha, whose compassion of Saturday night had turned into a more warlike mood.

'Mr Suckbitch has asked me to go to Sidmouth with him. We might see the Armada.'

'I'd like to cut their cocks off and hang them round their

134

necks,' said Aunt Martha, presumably confining herself to the Spaniards this time.

'Mrs Pook,' called Mr Suckbitch, who could hear her voice but not see her or indeed catch the words, 'Rosalind will be quite safe.'

Aunt Martha came into view looking rather disappointed, but the thought of bloodshed had so mellowed her that she said 'Oh, I reckon the child might as well go,' quite amiably. So they set off. Mr Suckbitch led Mab down the yard till she was off the cobbles.

'Mr Suckbitch,' said Rosalind, settling herself on the pillion and putting her arms round his waist, 'where are they? How far have they got?'

'They're past Plymouth.'

'You mean they just went straight past? Without attempting to land or attack?'

'Yes. They obviously discussed it, though. There were comings and goings to and from the flagship for hours. The citizens of Plymouth were furious when they sailed on. They were all ready for them.'

'Everybody's ready. Obed was telling us yesterday that they've even got a gun at Exmouth. And it's only a collection of fishing huts. And there's that great sandbank across the estuary. Obed nearly laughed.'

Mab, walking carefully, turned into the steep hill that led down to the river.

'What would be the next port they'd try, if they did?'

'Weymouth, I imagine. But they won't.'

'Mr Suckbitch, how do you *know*? Has an angelic messenger appeared to you?' Rosalind, rising steeply from her depression of the two nights before, was getting slightly above herself.

'No, my dear,' replied Mr Suckbitch mildly, 'just a messenger.' Rosalind concluded that gentlemen were kept informed of events in a way that yeomen were not.

The cool of night was still present in the air and something of its darkness too, as Mab picked her way downhill. The river was bright grey and silver and the weed trailed sombrely in it.

135

'Which way are we taking to Sidmouth?' asked Rosalind as they started up the hill on the other side.

'I want to go a little way east to Collyforches first, so after that I think we'll cut across to the ridge above Blannicombe and not go through Honiton.'

'Why ever Collyforches? Oh, I know. How silly of me. There's that one point there where you can see the sea.'

'That's right. Zachary has taken some of the men up there to keep watch. There's no point in their going as far as Sidmouth, and clearly if they all stayed down in the valley the first thing they'd see if anything did happen would be the Spaniards coming over the hill.'

Just before they got to Collyforches they heard loud laughter and talking somewhere to the right. Evidently Zachary and his men, vigilant though they were no doubt being and though they had certainly been up all night, were not taking their responsibilities too grimly. They were gathered in a field just off the road. A row of trees bounded the field on the south side, and above them, between two ridges, shone a triangle of the English Channel, not big enough to contain more than one galleon at a time but for that reason likely to emphasize it more.

Zachary came forward. 'What news, sir?' he asked Mr Suckbitch.

'Excellent news. A good story at least.' The men gathered round. 'Captain Fleming was the first to sight the Spanish fleet. Off the Scilly Isles it was. When he got back to Plymouth with the news on Friday afternoon the Admirals were playing bowls on the Hoe. Captain Fleming made his report and Drake just said, "We've time enough to finish the game and beat the Spaniards, too," and went on playing.'

Everybody roared with laughter.

'Was Lord Howard there?' asked Zachary.

'I imagine so. Yes, he must have been. Captain Fleming would have reported to him.'

'Trust Er to have the first word,' said somebody.

'And the last,' said somebody else.

Then they all laughed again, more heartily than before even, as the real beauty of the story dawned on them. As men of Devon, living near enough to the sea to know the state of the tides, they realized after a moment or two that, at the hour the news was delivered, the sea was just beginning to pour into Plymouth Sound and that before any ship could possibly get out of harbour – with a west wind blowing too – there would be time to finish a protracted game of chess let alone a game of bowls.

The men immediately began to improvise on the story. 'Well,' said Joseph Priddy, making for a gap in the hedge, 'the Spanish Armada can wait but my bowels can't.'

Under cover of the laughter and joking Dick Pulman came up to Rosalind. 'Is Alice nervous?'

'Good God, no,' said Rosalind. 'At least, I don't *think* so,' she added kindly, on reflection, in order to leave Dick some loophole for the tender concern he was clearly longing to feel.

'I'm afraid she can't have slept very well these last two nights,' continued Dick. Rosalind, who had hardly slept at all, began to feel less kind, but just then Mr Suckbitch, who had been talking to Zachary, came up to her and said they should be moving on. So they rode off to the west, with the wind full in their faces.

'Oh, dear, Dick Pulman does *fuss*,' said Rosalind, having to raise her voice now, which, like all country people, she could do with ease. 'Mr Suckbitch, why *didn't* they put Drake in charge?'

'You can't put a pirate in charge,' Mr Suckbitch's voice blew back to her. 'Not of other pirates, that is. They tend not to obey each other.'

Across the valley they could see Sparkhayes, white and well-kept on its hillside. Although they were only a mile away as the crow flies Rosalind felt a painful nostalgia for it as well as a protectiveness so violent that it surprised her. They soon turned left on to the ridge that spurred down towards Sidmouth and would carry them nearly all the way there. Mab who had a taste for the sea began to canter. Rosalind clasped her arms tightly round Mr Suckbitch's ribs.

'Mr Suckbitch,' she bawled, 'you feel like a tree.'

'A what?'

'A *tree*.'

'In what way?'

'Warm,' she yelled, 'like a tree trunk,' she drew breath for the grand conclusion of her simile, 'that's had the afternoon sun full on it.'

'My dear. What you say. Does me good. I've always wanted. To feel like that. But could you say it. At Sidmouth? We're screaming ourselves. Hoarse.'

'Oh, I've said it now.'

'Thank you. Very much.'

The hedges were no less gleaming and luxuriant than they had been farther inland. There were as many foxgloves and wild roses; there were as many yellow butterflies. But soon Mab was not the only one who could smell the sea. Hints of it came excitingly along the now warm summer air to the two human beings, and before long, across fields and woods and common land and bracken, they saw the English Channel, not the keyhole view of Collyforches, but a broad beautiful expanse, as though a door had been opened into a big room. There was not a ship in sight. The wind was falling and the white wave-tips had a mechanical look about them that showed they were the result of the previous night's squalls and not the herald of storms to come.

The road from Branscombe to Sidmouth ran along the cliff, through cornfields, at right angles to the ridgeway. They joined it and went down the steep hill so slowly that normal conversation became possible again.

'The beautiful cornfields,' said Rosalind.

'Yes,' said Mr Suckbitch as though he found the remark true but uninteresting.

'I mean, our men, our sailors, can see their next winter's food. While they're fighting, I mean.'

'You think that would spur them on?' Mr Suckbitch sounded not only interested now but involved. Rosalind had often noticed that he needed to know where his next meal was coming from.

138

'Oh, yes. When I saw Sparkhayes just now I felt I could pick up a pitchfork.'

'So did I, Rosalind, so did I, when I saw the church.'

'The *church*?'

'Moons lies behind it.'

They came to the ford, shallow but with deep brown water on either side of it, that had been the terror and delight of Rosalind's childhood, and into the narrow streets of the little town, with its smell of fish and the screams and shadows of seagulls.

'Now, Rosalind, I suggest you go up on to the cliff and wait for me there. I've got to go and see somebody. You won't be alone,' he added with a grin as they observed a crowd of citizens, neat as to dress but ragged as to formation, scurrying out of their houses and making for the cliff path. 'Like rats hoping to see a sinking ship. *Au revoir*, my dear.'

'*Au revoir*,' said Rosalind with an air.

She certainly was not alone. Before she had even set foot on the cliff path, a vagrant, such as she had never seen in Moon's Ottery, accosted her. She gave him a coin from her pocket, wanting to be liked even by a vagrant. He glanced expertly at it, realized the generosity without worrying about the motive and said with genuine cordiality, even while looking about him for the next patron, 'God bless you, maid.'

'Oh, not at all,' replied Rosalind thoughtlessly, and started up the path. The great beauty of the Sidmouth cliffs at this time of year was the enormous clumps of mustard. Rosalind knew it was properly called black mustard, but what was black about it she had never been able to understand, as it was yellower than buttercups and seemed to light up the whole landscape. As she climbed she remembered her mother's reaction to the comment of one of their men who had been to Sidmouth for the first time one July when she was a child: 'God's been shitting mustard,' he had said on his return with awe and amazement. Mrs Mutter had duly told him off for vulgarity and blasphemy but her daughters had heard her laughing in the dairy afterwards. As Rosalind toiled up the sultry path she felt that God had certainly been shitting mustard in the summer of 1588.

At the cliff edge to her right, seagulls kept appearing and disappearing, but the higher she went the more silent they became. The foliage was so dense and tangled as to shut out all view of the sea except for an occasional sparkle. Once at a rare gap she looked over but the beach was now so far below as to make her giddy. At last she came to the open space where she knew all the watchers would be gathered. The first thing she saw was a pile of weapons stacked on the grass by the entrance, an extraordinary assortment: arquebuses, muskets, pikes, even some longbows, as though several centuries were all going to war at the same time. The Sidmouth militiamen clearly felt it to be not only their right but their duty to command what was almost certainly the best view that anyone in England was likely to have of the Armada.

To the east the tall bright-red cliffs stretched away in folds to a point where they became covered with greenery, on the other side of which they emerged pure white and so continued up to Beer Head. All her life Rosalind had disliked and distrusted white cliffs, feeling that the correct colour was red and anything else was an aberration. To the west lay Sidmouth with its fringe of beach, ending abruptly in a less spectacular series of little promontories and headlands – Hern Point, Brandy Head, Danger Point – bright-red but less showy, covered with homely fields.

Limited as was Rosalind's experience of the world, village life had taught her to distinguish from a crowd of know-alls any person who really did know. On this occasion she was helped by her quick hearing. In the absence of ships a man was identifying to his friends all those who joined the crowd. 'There's Farmer Mutter's youngest maid,' he said. Glancing at him, in what she hoped was a casual manner, she realized he was someone she herself did not know and accordingly gave him full marks for omniscience, almost full marks, that is, unless he was using the superlative ungrammatically. She edged towards his group.

It was useful that she did so, for at that moment there appeared from behind Danger Point the first ship of the day, or rather two ships: a galleass, her bank of oars flashing brightly and vigorously, towing what must have once been a galleon, a sad sight now, misshapen with her stern castle blown away, smoking blackly and wallowing low in the water.

'Ah, there she is,' said the man who knew. 'I was wondering.' His tone was purely omniscient and gave no indication whether the wreck was a cause for mourning or rejoicing. 'The *San Salvador*,' he went on. 'She blew up last night and had to be abandoned. Looks as though she's being towed into Weymouth.'

'Who blew her up then, Harry?'

'One of her crew.'

His friends laughed derisively. 'Own goal,' said somebody, and they all laughed again.

'Half of the buggers jumped overboard.'

'Which half then, Harry, top or bottom?' More laughter.

The morning wore on. The smoke of the *San Salvador* merged into the greyness beyond Beer Head, and nothing else happened. 'A fine time to leave me,' thought Rosalind, beginning to feel lonely and frightened and thinking better of her scorn at Dick Pulman's fussy attentiveness to Alice, but at last Mr Suckbitch appeared at the top of the path, skirting the pile of weapons. She went up to him and they stood together apart from the others.

'They're nearly here,' he said in a low serious voice. 'They'll be coming round the point in a few minutes.' Rosalind began to shiver and he took her hand.

A yell went up from the crowd. Round the headland came the Armada: the Invincible. Rosalind understood then and for ever afterwards the meaning of the word; it had nothing to do with whether you were actually conquered or not. The beauty, the heaviness, the height of the ships was terrifying and definitive. Their slowness surprised her, you could walk as fast. Somehow, against all her previous observation of sailing ships, she had expected the Spanish fleet to come dashing and scudding up the Channel, but in fact they came as slowly and inescapably as a nightmare. She had also expected them to come in a line, something like a team of horses, but here they were in a wide crescent, seeming to block the Channel, as though against all nature a new moon had expanded to fill the sky.

'Is that the flagship?' whispered Rosalind, pointing.

'Yes. The *San Martín*.' Mr Suckbitch spoke with inexplicable feeling.

'Why are they in that curved shape?'

'You'll see as they get a little farther past. You can begin to see now. If any of our ships tried to get in and disrupt the formation those two backward wings would close in like a pair of pincers. That's where they've placed some of their strongest ships of course. It's no more than defensive, but it's clever.'

'But where *are* our ships?'

'Your question is about to be answered,' said Mr Suckbitch, as cheering began to break up the complicated silence that the passing of the Armada had induced: a cheer for Lord Howard in the *Ark Royal* with its embroidered sails and Byzantine turrets, leading the fleet in line ('en ala' Rosalind heard the man who knew describing it); a cheer for Hawkins in the *Victory*; a cheer for Frobisher in the *Triumph*; then silence while everybody drew breath for the loudest cheer of all.

'Where's Drake?' It was Harry's first and last question of the day. But the Vice-Admiral's absence seemed to cause no alarm, merely excited speculation. It was inconceivable that Drake should have come to any harm. It must be some brilliant ploy, the meaning of which would be revealed later.

'El Draque,' said Mr Suckbitch to Rosalind and began to laugh.

'Why? What? Tell me.'

'Well, apparently yesterday afternoon about the time the *San Salvador* blew up, the *Rosario* collided with another ship, lost her bowsprit and couldn't proceed. They tried to tow her but the cable snapped. So they had to leave Pedro de Valdés to it, and as far as anybody could see – the light was going, you know – he wasn't getting on with the repair work any too quickly. Well, as night fell,' Mr Suckbitch laughed again, 'Drake decided to leave the fleet for an hour or two, it seems.'

'What, without telling Lord Howard?'

142

'Without telling Lord Howard. You may remember what I said about pirates. He was supposed to be leading the fleet, too – a signal honour – and they were all following his poop lantern. He must have extinguished it and just disappeared.'

'But what *will* he tell Lord Howard?'

'Oh, he'll have some marvellous tale. He saw some mysterious ships which could have been Spaniards attempting to land, or something like that. He felt it his duty to investigate and in the course of his researches – at dawn, I imagine – what should he come upon but the *Rosario*?'

'Oh, no. No. A very wealthy prize.'

'A very wealthy prize indeed. Now safely in Torbay.'

'And the captain? Pedro . . .?'

'De Valdés. On board the *Revenge*.'

Mr Suckbitch could not possibly have timed his story better. ' 'Tis Er,' shouted someone, and roar upon roar went up as the *Revenge* flipped jauntily round Danger Point, nimble and fast, zealously catching up the fleet, conscientiously bringing to the Admiral a highly important captive.

'A strange view de Valdés must be having of his own fleet,' said Mr Suckbitch. The Armada was now well on its way to Beer Point and they could all see into the concave side of the crescent formation, stately and lethal.

'But Mr Suckbitch, why are we just *following* them?'

'My dear, what else can we do? At the moment? There was some sporadic fighting yesterday. There'll be some more today or tomorrow. But we can't do much to disrupt that formation, though they'd like us to try. Lord Howard is a wise man. He knows what he's doing.'

'I see about the pincers, of course. But why didn't we meet them head on, off Plymouth?'

'Oh, that was the cleverest thing of all. Not to, I mean. We're holding the weather-gauge now, you see. Howard must have stood out to sea right in the path of the Armada and then doubled back in some way and come up behind them.'

The afternoon was well advanced now and the ships were blurring into the distance. The watchers on the clifftop began to move. Harry and his friends chatted their way down the path. The militiamen disentangled their weapons and turned towards their homes. There would be no fighting for them today. Let the men of Hampshire and the men of Kent carry on.

Rosalind sat down, ungracefully. 'I'd like to wait a bit, if you don't mind, Mr Suckbitch.'

'I'd like to, too. Don't cry, my love, though I know how you feel.'

'I don't want to sound like Aunt Martha.'

'There's little danger.'

'What a funny thing to say in the circumstances,' Rosalind spluttered.

'What did Aunt Martha say?'

'That after all 'twas somebody's boys. All of them.'

There was a pause. Then Mr Suckbitch said, very sadly, 'There's a great deal of ambition out there, a great deal of pride, but less cheerfulness I should think in the *San Martín* than in the *Revenge*. Francis Drake is a confident and a lucky man. Medina Sidonia is neither.'

'You know the Duke well?'

'I knew him, yes. Not very well, naturally. The difference in our ranks precluded that, though an Englishman abroad can move more freely than at home, of course.'

'Oh, of course.'

'He was affable to me.'

The wind was freshening. 'Come, my dear, it's getting cold. We don't want Mrs Clapp giving you good advice tomorrow.'

They began to walk westward along the cliff. After a few steps Mr Suckbitch paused.

'Don't dream about murdered men tonight, or if you do, spare a dream for those whose honour is to be wounded, whose pride – proper pride – is going to be destroyed.'

'I will, I promise I will, Mr Suckbitch, but I have to tell you that, if it were me, I'd rather live with wounded pride than be dead.'

'So would I, Rosalind, so would I.'

He gazed eastward again. The tall Spanish ships were still in sight, bunched against the sky; and he looked as though his thoughts were with the flagship where the Duke of Medina Sidonia was standing, that dignified, unlucky prince who had been affable to him.

They had a cool ride home. The air was full of white moths that wriggled and landed like snowflakes. Mab looked as though she had been to the North Pole. As they got to the descent into the Otter valley, they saw three riders ahead of them, one on a grey cob and two on bay rouncies: Dick Pulman and his brothers going back to get in the harvest.

11

AN unreasonable calm settled over the Otter valley, as though in passing the Devon coast the Armada had sailed out of the inhabitants' lives for ever. On the Monday evening those with quick ears or lively imaginations heard firing in the distance, and on Tuesday morning news got through that there had been some sort of engagement off Portland Bill, but nothing much seemed to have happened, any more than it had off Eddystone, so presumably the Spanish fleet was still advancing up the Channel in formation, towards its reinforcements at Calais, towards the Thames, towards London, with the English fleet still watchfully following. A moment's realistic thinking would have made people aware that the next view they had of the Spaniards might be of them marching systematically westward, to colonize and govern, as so many races had done before them, but nobody seemed to be thinking realistically. Ever since the invasion had been talked of, dwellers in the southern counties had been consistently scornful of those who lived in the north, well out of harm's way, but now if they thought of them at all, it was with something like fellow feeling.

It was, however, the calm not of fulfilment but of anticlimax. Throughout the community, personal worries, which had receded in the presence of danger, came flooding back. There were so many calls on Mrs Clapp's skill – people bleeding or failing to bleed, copiously vomiting or unproductively retching – that she ran out of herbs and, with a mixture of triumph and annoyance, had to borrow some from Mrs Bash. Mr Hall was similarly embarrassed by appeals for spiritual advice; old guilts loomed up to torture people, and Mr Hall was so anxious to seem not to be hearing confessions that he entertained all penitents in the parlour and offered them refreshment, so that he ran out of malmsey. Several housewives, legally serving fish on Friday, fell into a panic that they might be considered papistical. Toby Rolle trundled his cannon back home and started on a series of prostrating headaches.

At Sparkhayes and Sweethayes, John Mutter and Dick Pulman were preparing for the harvest, which looked like being an exceptionally good one. Alice, now unacknowledged heiress of the two farms, was both complacent and hard-working. Rosalind, hard-working, too, but the reverse of complacent, resumed whenever she could her walks down to the river. She was now feeling the pain she had expected to feel on the anniversary of her mother's death, but it was beginning to be complicated by resentment. She blamed her mother for dying. 'A fine time to leave me,' she said aloud as she walked, 'a fine time to leave me,' echoing the words she had used about Mr Suckbitch on the cliffs at Sidmouth, words she had never consciously needed in her life before.

On the third evening after her return from Sidmouth she was walking down the lane in the dusk. She was weary. She had been busy from first light getting ready the provisions that would be required for those cutting the corn. Farmer Mutter took on extra men for the occasion and they would all be out in the fields early and late, with the women carrying food to them. It was some time before she could get the smell of cooking out of her nose or, she felt, her clothes and hair. It was a wholesome enough smell but did not go well with the raw, untamed though sweet odour of the evening lanes and fields that presently stole through to her. The usual summer mist was over the valley, delicate not thick, but mist all the same, and she was sufficiently honest to reflect that at least she could hardly blame her mother for risking death by going down into the evening mist, popularly supposed to be such a killer, when she was doing the same. But she had no dependents, nobody to leave.

A man was standing on the bridge. As she approached, he walked slowly and quietly towards her, his hands spread out, not in Mrs Rolle's boundless gesture of immensity but as though to indicate modest harmlessness. It was the way in which any intelligent person on a farm – as opposed to those who shouted and waved their arms – would go up to a nervous animal. About two yards away he stopped and looked gravely at her. '*San Salvador*,' he said.

Rosalind stared; first at his face which was a peculiar colour. Pallor she would have expected in someone who had had a narrow escape from death four days before and had presumably been living rough and on the run ever since, but this colour was quite new to her, a sort of pale brown, almost grey, though it was not the grey of ill-health. The men of the Otter valley were ruddy and sunburnt in youth and prime, and pink even in old age. Mr Suckbitch, it is true, was comparatively pale, but it was the explicable pallor of someone who spent much time indoors, and went for walks rather than spending long days in the fields. Mr Drewe was deadly pale, but that was straightforward bloodlessness.

She then looked at the stranger's clothes. They had once been fine but the colours had run and the braid was tarnished. Moreover they were badly singed. In fact he looked quite theatrically like someone who had jumped out of a burning ship. She did not bother to ask him if he spoke English. It was obvious that a man in his plight would, if he could, say something more ingratiating than simply the name of his ship.

She pointed to the parapet on the bridge. 'Sit,' she said, 'stay,' as if she was talking to Rex and Lass, the only difference being that they would not have obeyed and this man did. She noticed the grace with which, even in these circumstances, he sat down. Then she hurried back to Sparkhayes. 'Oh, God,' she thought, 'do I have to spend my entire time running uphill?' and then had to pause for a moment to laugh, as the question sounded like some motheaten speculation about life. She would tell Mr Suckbitch.

As she entered the courtyard, a candle was still burning in her father's bedroom, but it was to Obed's door that she ran. It opened as she approached. Obed was obviously just going out

148

on some final visit of inspection as his lantern stood ready and he had picked up his dagger.

'Oh, Obed, there's a man.'

'I reckon I'll need to know a bit more than that, maid.'

'Down by the river,' she said, and pointed.

'I reckon I knows where the river be to, after sixty years. What sort of man then?'

'A foreigner. A real one I mean. Not just somebody we don't know. He says he's from the *San Salvador*. A Spaniard.'

'Come on then, maid. Best have a look at un.' Obed stuck the dagger into his belt and took up the lantern.

The Spaniard was sitting exactly as Rosalind had left him, looking strangely at home. He got up as gracefully as he had sat down, and bowed. Obed, without imitating his courtliness, but equalling him in dignity, stood absolutely still and gazed at him. 'Mm,' he said at last and turned to Rosalind.

' 'Ee certainly do look as if 'ee'd been at the wrong end of an explosion. Best take un back to the barn for the night.'

'Right. Let's.'

'Come,' said Obed to the Spaniard, and the stranger accompanied them. At Sparkhayes, the house was now in darkness except for a candle in the passage.

'No call to trouble your father tonight. I'll give this chap some blankets and dry straw, if you goes up and gets un something to eat and drink.'

Rosalind moved quietly through the sleeping creaking house with her candle. It was easy to select food from the stocks she had assembled earlier in the day. She gave a little thought to the drink and decided that some of the elderflower wine, that she had prepared for the haymakers in June, would be the most refreshing thing for a man who had had his bellyful of salt water. Obed took these provisions into the barn.

'Off to bed then, maid,' he said as he came out and closed the big door behind him. 'Can't do anything more tonight. First thing tomorrow, I'll tell your father, and 'ee'll send for Mr Suckbitch, like as not. 'Ee speaks Spanish. The only one who do.'

149

This was true, Rosalind thought as she went to her room. The younger men, she had heard, were learning Italian; certainly Mr Drewe's son spoke it fluently, according to his own account and his mother's. Mr Drewe himself was no linguist, even his English being rather costive. Mr Hall limited himself to professional Latin. Mr Rolle spoke a little airy French. And that was all.

While the girls were dressing next morning, Rosalind told Alice the story. She spoke as though it was the most natural thing in the world and Alice received the tale in the same spirit, though in fact nothing half so strange and exciting had happened to either of them before. As soon as breakfast was ready they set aside some food and drink, and with the most cursory of explanations to Aunt Martha, went down to the barn together. Nicholas wanted to go with them, but Aunt Martha seemed to think that Spaniards were in some way catching and forbade him to, in spite of his whining.

The barn door was heavy and awkward, so Rosalind handed the plate and pitcher to Alice before starting, with a proprietorial air, to open it. Normally she might well have left the task to Alice, who never expected her sister to wait on her, but that morning a sense of showmanship inspired her. As usual, after a lot of heaving and shoving the door did the last two feet in a clattering rush, carrying Rosalind in with it. Recovering herself, she had a sideways view of the Spaniard getting up lithely from the straw, and was struck again by the quality of his movement, which was different from anything she had seen before. Dick Pulman and even the older men in the valley moved rhythmically and effectively when they worked, but this man's actions and gestures seemed to exist in their own right, to draw attention to themselves, and yet at the same time to be unconsidered, even unconscious.

Although it was still early the morning was bright, and as Alice stood in the doorway holding the plate and pitcher she appeared to be luminous, like the angel in one of Mr Suckbitch's pictures. She was staring at the Spaniard, not rudely but contemplatively. He was staring at her in the same way. Thanks to Obed's hospitality no doubt, he had washed, combed his hair and beard and even smartened up his clothes. After a few moments he bowed low to Alice, and later to Rosalind when he caught sight of her in the shadow by the wall. Alice handed him what they had brought.

'He looks more like himself this morning,' she said as they went up the yard again.

'How do you know? How do you know what that ever was?'

'Rozzy, what's the matter with you? It's only a way of putting it.'

Immediately after breakfast, Obed set off for Moons, as Farmer Mutter, though unwilling to bring his friend out at an hour that Mr Suckbitch usually reserved for happenings like the Armada, felt that the time had come to summon an interpreter. While Alice and Rosalind were clearing the hall, Rosalind kept peering out through the amber window.

'You seem very interested in the Spaniard, Rozzy.'

'Of course I'm interested. He was my find.'

'Finders isn't keepers, you know, with men.'

'Just because you're going to marry old Dick Pulman, who isn't all that much of a mystery, you needn't think you know everything about men.'

'Dick Pulman has depths.'

'So has the ford at Sidmouth.'

'You see. The water's very deep there. You used to be terrified of it as a child. I never heard such howling.'

'Not at the actual ford it isn't. Just about two inches. It's only deep at either side.'

'My dear Rozzy, you must have been associating with some very pedantic people.'

'If you mean Mr Suckbitch, as I presume you do, at least he isn't an open book.'

'No, just a book.'

Rosalind glared.

'Anyway, who said I was going to marry Dick Pulman?'

Rosalind was jolted out of her anger by genuine surprise.

151

'Why, everybody. All the village. Father. Aunt Martha. Everybody.'

'Have you ever heard *me* say it?'

'Well, no.'

'Then wait till you do.'

They heard noises coming into the bottom of the yard and, reconciled by curiosity, they hurried to the front door and looked out. Mr Suckbitch and Obed were dismounting and Farmer Mutter was going forward to meet them. After a short consultation Mr Suckbitch went into the barn alone. The girls did everything they could think of to stay out in the front courtyard: shook out crumbs, fed scraps to Praise-the-Lord, even started weeding between the cobbles. At last Mr Suckbitch reappeared.

'Come on, Rozzy,' said Alice. 'We've a right to know.'

They joined the group in time to hear Mr Suckbitch say '. . . so I really think you should let him stay, John. Good morning, Alice. Good morning, Rosalind.'

His nod to them both was as cool as it could be. Rosalind had not seen him since the day at Sidmouth and was bewildered by this apparent dissolution of their good understanding.

'He's in danger at large,' he continued.

'Surely not,' said John Mutter. 'I'm willing enough to keep the chap. But the Armada's gone by and he's on his own. Surely nobody would take against him, as it is.'

'No, precisely, as it is, they wouldn't. But wait till English blood has been shed. They'd murder him.'

'Would he work?'

'Yes, indeed. He's offered to. He's got land of his own in Spain. He understands farming and isn't above soiling his hands any more than you are, John.'

'Well, I've certainly got a bit behindhand, with William being up at the beacon all this time. He's a fine lad, turned out to be, William has, and I'm grateful to him, but there's no denying I've had to let a good few things slide. I don't mind letting this chap stop. What do you say, maids?'

'I agree,' said Alice.

'What's he called?' asked Rosalind.

Mr Suckbitch rattled off a long name.

'Oh dear, can't we just call him San Salvador?'

'Now, don't be whimsical, Rosalind.'

'I wouldn't need to be whimsical, Mr Suckbitch, if you'd take the trouble to speak the name more slowly, or to repeat it, or even to write it down for us to see. In your *notebook*, you know.'

'Rozzy, you've been too pert since your mother went. Too pert by half,' said her father.

'I couldn't catch the name neither,' announced Obed. 'I idn' educated but I idn' maze. And we got to call un something.'

Mr Suckbitch looked distressed. 'I gave the wrong impression. I'm sorry. I *will* write the name down, Rosalind, but I do my notes in the evenings now and I haven't got my book with me. In the meantime couldn't you perhaps just call him Señor? Or Señor Xavier. That's his Christian name.'

'I'll endeavour to be correct,' said Rosalind and flounced up the yard as well as anybody could flounce on cobblestones and banged the front door, but not before she heard her father say apologetically, 'Nobody understood that little maid except her mother.'

The village approved the arrangement about the Spaniard. Mr Drewe turned it over in his mind and condescendingly nodded agreement. Mr Hall said, 'I was a stranger and ye took me in,' rather absent-mindedly, but added with enthusiasm that it was a great thing to have extra help at harvest time. The last comment was echoed by all the farmers in the valley, who began to wonder if John Mutter had been left in with the bread after all. The Spaniard was removed from the barn and promoted to the apple loft, a fragrant space above the dairy. It took up the width of the house and the roof sloped down to the floor both to the north and the south, so that a man could stand fully upright in only a small area in the middle of the room. There was no sense of constriction, however, for a tall window in the thatch looked over the courtyard and fields, right down the valley towards the sea. On a clear night you could see lights moving down in Monkton and up on the ridge that divided the Otter valley from the Channel. For the first few days, when nobody expected him to work, the Spaniard spent most of his time gazing out of this window. Whenever the girls were in the yard or the front field they could see his pale meditative face framed in the reeds of the thatch.

'Shall we wave?' asked Rosalind.

'No. I doubt if he can see anything nearer than Spain.'

Harvesting began. The atmosphere in the fields was cheerful, though there was an undertone of haste, as the wind was veering and the weather might be going to change. Alice, Rosalind, Aunt Martha and Mary went to and fro all day with provisions, so the girls had every opportunity of seeing how Señor Xavier was being received by the rest of the community. Though every farm was largely taken up with its own harvest, there was considerable coming and going at this time, disguised as neighbourliness or undisguised as curiosity. The reputation of each farmer depended on his crop, and there were plenty of people who found time to bustle about reporting to everybody on how everybody else was doing.

The Spaniard, looking elegant even in clothes provided by the combined rummaging of Farmer Mutter, Obed and William, worked with the best, in spite of his recent experiences. This was the quickest road to general benevolence, and as he scythed away hour after hour while the sun rose and sank, there were comments of, 'Well done, lad,' and 'Bugger idn' afraid of work, eh?' from those who momentarily straightened up and looked about them. He was willing to learn, too. Farmer Mutter, who assumed an air of authority at harvest time which he could not summon up during the rest of the year, showed him the traditional local way of cutting corn: much nearer the ground than was usual in other parts of the country, the object being to ensure a supply of really long reeds for thatching. The method was more difficult and more tiring, but the Spaniard soon mastered it.

As she left the field with an armful of empty cloths and dishes after the midday meal, Rosalind let the others go on and paused to gaze at him as he scythed up his path the golden field away from her. She had been standing there rather a long time when she was conscious of Obed beside her.

'He's adaptable, isn't he, Obed?' she said in her school-mistressy voice, trying to sound detached.

'Mm. Turn his hand to anything, that chap.' Though the words were congratulatory, Obed's tone was dour, surprisingly so coming from a man who was remarkably generous about other people's achievements.

The fact that the Spaniard could speak to nobody mattered very little in the harvest field, where action had taken over and words were barely necessary. His expression was in keeping with the harmony of these fruitful summer days. Surliness or even anxiety would indeed have jarred, but he managed at all times to look amiable and at ease. He never actually smiled. Rosalind often wondered what he would look like if he did: how his lips would part, what sort of teeth he would have. Her own community suddenly seemed like a bunch of grinning, cackling idiots, beside him.

His communication with William and Mary was as good as, perhaps better than, that of the others. They realized he could not talk and were drawn to him. He realized their condition, and looked at them with a peculiarly intent gaze which seemed to convey something to them, perhaps the fact that he took them seriously. He never mimed to them in the representational way that the villagers did but used gestures that were eloquent in themselves, and abstract. Rosalind felt that if, against all probability, *he* had had to mime the lighting of the beacon at the approach of the Armada, he would have done it success-fully without representing ships or the Channel, a bonfire or a tinder-box.

On the evening of the first day of harvest Rosalind was sitting in the courtyard shelling peas, feeling more at home than she had done for weeks. Though she was less weary than she had been, she had no particular wish to go down to the river that night, and thought she would do better to get on with the next day's food. Praise-the-Lord was walking round the outside of the house talking to himself, as was his habit. He had an extraordinarily articulate mew: many of the noises he made sounded like words; tonight he seemed to be saying 'only'. His voice was soon joined by that of an owl, somewhere on the hill behind the farm, who wailed desperately and unceasingly. Rosalind feared the sound; she had never been able to rid herself of the childish mistake that it was bats that hooted. She was just beginning to wonder if she could stand this weird coincidental duet any longer, when the owl suddenly fell silent and the percussion of horse's hooves took its place. Rosalind knew this meant the approach of Mr Hall and went indoors to fetch her father.

As everybody knew, Mr Hall was making a round of the farms to arrange about the delivery of the tithe corn. This did not indicate rapacity on his part – he would get the corn in any case – but a desire for seemliness. The lanes that led to the tithe barn were all very narrow and awkward, and one year the teams of two waggons had simultaneously refused to give way. There had been a free fight and a considerable amount of corn had been spilled. So now Mr Hall composed a timetable and everything went smoothly. The farmers appreciated his consideration in calling on them at the end of the day, instead of interrupting work in the field or summoning them to his house.

Farmer Mutter was nodding neck-breakingly in his chair but when Rosalind told him of Mr Hall's arrival he went out to greet him with alacrity, much greater alacrity than if he had come on some spiritual mission (which in fact he was very little likely to do). A man could communicate with his God unaided but to take corn to a tithe barn needed a mediator. It was some time, however, before they came to the subject of corn.

'News,' said Mr Hall as his host ushered him in, and John Mutter and his daughter remembered the Armada. In his mild voice Mr Hall told them an exciting story. Pamra ('I'm sorry; it's catching'), Parma had not kept his tryst, nobody knew why not, but Medina Sidonia had waited at the rendezvous all the same, having little alternative. This had been the opportunity the English fleet had been looking for. With the wind still blowing from the west they had launched fireships into the

156

great crescent. No Spanish ship had caught fire but that was not the point. The impregnable formation had had to break up to let the fireships through and now at last Drake and the others could get at their enemy, and nobody doubted what the outcome of that would be.

' 'Tis the end of the war then, you reckon,' said Farmer Mutter.

'The end of this Armada, I do believe,' replied Mr Hall. 'But the beginning of the war.'

12

THE very day after the harvest had all been gathered in, the weather broke. The wind now blew strongly from the south-east, a gale sprang up, and blinding squalls of rain strode across the stubble-fields. A villager who had been up to the farm at Collyforches reported, on his bedraggled and breathless return, that the sea had changed colour and the waves had changed shape.

Nicholas and Margaret caught messy, snivelling colds, and Rosalind went down to Mrs Clapp to fetch something for them, ordered to by Aunt Martha but glad enough to get out of the sound of their irritating coughs. Squelching across the village green on her way home she saw Mr Suckbitch and Mrs Drewe squelching towards her. They were past the Moons turning so she presumed Mr Suckbitch was escorting Mrs Drewe to the manor gates and so it proved. Mrs Drewe boomed something that sounded like, and probably was, 'What weather', at Rosalind who yelled back agreement, hoping that the comment called for it, and went on her way, pulling her shawl further over her head and trying to pick off the wet strands of hair that clung to her face like leeches. Mr Suckbitch soon caught her up. They had not met since the tiff in the courtyard and the manner of both was as constrained as was compatible with talking in a blustering wind.

'Come up to Moons and let Mrs Bradbeer make you a hot drink before you go on to Sparkhayes.'

'Thank you. I'd like to.'

By the time they got up the hill the current rain-squall had passed over and as they entered the gates of Moons, the two heavy horses that drew Mr Suckbitch's carriage through the rough lanes were being led out to the front of the house, their fetlocks streaming on the wind like weeds in water and their habitual kindly smiles broadened by the exciting turbulence in the air. The carriage was already there, looking slightly less shabby than usual with the glimmer of rain on it. Rosalind wondered very much why Mr Suckbitch was going to London, and at such a time, but did not feel like starting on any natural enquiries about his journey. Mrs Bradbeer, when she had settled them in the parlour with their hot drinks, went off to finish packing up food for the road. Mr Suckbitch always travelled with stacks of provisions, as though London was a desert with no oasis or palm tree anywhere. He never finished them, no one could, but each time he meticulously brought back the remains even if they had gone mouldy, which partly accounted for the stale smell of the carriage.

'It'll be very blowy on the Plain.'

'I'm not going over the Plain this time. I thought I'd take the south route and have a look at Wilton House on the way. I haven't seen it for ages and it's so beautiful.'

'It's a pity Sir Philip Sidney's dead. He was a relation, wasn't he, and often there? You could have given him Mr Rolle's kind regards.'

'I don't know any of the Pembrokes, alive or dead, but they let you look round.'

'But won't it delay you? Mr Rolle says it's a huge house.'

'Yes, but I may have to kill time anyway. There's someone I have to meet in Salisbury, and heaven knows when he'll get there. I know when he's starting off – I had a letter yesterday – but the roads from London, once you get out of the city, are almost as bad as these.'

'But if you're going to London why can't you meet him there?'

'Because he's on his way down here.'

'Then why . . . ? Oh, never mind.'

'Can't I meet him down here, you were going to say.'

'No, I wasn't. Well, yes, actually I was, but I thought better of it.'

Rosalind sipped her hot drink. 'Mr Suckbitch, why were you

159

cross the other day? In the courtyard, when you said I was whimsical.'

'I was worried,' he said crossly.

'What about? I mean, may I ask what about?'

'It may be outside your experience, Rosalind; I don't know. Have you ever felt that in following a certain course of action you had to cozen *somebody* and couldn't decide whom?'

'No, I haven't. No, never.'

'I can't tell you the details because it's a personal matter but that was the problem I was worrying about.'

'It sounds terrible.' At a loss, Rosalind sipped her drink again. Mr Suckbitch, who as she had frequently observed seemed unable to sip, had already swallowed his. 'How is Xavier getting on?' he asked as though trying to change the subject. Rosalind understood that he was using the Christian name by itself deliberately and was gratified.

'Oh, fine. He worked very well at the harvest. He did scything mostly. He's very good at it. Tell me, he's not really a farmer, is he?'

'Why, what do you think he is?' Mr Suckbitch looked startled.

'I mean, not like Father and Dick. More like a lord, I should have thought, but one who can do everything his men can, probably better. Not like Mr Drewe.'

'Very nearly right. He tells me he's the younger son of a lord who has a large estate outside Toledo.'

'Will you show me on the map some time?'

'Certainly. When I get back. I ought to be loading up the carriage now, if you'll excuse me.'

As they went towards the front door together he recited, in a conversational way: 'Purse, dagger, cloak, night-cap, kerchief, shoeing-horn, wallet and shoes.'

'I can see it's a list of what to take, but it sounds as though there's more to it somehow.'

'So there is. It's all in hexameters. Fitzherbert. He's not one to teach us only what not to leave behind in the inn, if he can teach us poetic metre at the same time.'

'Please say the line again. I could hear there was something but I didn't realize it was a hexameter.'

'I'll give you the next line: Spear, mail, hood, halter, saddle-cloth, spurs, hat, with thy horse-comb.'

'So it is,' cried Rosalind, delighted. Mr Suckbitch smiled at her pleasure, but as he looked down the hill he suddenly became gloomy and irritable.

'For days nothing comes up this lane, but whenever I set out on a journey it's instantly like the queen's highway and I get held up.'

'Oh, Mr Suckbitch, how could that possibly be? As you say, nothing comes up this lane unless it's something you've ordered and are expecting. Moons is the last house, and the Luppitt traffic goes along the top. And if something did come up unexpectedly it couldn't do it *every* time you wanted to drive down.'

'It could and it does.'

'But do you take any notice of the times you set out and it doesn't?'

'I would, if it ever happened.'

'But, Mr Suckbitch, if you really believe that, how do you account for it? Is it the devil or some evil spirit? And why should it pick on you?'

'You don't understand, I'm afraid. Now, my dear, I really must be getting off. The days aren't as long as they were.'

As Rosalind got to the bottom of the hill, sure enough a cart was just turning into the lane. It was only a two-wheeled tip-cart but there would certainly not be room for it and Mr Suckbitch's carriage to pass each other without considerable manoeuvring. Rosalind giggled half the way back to Spark-hayes.

August was nearly over before the weather began to clear. There had been no more news of the Armada, no reliable news, that is, only a plethora of rumours so wild and contradictory that even Farmer Mutter could not believe any of them. Of one thing only everybody was convinced, by means of their own observation: that with the wind blowing so strongly in the direction it had been, the Spanish fleet could hardly be coming back again down the Channel, so as far as most people were concerned it might just as well have vanished. There was certainly nothing to be done. About the question of land-fighting, information was much more plausible. Parma, who had clearly not been escorted across the Channel by Medina Sidonia, had not arrived on his own either, which had at one time seemed a decided possibility. The English army had been mobilized at Tilbury, the Queen had gone to inspect the troops and had made a speech, the most vivid phrases of which made their way into the Otter valley, to be used or abused by those who had a taste for phrases. 'Let tyrants fear' was adopted by Zachary Gollop and applied to anyone who crossed his path, while Mr Rolle soon assembled a repertoire of jocose remarks about the hearts and stomachs of kings.

The heat of the summer did not return. When the outdoor work of the farms could be resumed, it was in autumnal sun, with days that were cool though often golden. The agricultural year started in the customary way with the rams being put to the ewes. For this, the date that had to be avoided all over the country was the fourteenth of September, which, as the Feast of the Exaltation of the Holy Cross, had been the traditional day in the time of the Old Faith for the coupling of sheep. The farmers of the Otter valley always chose a day in the first half of the month. It meant that their lambs were born slightly earlier than in other shires and indeed than in other parts of Devon, but as the winters were relatively mild and the pasture exceptionally rich this did not matter. Towards the end of September came the sowing of the wheat and the rye, and on the day when that was finished everyone felt that the cycle of the farm had truly begun.

The next day was Sunday and the bells, now free to ring again, were pealing cheerfully up the valley as the Sparkhayes household walked down to church. When they came to the last bend in the lane, however, there was a sudden strange jangle as if someone had taken the tower and shaken it and in the course of a few minutes the bells clashed clumsily and inharmoniously into silence. The explanation was apparent to the Mutters as soon as they emerged on to the village green. The churchgoing groups were excitedly gathering at the lych-gate where Mr Drewe was making some sort of announcement, and the ringers had presumably abandoned their bells in haste in order to join them; some busybody must have pounded up the stair to the ringing chamber with news. Mr Drewe's speech seemed to be causing a sensation out of all proportion to his listless delivery. Alice and Rosalind ran on ahead but by the time they arrived he had finished and gone into the church.

There was no lack of informants, however; the girls were soon in command of the facts. At last there was official news of the Armada, or what had been the Armada. Soon after the incident of the fireships, the Spaniards, driven by the wind and with the English fleet behind them, had had no choice but to sail away northwards along the east coast of England, buffeted and beset by the evil weather. They were badly mauled; the English fleet was barely damaged and, in spite of shortages of ammunition and food, was behaving very cockily. Lord Howard – he was being mentioned now almost as often as Drake – had followed the Spaniards as wisely and as watchfully as he had followed them up the Channel: past Hull, past Newcastle, past Berwick, till they were off the coast of Scotland. It then became so obvious that the Spanish fleet was incapable of landing anywhere or of doing anything at all but dragging itself back to Spain – and even that looked doubtful – that the English fleet had turned away and put into the Firth of Forth, and left their enemies to it: the final decisive gesture of victory. The Armada had disappeared into the wind and rain, heading for the ruinous north coast of Scotland.

The ringers, who had hurried back up the tower again after hearing the news, now rang a brief triumphant peal as the congregation pressed into the church. Hardly anyone took in a word of the first part of the service but by the time Mr Hall entered the pulpit to deliver his sermon they were ready to attend.

'*So let all thine enemies perish, O Lord.*

'Dearly beloved brethren, we meet here today, as we should have met in any event, to celebrate the goodness of God. I need not repeat what you have already been told this morning: that God has in recent days been good to us in no ordinary measure, that he has scattered the foes of our country and utterly put them to flight. In the puddled waters of adversity we have been shown the reflection of his face and after the dark hours of eclipse we have seen him brightly at last. I could wish that the proud task of leading our rejoicings had fallen to a worthier person than I, but your own actions and intentions will support me; to them I confide myself. The laurel wreath like the shroud fits everybody by expanding or contracting itself to each one's size. Let us all give thanks together.

'*So let all thine enemies perish, O Lord*. These words were spoken by Deborah, who was a judge of Israel, in her hour of victory. She had gone up to Mount Tabor with her captain Barak and all his host, to discomfit Sisera and his nine hundred chariots of iron.

'When we see and hear valour in a woman we necessarily set more store by it than when we find valour in a man, who by birth and upbringing is formed for gallant deeds. How can we sufficiently praise and give thanks to God for our Gracious Lady Queen Elizabeth, who, like Deborah, has shared the toils and dangers of war with her captains and with her subjects, and who rode to Tilbury with Robert Dudley, Earl of Leicester, just as Deborah accompanied Barak to the battlefield, to inspire and encourage her troops? In the catalogue of female wonders she is a glory both to our nation and to God whose instrument she is, a chosen arrow drawn from the quiver of the Lord. Heart, stomach, wit and mind, all the organs of her body are his and the music they make is by him.

'To echo the words of that Deborah of old must be our first duty: *So let all thine enemies perish, O Lord*. But, Deborah. . . .'

Rosalind had never followed a sermon so far in her life and even now when she lapsed into her own imaginings they were concerned not with fantasies of lovemaking but with the implications, both glad and painful, of what had actually happened in her own world. As always, the peroration brought her back to her immediate surroundings.

'Finally, dearly beloved brethren, let us remind ourselves of another passage in the victory song of Deborah. The triumphant prophetess spares a thought for the enemy; she considers the sufferings of the mother of Sisera *who looked out at a window and cried through the lattice: "Why is his chariot so long in coming? Why tarry the wheels of his chariot?"* Brethren, I have served God in this parish in the reigns of three monarchs and in two separate fashions. We do not now worship God as our late enemies do. We receive our absolution nearer at hand than Rome and less wasted in the carriage. But let us not be numbered among those who go to heaven against each other's wills. Our Queen once replied to an ambassador who was persuading her to return to the faith of her sister and of her grandfather that, even as it was, she hoped to be saved as well as the Bishop of Rome. She would, I think, hope equally that the Bishop of Rome might be saved as well as herself. Reflect, dear brethren, that in this mortal life there are no evergreens; death like this late tempestuous autumn will shake us all by heaps into our graves. And under five feet of earth the Duke of Medina Sidonia will sleep as free from care as Lord Howard and Sir Francis Drake, though the oak tree springs above their graves and the orange tree above his.

'Brethren, mercy speaks in a sweeter and more audible accent than victory. May the wings of the cherubim, like a cool, comfortable shadow, shelter us one and all from the scorches of the last judgement. Blessed be the Lord God of Hosts who has given us the victory over our temporal foes. May he also give us the victory over our last enemies, hell and death, and may we all, conquerors and conquered, be merry together in his eternal hall.

'In the name of the Father, Son and Holy Ghost. Amen.'

The congregation came out of church more subdued than they had gone in. Alice and Rosalind talked to each other in low voices.

'Rozzy, do you suppose Mr Hall had that sermon ready all summer in case of victory?'

'Mr Drewe may have told him last night and then he could have sat up writing it.'

'Then I think Mr Drewe might have gone round the valley and told the rest of us too and put us out of our misery.'

'Well, Alice, we weren't in it particularly, but I agree, so he might. Actually, I expect Mr Hall had it ready. Mr Suckbitch says that in London when famous people are seriously ill or very old or condemned to death, the printers get broadsheets ready so that they can be handed out on the day.'

'Do you think Mr Hall had a defeat sermon prepared then, or one on the death of Drake or something like that?'

'The death of Drake he could have adapted from the death of Sir Philip Sidney and a defeat one he'd hardly have had time to gabble out before the Spaniards arrived, so probably not.'

They heard a shout behind them and turning round saw their father approaching, accompanied by Mr Hall.

'Mr Hall here says Zaver ought to be told.'

Rosalind choked with fury at her father's pronunciation of the name. At the beginning, following Mr Suckbitch's lead, he had said Havéer, like everybody else, but unfortunately he had recently seen it written down and had mulishly insisted ever since that a name spelled like that was obviously pronounced Zaver. She had tried to reason with him but it had made him more obstinate, and reproachful, too, that all her education had failed to show her that X was pronounced Z and not H.

'Oh, dear,' said Alice to Mr Hall, 'of course he ought. I'm afraid I didn't think.'

'But how?' asked Rosalind. 'I mean, in what language? With Mr Suckbitch away.'

'Latin,' said Mr Hall. 'I can't rattle away in conversational Latin as Her Majesty can but I know from the Vulgate all the words about ships and tempests and the sea. My very lack of fluency may help to break it to him.'

When they reached Sparkhayes Mr Hall went straight up to

the apple loft, and the girls could hear the stilted rhythms of his church Latin. He came down looking sorrowful.

'He's taken it very much to heart. So many of his friends, you know. There probably isn't a noble house in Spain that won't have lost somebody.'

'Is there anything we can do?' asked Alice.

'Let him stay where he is at present. Don't let him come down to the hall. Rosalind, you're the cook nowadays, I hear. Could you take him up something to eat, something special perhaps?'

'Yes, of course. But, Mr Hall, there's one thing. Xavier will be perfectly safe now, won't he?'

'Much the same as before, I think, Rosalind. The war isn't over, you know.'

'But the Armada was the only way the Spaniards could land on English soil, and it's been destroyed.'

'Philip of Spain has always said that if this Armada failed he could easily muster another. That may be true.'

'Yes, I see. Xavier came when the Armada had gone by, so if another one was on its way, he'd actually be worse off.'

'I'm afraid so. He would certainly need to be in some stronger position than he is. Your good father's employment of him wouldn't be enough.'

When Mr Hall had gone, Rosalind climbed the ladder with a plate of the best delicacies she had in her store. She knocked and entered the loft. The smell of recently picked apples was overwhelming.

'Señor Xavier,' she said.

He was standing at the narrow window, apparently staring down the valley, with one arm resting on the lintel and his head on his arm. He did not move. Rosalind waited for a while, noticing distractedly the beautiful pile of tithe apples set aside on a trestle table, and wondered if Mr Hall had, however distractedly, noticed them, too.

'Señor Xavier,' she said again. Still he did not move. She put the plate down on the table beside the tithe apples, and took a few steps towards him.

She tried a third time: 'Señor Xavier.' With a feeling that

167

what she was doing was momentous she raised her arm, which seemed all at once unmanageably heavy, and put her hand on his shoulder. If he moved at all then it was to give the faintest of shrugs; he did not turn. Rosalind looked past him down the long valley and imagined she could trace in the autumn air the path her mother's soul had taken on the night of the passing bell.

Leaving the food on the table, she descended the ladder.

13

THE next evening Rosalind went down to Mrs Clapp's and was as usual invited into her working parlour. The days were perceptibly drawing in now and the room was grey except for the circle of lamplight.

'Well now, dear, who is it this time? Aunt Martha or one of the children?'

'It's me, Mrs Clapp.'

'Why, dear, what's the matter? You are a bit peaky now I come to look at you properly. Had a quarrel with your little friend that visits you once a month, eh?'

'Oh, no, Mrs Clapp, it isn't that.' Rosalind was in a state of such agitation and distress that she could say no more but just sat looking wretched.

'Now, Rozzy, you mustn't upset yourself.' In the middle of her words of consolation Mrs Clapp turned to stir something. 'There's nothing to worry about.'

'Mrs Clapp, I'm not on my deathbed.'

The white witch veered round and stared at the girl, as though Balaam's ass had spoken (so Rosalind thought even in her anguish), or at least not quite that: Mrs Clapp had always known Rosalind to be highly articulate so it was more as if Balaam's ass, after you had thoroughly got used to the fact that it could talk, had suddenly said something surprising.

Mrs Clapp forgot the brew she had been fiddling with and gave Rosalind the kind of attention she had never given a patient before. Her face, pickled by years of professional healing, was transformed at the first encounter with rallying that she had ever recognized as such. She looked as she might have looked before she took up medicine at all or as she still might have looked if she had not been living alone so long – she had been widowed early – with no family or close friends to keep her human. She had always been accounted an honest woman; now she was visibly so. Rosalind felt free to explain her trouble.

'Mrs Clapp, I'm in love, with someone who doesn't – who doesn't –'

'Love you.'

'Who doesn't even *see* me.'

'That's bad then. Seeing you can't speak to him.'

'You know who it is?'

'Of course, maid, of course. Everybody does. You colour up so when he's named.'

'Oh, dear.'

' 'Tis nothing to be ashamed of. I wouldn't give twopence for a woman who went to her grave without ever having put her heart in the wrong place, as you might say.'

'You think it *is* in the wrong place then.' Rosalind went cold.

'I'm afraid so, dear. *He's* not the one.'

'Why not?'

'I'm not saying that anybody has to have words. Look at your William and Mary, look at that cat of yours, that Wat – and I know what you call him between yourselves, you naughty maids – you and he are as close as black witch and familiar, without a word spoken. 'Tisn't because you and this chap can't talk to each other yet. If 'twas right there'd be a way. But I'm thinking you need somebody you can have a bit of conversation with right from the start; 'twould happen that way, I mean. You don't talk the hind leg off a donkey, I'm not saying that, but you're quick with a word. If someone says something you'll cap it like. Look at just now. And you can hold your own – *I've* heard you – with folks that are much better educated than yourself.' Mrs Clapp gave what was for her a meaning look.

'You do believe in love potions, don't you?'

' 'Course I do, and 'course they work. It needn't be a potion either. There's juice you can put on a man's eyes when he's

170

asleep, and when he wakes up, if you're the first person he sees, he'll fall in love with you all right.'

'Then why won't you – you know what the juice is?'

'I know what 'tis but I won't. 'Tis man-handling nature. I'm a white witch, not a black one. Besides, do you really want a man who loves you just because he's had a bit of juice squeezed on his eyelids?'

'Yes.'

'I know, dear, I know. But you won't always think so. It's got to happen naturally. And 'twill, believe me.'

'But *you* don't let *everything* happen naturally. You'd have saved Mother from death if you could. You came to her at once, and you brought a bag of things made out of herbs.'

'Herbs are natural, see. Nothing grows in vain and they can help. Keeping warm and clean is natural and that helps, too. I often tell people to do that. 'Tis when you start changing the wind or killing other people's cattle or, like I was saying, forcing people to fall in love, that you turn as black as hell. And then they have to burn you, see.'

Rosalind was sufficiently interested in this point of view to forget her misery for a while. She wondered whether Mrs Clapp had evolved this philosophy to explain her own ineptitude in the face of emergency or whether her apparently supine behaviour was the logical outcome of her beliefs. The white witch saw that her words had in some way helped and followed up the improvement by suggesting that though she was not prepared to give her client what she wanted she could give her a cordial which would make her feel calmer. Rosalind accepted it, thanked her sincerely and went home in the deepening twilight. There was something in what Mrs Clapp had said which comforted as well as interested her, though she was as much in love as ever with Xavier, who never seemed to see her.

Mr Suckbitch returned to Moon's Ottery in mid-October, when all the farmers in the valley were stacking logs in a week of fair weather which might well be the last before winter set in. Rosalind was anxious to see him, so anxious that she examined her motives and decided it was because he was the one person in the valley that she could be quite certain did not know of her love for Xavier. Mrs Clapp's statement that everybody knew about it had shaken her, though she realized it was something of an exaggeration. She could think of two exceptions to start with: Aunt Martha, who did not pay little girls the compliment of believing they fell in love, and her father, who would not take the responsibility of noticing anything which might seem to call for parental guidance. Alice she was not sure of; her sister gave no sign, either by way of direct comment, which would have been unlike her, or by teasing, which would have been very like her, that she had grasped the situation, and they never had the sort of conversation about Xavier which would have made Rosalind show her feelings, voluntarily or involuntarily. But of Mr Suckbitch she could be sure; he had been away during the whole critical time, and even now that he was back it was safe enough, as he was not a person to whom people gossiped, or if by chance they did he remembered it all the wrong way round.

It was not the shame of having a past passion recalled that she dreaded. She had never been in love before, but she had enough imagination to see how foolish a woman might feel when and if ever she fell out of love: how unattractive, how fat, how ill-chosen the object of her passion might now seem to herself and have seemed to others all along. But hers was a very present passion. She thought of Xavier all day and saw everything in terms of him. Whenever she could, she contemplated his gracefulness and his melancholy pale-brown face. She could see, hear, smell, taste and touch him from afar. Strangely she did not dream of him at night. She would like to have done; it would have been better than waking up in the soft darkness, as she now habitually did, and hearing Alice's breathing which seemed to have taken on an unbearable sensuous quality.

It had not needed Mrs Clapp's remark to suggest to her that it was a hopeless passion. She had read stories where those in love, for various quite credible reasons, gave no indication of their feelings, but she doubted if this happened in real life. Nobody had ever been in love with her, she was sure, but she

172

was equally sure that if anybody had been he would have done something detectable about it.

One morning, a few days after they had heard of Mr Suckbitch's return, Rosalind set out for Moons, determined to use all her ingenuity and energy to prevent Xavier's name coming into the conversation, as she knew she would blush if it did, and even Mr Suckbitch might notice if her face suddenly went scarlet, or she would think he must have noticed and become awkward in her manner.

As she walked down the lane each farm she passed was giving off a low booming sound as log was piled on log. The air was crisp but not cold enough to have subdued the smells of the valley. She enjoyed the crispness, and positively gave thanks for it when she saw Mr Suckbitch coming round a bend towards her. It was so much easier not to blush out of doors especially on a cool day and, if the worst did happen, heightened colour could always be put down to healthy exercise. She stepped up her pace, so as to give greater plausibility to this explanation, should it be needed.

As the distance between her and Mr Suckbitch narrowed, Rosalind thought how English he looked. This had never occurred to her before, as her usual reaction had been to contrast him with the other men in the Otter valley, but now more exotic standards had broadened the comparison. It was not just a question of race either; species came into it. Xavier reminded her of one of the deer in Mr Drewe's park. Mr Suckbitch resembled one of the solider fauna of the region.

After the first greetings, Mr Suckbitch said he was on his way to Sparkhayes to see her father, so Rosalind, whose only destination had been Moons, turned back with him, and immediately plunged into speech.

'I was sorry about the Duke of Medina Sidonia,' she said in her hostessy voice, which she had not used to Mr Suckbitch for over a year.

'Yes.' He sighed. 'This will break him. The responsibility, the failure, on top of all the doubts he must have had from the start.' He sighed again.

173

'Will his religion help him?'

'Possibly.'

'His learning? Surely learning gives a person strength?'

'Have you ever found it to do so?'

'Oh, yes.' The conversation, she thought, was developing on safely impersonal lines, impersonal, that is, compared with the subject of Xavier. 'Quotation helps. When Aunt Martha is being very unpleasant, I say to myself:

> Then shalt thou know beauty but lent
> And wish and want as I have done.'

'That doesn't sound very appropriate to Mrs Pook. It sounds more like when Alice is being unpleasant.'

'Oh, Mr Suckbitch, you mustn't be so literal. It's just an expression of vengeance and final triumph. Besides, Alice is never unpleasant. Alice and I are allies. Aunt Martha is the enemy. She brings about the tragedies.'

'Mrs Pook has made you suffer, I know, but. . . .'

'You haven't heard what happened the Sunday before last. We were in church and the Goslings came next to Nicholas. Well, you know they're supposed to have been in contact with the plague. Oh, you probably haven't heard but they are. Aunt Martha made me change places with Nicholas. She doesn't care if *I* get the plague. And afterwards she told me that it wasn't because she loved me less than Nicholas.'

Rosalind's anecdote succeeded beyond her intentions. Mr Suckbitch looked as if he would like to murder somebody, preferably Aunt Martha.

'Mrs Pook is a wicked woman.'

'Of course, I do annoy her, on purpose sometimes.'

'You provoke her, I know. I've heard you. But that's no excuse.' He glared for a while, then went on more calmly, 'But I was disputing your use of the word tragedy. Your aunt makes you suffer, but as though she were a pitchfork or a runaway horse. You may goad her or you may simply be in the way. You don't cause her.'

Once again Rosalind had met a point of view which took her

mind off her heart. She walked along so deep in thought that Mr Suckbitch's next remark did not have an immediate impact.

'Talking of learning, I'm going to ask John if he doesn't think Xavier ought to have some English lessons.'

Mr Suckbitch was looking straight ahead so Rosalind had no need to busy herself with some interesting sight on the other side of the hedge, and in fact by the time she had got back from the nature of tragedy to Xavier's English lessons, she did not blush at all.

'And you'll be the teacher, of course?'

'I think it'll have to be me, as the only Spanish speaker. Theoretically, I know, you can teach a language using nothing but the language you're speaking. You know, parts of the body: the head, the neck, the chin, the elbow. Pointing to them. But I wouldn't rely on it myself.'

'Anyway, Xavier might want to talk about things you can't point to. And he certainly wouldn't want to talk about his chin and his elbow.'

'You think it's a good idea?'

'It's an excellent idea.'

November was a busy month for Rosalind, though her activities were different from those of twelve months before. There was no question of a pageant this year; for one thing the Drewes were going to be away. Mr Suckbitch was openly jubilant. For him it had been the effort of a lifetime. Rosalind was only slightly disappointed. Much as she had enjoyed writing her scenes and looked forward to writing more at some other time, she felt she could do with a break. This year, now fully recognized as the cook, she had to cope with the heaps of offal from the beasts that were being slaughtered before the onset of winter.

So autumn wore away. October passed calmly and windlessly into November. Smoke went up straight, and the fallen leaves lay still on the ground in the shape of their trees. Xavier worked willingly but not always as successfully as in the harvest field.

'Do you know, Rozzy, Xavier nearly fainted this afternoon.' Rosalind had hardly left the kitchen all day and Alice was keeping her abreast of the news.

'How? Why? Was he hurt?'

'Not in his body but in his *mind*,' said Alice importantly and then grinned at herself. 'It was when they were killing that last sheep. Xavier was supposed to be holding on to them, while Father and Obed cut their throats, and this particular sheep was putting up a real fight and it seemed as if Xavier couldn't stand it any more and he let go. Much worse for the sheep of course in the end.'

'You know, Alice, the slaughtering does seem to have been especially bloody this year. I've never done the offal before, but it has seemed bloodier.'

'Well, I felt a bit faint myself, and goodness knows I've watched enough animals being killed in my time. I thought perhaps I was seeing it through Xavier's eyes.'

'But that's the strange thing. Why should his eyes be like that?'

'Oh, he may have missed the slaughtering on his father's estate. I get the impression he could more or less choose what he did.'

'Yes, but he couldn't have missed the slaughtering on the *San Salvador*. Half of them were blown to pieces. One sheep would be nothing to it.'

'That's true, Rozzy. Oh well, there's no accounting for it.'

'Unless he cares about animals more than he cares about men. I often feel like that myself.'

'Remember to say so when Father's listening.'

'So what happened? Did Xavier fall down?'

'No. He went very white and groped his way to the door. I didn't know what to do. In the end I just put my hand on his shoulder.'

'And did that help?'

'Ugh,' said Alice, looking down into a pail of offal. 'I see what you mean, Rozzy.' She raised her head. 'Yes, it did seem to.'

The weather continued fair and Rosalind saw little of Alice who was working out of doors. She did not see much of Xavier either. She imagined that he must go to bed early for often when she went out into the courtyard in the evening, after a day in the kitchen which still smelled of blood, there was no candlelight in the apple loft.

Towards the end of November, Alice got up unusually early one morning and was out of the room before Rosalind was fully awake. In a few minutes she was back again, not as though she was dithering or restless, however, but as though she had come to some resolution. She sat on the bed.

'Rozzy, I want to tell you something.'

Rosalind sat up, wrapping the bedclothes round her. 'What, Alice?'

'Xavier is in love with me, and he's asked me to marry him. When we can, you know.'

'Don't be daft. How can he ask you to marry him? He can't talk English.'

'There are ways.'

'And are you going to?'

'Yes, I think so.'

'What about Dick?'

'I explained to Dick that I couldn't marry him, some weeks ago when he asked me to.'

Rosalind had no more to say. She sat silently, clutching the bedclothes. Alice, apparently, had no more to say either, and they stayed where they were as the light grew stronger. At last Alice spoke.

'Rozzy, are you on my side? There'll be all sorts of objections.'

'Yes, Alice, I'm on your side.'

Alice kissed her and went out of the room. Rosalind got up and dressed. It never occurred to her to plead illness, yet she was irrecoverably wounded, though nobody noticed. She went about her duties with a heart as frozen as though in fact she was dead, and the air around her felt dead, as though she could not have breathed it even if she had been alive. All that day one sentence lay in her frozen brain: 'Nothing can ever be so bad again. Nothing can ever be so bad again.' And indeed nothing ever was.

Alice spread the news in the course of the day, producing exactly the objections she had anticipated, together with a great deal of bustle. Farmer Mutter, quite unable to cope, rode off, most uncharacteristically, to see Mr Hall. His instinct to consult the parson instead of falling on his knees in private prayer was a measure of his confusion. Aunt Martha, equally unable to cope, was nevertheless full of comment.

'You maids. I don't know.'

'Why the plural, Aunt Martha? I'm not marrying a Spaniard.'

'Squitter-books don't get married,' said Nicholas. Aunt Martha, annoyed at the word 'plural', smiled approvingly. Rosalind found herself quite indifferent to their hostility.

'Whatever must Jane be thinking?' pursued Aunt Martha, adding as nobody made a suggestion, 'After all 'tis a lord.' Rosalind felt that this fact might not carry much weight in heaven, but had no wish to make the point, and it was too much effort to speak.

'Here's your father back. With Mr Suckbitch. He do look bad, sure enough. Caught something up London, I reckon.'

Mr Suckbitch looked normal enough to Rosalind, though he said so little that she wondered why he had come. Her father on the contrary was much more talkative than when he set out. He told the girls about his conversation with Mr Hall, and Mr Suckbitch, who must have heard it all on the way up to Spark-hayes, listened again. 'Funny, first thing he said was "Why not?" when I'd've expected un to say "Why?" ' After this reassuring start Mr Hall had apparently gone off to demolish the difficulties individually and unanswerably. 'Papist, he said, why we was all papists till recently and Alice'll be living in a papist country. The war, he said, Alice'll be safe, in Spain married to a Spaniard.' Even on the subject of what Mrs Mutter would have said Mr Hall had been sanguine.

Obed was silent as to his opinion of the engagement and offered congratulations to nobody. He did not seem in the least hostile however; he simply behaved as though all those things had already been said, and went on to exercise his usual matter-of-fact benevolence. Seeing that William and Mary were puzzled by the excitement, he took on the task of explaining to them what it was all about.

Xavier was everything that was graceful. It was hard to realize that he was not making pretty speeches, thought Rosalind, as he kissed her hand when she held it out to shake his in congratulation. Alice had no expression on her face but beauty.

By the evening it was clear that Mr Mutter was not only reconciled to the idea but delighted with it. After all, his future son-in-law was of noble birth. Not many yeomen farmers could say that. His immediate hopes for Sparkhayes looked like being dashed, it is true, but he soon began to wonder if perhaps they might be fulfilled in Rosalind; she was so much less odd these days she might attract a steady young farmer after all.

One thing he did insist on was a proper betrothal ceremony. The actual marriage clearly could not take place till Xavier had made some contact with his native land and his relations. But betrothal rites there must be. Arrangements were made. Rosalind prepared some choice food. Mr Suckbitch spent half an hour up in the apple loft coaching Xavier in his words and actions, and was then enlisted by Farmer Mutter to attend the ceremony in case any interpretation was necessary.

So one evening by candlelight the household gathered in the parlour. The fire had been lit but the room was cool, for the fire, so seldom used, had started by smoking evilly and the cross-draughts skilfully engineered by Rosalind and Mary had only just cleared it. Farmer Mutter was in a highly emotional state, blowing his nose and alluding to his dead wife, and behaving as possessively to Alice as though he was the future bridegroom.

Obed, whose natural reticence seemed to have hardened into taciturnity in the last few days, took up a position in front of the panelling at the end of the room, looking as though he too had been carved out of wood, but had later been coloured. The only person he spoke to, and then in a low growl, was Mr Suckbitch, with whom, to Rosalind's knowledge, he had already had a long discussion in the courtyard. William and Mary, William holding the baby, made a family group in one corner. the adults amiable but still puzzled. They detected in what was going on some similarity to their own wedding, some difficulty in communication which was being solved by the goodwill and effort of others, yet there seemed to be no need for miming; there was clearly going to be nothing like William's spectacular grave-digging performance. Aunt Martha kept telling Nicholas and Margaret to keep still, pushing and pulling them about to emphasize the point. Mr Suckbitch having checked that his pupil was word-perfect, came and stood by Rosalind.

Farmer Mutter, with his back to the surly fire, gave a signal and the engaged couple came and stood in front of him, both very composed. Alice spoke first, giving Xavier her hand.

'I take you for my future husband. I give you my hand and my faith.'

'I take you for my future wife. I give you my hand and my honour,' said Xavier carefully. 'Half an hour to learn two sentences,' Rosalind could not help thinking. As he had not yet had many lessons from Mr Suckbitch, and his was not the outgoing type of character that learns clownishly by making ridiculous mistakes, it was the first time that some of those present had heard him speak, and their expressions showed what a novelty it was. For the second time in a few weeks Rosalind, who seemed incapable of a charitable reaction, thought of Balaam's ass.

The couple then kissed, in an offhand manner compared with the way in which Mr Mutter afterwards embraced Alice. Rosalind stepped forward with the ritual drink: wine, presented by Mr Suckbitch, in glasses, provided by Mrs Bradbeer. 'Cider in pewter tankards, if it had been Dick,' thought Rosalind, who knew that her father, with complacent anxiety, had consulted the Moons household as to what the son of a lord would expect. Alice and Xavier drank to each other.

The feast in the hall was long and apparently joyful. Those

who could say grace, said it; those who could sing, sang; those, like Obed, who aspired to do neither, drank deeply. Rosalind felt she would never forget the sight of Xavier standing in front of the hall fire, which burned so generously and clearly compared with the one in the parlour and which brought out so luxuriously the scent of the food she had prepared: relaxed and elegant, as beautiful in his own way as Alice in hers, looking upwards ('Like Praise-the-Lord. Oh, dear, I must stop this'), he sang an alien and mournful tune that stirred the blood. And so Alice and Xavier were betrothed.

It was now Rosalind's chief aim to be as much out of sight of them as possible. It would be many months probably to the marriage and the departure of Alice and her husband for the olive groves and the foaming wide river of Toledo, and the smooth sunny courtyards with the potted plants and the fountains, that Mr Suckbitch had described. In the meantime, to see them together – working in the fields or barn, sitting hand-in-hand by the fire in the hall with Farmer Mutter hovering over them while they clearly wanted to be alone, walking over the cobbles, leaning on the gate – was something she would spare herself if she could. She would also spare herself the occasions when they were nowhere to be seen; that was worse. Not, it turned out, that they were always together at these times. Xavier must have roamed about by himself as well, for once or twice Rosalind found Alice alone in the dairy or the hall, completing some task. But she always had the agony of imagining they were together. It was quite easy to keep out of the way. She was genuinely busy in the kitchen for hours on end, and after that she could go on errands, even if she had to invent them herself. Nobody seemed to notice her manoeuvres, except Alice.

'Xavier is delighted to have you as his sister, Rozzy,' she said one evening in their bedroom. 'He admires you so much.'

'Bullshit,' replied Rosalind.

On one of her self-made errands she saw Mrs Rolle, Turk snorting at her heels, coming up to her. The engagement had caused such a pleasurable stir in the village that she was quite used to people coming up to her, but she had not expected it from Mrs Rolle. She observed, however, that Mrs Rolle was looking far from pleasurably stirred.

'Rosalind, there's something I feel I must say to you, if you don't mind.'

'I expect I can bear it,' replied Rosalind reflectively and in all seriousness.

'You may be doing Alice an injustice.'

'In what way?'

'She does know how you feel, Rosalind, and it distresses her very much. She came to see me about it a few days before her engagement.'

'I don't know why she needs to go around parading her interesting conscience. She has every other pleasure. And why you, Mrs Rolle? I don't mean to be rude, but why? Or is she consulting everybody?'

'No, only me. She realizes from something I must have carelessly let slip once, or perhaps just implied, that I wasn't able to marry the first man I loved. So she thought I would understand what you were feeling and could advise her. And after all, she could hardly turn to your father or your aunt.'

'What did you say?'

'My dear, what could I say? Only the old, old platitudes. That if she rejected Xavier it wouldn't mean he would transfer his affection to you. That a woman can love a second time, perhaps better and more realistically. That sort of thing.'

'Was Mr Rolle there?'

'Oh, no. Alice and I saw to that,' said Mrs Rolle with unusual candour.

'Because he would simply think that a girl as pretty as Alice had a right to anything and anybody she fancied.'

'Yes, I'm afraid he would.'

'He must despise me.'

'Ah, no, that's where you're wrong,' Mrs Rolle spoke much less tensely now and even smiled. 'He admires you. All the village does. You see, you've behaved with such composure, that they're thinking they must have been mistaken. They think

182

it must all have been a clever plot: that you and Alice were putting up a show to blind everybody to the real situation.'

'But why ever should we do that?'

'Why indeed? But people love a plot, you know.'

'And Mr Rolle thinks that too?'

'Certainly. He puts you in the same category as Zachary Gollop, a cunning contriver, a sort of Machiavelli. He likes to feel there are clever people around him. It makes him secure.'

'So nobody's laughing at me?'

'On the contrary; and if you keep it up nobody ever will.'

'Oh, Mrs Rolle, thank you, you don't know what you've said, or rather you do.'

'Yes, my dear, I do.' She paused and then added, 'I married six months later,' and set off home as briskly as Turk would go.

Knowledge of Alice's scruples did not help Rosalind at all. She could not see that scruples were any recommendation if you went on doing exactly as you would have done without them. But to realize that at least she was not an object of ridicule or patronizing pity did much to carry her on into the bleak weather of December. The days were now so short and dark that it was almost immaterial when one went out of doors, or went to bed or got up. The hour of dusk was often no greyer than noon had been. Perhaps because Christmas was approaching she felt a return of her previous compulsion to walk down to the river. She now had two losses to celebrate. Her *amour propre* had been saved, she gratefully realized, but the pain of losing Xavier, together with the misery of being driven to hope that he would go out of her life as soon as possible, never left her and never let her rest. She wondered, respectfully, how Mrs Rolle could possibly have recovered in six months.

About ten days before Christmas she set out for the river one evening. It had been a misty day, with drops running down the thatch, rolling from one piece of straw to the next, like beads. All morning the mist had been a diffused haze which made any man or animal moving in the fields seem huge, silvery and transparent. The trees looked like metal with holes in it. In the course of the afternoon the mist sank to show the opposite

183

hill. Thickening as it sank, it settled in the valley along the line of the river.

Rosalind left the house at what she assumed was her usual time but found when the lights of Sparkhayes were behind her that in fact night had fallen. This unnerved her; she had always been badly frightened if she discovered that it was later than she thought. But there was no reason to turn back. She would be as safe by night as by day, and what she could not see she could hear. The hedges were tall and black on either side of her and bats flipped across the lane. The lights from farms on the opposite side of the valley were quite clear. She glanced round and saw the lights of Sparkhayes too, with the black shape of Beacon Hill rising above it. On her right a little stream in the ditch lapped like a cat, as it made its way to the river.

The road went more steeply downhill as it approached the Otter, and soon Rosalind could see ahead of and slightly below her the whiteness of the track of mist that snaked along the water. The inhabitants of the valley were proud of this phenomenon which certainly could not be matched by other reaches of the river. ' 'Tis like a wall,' they used to say, and so it was, as Rosalind knew from childhood days, when Farmer Mutter had taken his daughters down to see it. They had been impressed. Rosalind had argued that no wall could be stepped through so easily or be so wide but she acknowledged that its abruptness, its height and its power to cut the landscape in half made it very like a wall.

She was walking lightly that evening in spite of her cares. As she came up to the mist she paused, to adjust her senses. For the next thirty yards or so she would need to hear her way. To one who knew the road and the bridge as well as she did this would not be difficult. After a few seconds' hesitation she stepped out of clear night air into the white mist. And now she guided herself entirely by the sound of the river. On the left of the bridge, the water was deep and flowed silently almost on the level. It emerged on the right as a small rapid, and struck on a stone with a high note in the middle of its general noisiness, before it poured down to the sea, gallons and gallons of it, on and on, for ever and ever. As she walked, unfaltering, through the damp whiteness, keeping an even course between the calm and the tumult, Rosalind cupped her ears in her hands, as she had done when a child, and the high note became a song.

In a few minutes she was out of the mist, between high hedges and black trees again, on the other side of the valley. The road, after the sharp left-hand bend, now ascended as steeply as it had descended. She never went far up it, feeling herself to be on alien ground, but the experience of going through the wall was one that could not be immediately repeated so she always liked to climb well free of the mist and look across at the lights of Sparkhayes before returning.

As she stood there, she suddenly thought she heard footsteps coming down the road from the direction of Sparkhayes. She listened intently and was soon sure. She was greatly surprised. Her first idea was that it could be Obed. He had followed her down to the river the evening she had got drunk and in recent weeks he had been silently watchful of her. But it was not Obed's unhurried tread. These footsteps were moving fast, almost running and sounding full of life and enjoyment and controlled energy. They were Xavier's, she became certain. She had listened to him so often even when she could not see him.

The footsteps got nearer and changed pace slightly as the hill dropped more sharply. Then they stopped and Rosalind guessed that Xavier had paused on the other side of the mist, as she herself had done. She raised her voice in her country girl's shout.

'Xavier,' she called.

There was silence for a full minute and then Xavier's voice came across the mist to her.

'Please?' he shouted courteously back.

'I'm over here. On the other side of the mist. Come and join me.' She doubted if his English had progressed as far as this, but hoped that the tone was comprehensible. Apparently it was, for after another pause the footsteps moved forward, though less confidently than hers had done, and she guessed that Xavier must have entered the white wall.

185

And then a sudden commotion broke out from within the mist: a scuffling, a gasping, a cry of protest, a snarl of violence, the thumping of fists on flesh, a grunting, heaving and cracking, and at last a terrible yell. Then a body fell to the ground. Rosalind tried to move towards the mist but managed only a step or two before she tumbled unconscious into the grass at the side of the road.

Here she was found two hours later by the Pulman brothers, riding home. She had begun to recover her senses, but she was deadly cold and could not speak. The brothers, however, were men of few words. Without a single question they got her up on to one of the horses and turned back towards Sparkhayes. The mist had now completely lifted and the brothers' lanterns lit up the road. Rosalind could see that there was nobody at all on the bridge.

She was never to recall the details of her return home. She remembered Mary working the bellows and blowing the hall fire into such a blaze that it outshone the candles. She remembered Obed and her father clasping and shaking the hands of the Pulman brothers over and over again and pressing them to food and drink. She remembered William lugging a mattress which he placed on the floor in front of the fire. And that was all.

In the blackest hour of the night she roused. She was lying on the mattress, wrapped up in blankets. The fire had been kept up and William and Mary were sitting watching her, one in each chimney corner. The others had gone. She became conscious of a dead weight on her stomach. It was Praise-the-Lord, watching her too. She knew that her voice had not come back, but she had a strange, comforting vision of four speechless creatures companionably staring at each other in firelight. Then she fell asleep.

At dawn she roused again, fully enough this time to know what she had to do. She struggled to sit up and Mary came eagerly forward to help her and offer her a drink. She could swallow but she still could not speak, so she made signs to Mary asking for pen and paper. When they were brought, she could hardly write. Her hand had no strength or control and her eyes would not focus, but sweating and shaking and exerting her utmost will-power she wrote two letters. One she addressed to Alice: *Xavier is dead.* The other she addressed to Mr Suckbitch: *Xavier is dead. I killed him.*

14

AFTER writing her letters Rosalind fell into a kind of stupor. When daylight came and the household began to stir, Aunt Martha, torn between resentment at not having been called to help in the night and resentment at being expected to help now, steered her upstairs to her bedroom, as Rosalind could walk well enough in a somnambulistic way. Alice was not there nor had Rosalind seen her downstairs. She did not know if her sister had received the letter. She could barely remember writing it, and she had certainly been in no state to make arrangements for either of the letters to be delivered.

The sun was nearly as high as it ever got in December when Aunt Martha came up with a hot drink in her hand, followed by Nicholas grizzling about something. Rosalind, though dazed and giddy, managed to sit up with no help from anyone and took the drink shoved at her. Aunt Martha went to the window to see what was to be seen from this relatively unfamiliar vantage point. She had apparently been told that Rosalind had lost her voice, for she went on talking about what she could see as though she were describing a hurling match to a blind friend, and not at all counting on any contribution from her niece. She had observed Obed coming out of the pig-sty and Farmer Mutter entering the barn before she was rewarded with anything unusual.

' 'Tis a carriage, seems, coming up from the village, must be, can't Mr Hall walk then like the rest of us? Or perhaps 'tis Mrs Clapp giving herself airs, on foot's good enough for Mrs Bash. Ah no, 'tis Mr Suckbitch's, must be off to London again, getting desperate poor chap, why don't he take a wife, widows enough after un I reckon. 'T have stopped, wheel gone then, no, one of the horses is pissing, ah, if we was all as innocent as an old horse, eh? 'Tis turning into our bottom lane, somebody's getting out, 'tidn' 'ee though, 'tis that Mrs Bradbeer, better go and see what 'er wants. Pull yourself together then, Rozzy, we've all got our troubles. Come along, Nicholas.'

It was not to her aunt, however, that she heard Mrs Bradbeer talking in the courtyard but first to Obed and then to Obed and her father together. The conversations went on for some time and sounded worried and unsatisfactory. At last Mrs Bradbeer came indoors and up to the bedroom. She was carrying what looked like one of Mr Suckbitch's notebooks and a pencil.

'My love, I'm sorry to see you like this. Now, I know you can't talk. They told me. And I certainly don't want to nag and worry you, but you see we're all in the dark. Nobody knows what happened but you. When Mr Suckbitch got your letter – Obed brought it – he asked me to come up and see you at once. I'll tell you later' – Mrs Bradbeer was following every expression on Rosalind's face – 'why he didn't come himself. And we must know, you see, for everybody's sake.' Rosalind looked surprised. She had thought that everybody now knew. 'Mr Suckbitch remembered that you like teasing him about his notebooks, so he sent you one, to see if you could write down what happened. Do you think you could?'

Rosalind nodded and held out her shaking and uncertain hands for the notebook. Fumblingly she took the pencil, too, and tried to coerce herself once more into the act of writing. Mrs Bradbeer arranged the pillows comfortably behind her and then sat down on the bed, looking very comfortable herself and as though there was no hurry at all.

'I went down to the river,' wrote Rosalind, with the simplicity of mental and physical desperation, all her tropes and figures of speech left apart in another life. 'I went through the mist. I heard Xavier. I called his name. They knew who he was. I asked him into the mist. They killed him in the mist. They took him away. I killed him.'

She sagged back against the pillows. Mrs Bradbeer put the notebook, with its distracted writing, into her pocket and took Rosalind's hand.

'Now, my love,' she said, 'did you know I came in the carriage?'

Rosalind nodded exhaustedly.

'And I expect you wondered why. I want to persuade you to come back to Moons with me. That's why I came by myself; we thought it would be more appropriate. You're ill and it's the sort of illness that's perhaps best treated away from home. There's a bedroom off mine that you can have. Your father and Obed think it's a good idea. Would you like to come?'

Rosalind nodded.

'That's good. We'll soon have you right. As it happens I'm just the person to look after you. A young relative of Lord Burghley's lost his voice after a shock and I know the cure. We'll get Mrs Clapp, too, though, shall we? We mustn't hurt her feelings. She's a good woman.'

Since her conversation with Mrs Rolle, Rosalind had often reflected how loyally and against what temptation Mrs Clapp had kept her secret, and she now nodded quite energetically.

Her father carried her down the courtyard, tears in his eyes. He loved his daughters devotedly but he knew he was too weak to deal with their troubles. Jane might have seen what to do. He did not. As the carriage drove off he returned miserably to the barn.

Settled in her pretty bedroom at Moons, Rosalind lay in the same strange trance as before, until the return of Mrs Bradbeer who had gone down to the village.

'Mrs Clapp was just off to Buckhayes where apparently three people have gone down with something exciting, but she's coming up to see you this evening. It'll be interesting to see which part she tells you to keep warm.'

Rosalind roused herself sufficiently to point at her throat.

'Oh, yes, of course. Now what euphemism will she have for that, do you think, if indeed a euphemism is necessary for a person's throat? The little red lane? No, too obvious and not half indecent enough.' Rosalind looked as though she had a point to make. 'Lane's aren't red, you mean. That's true. So it might do. Anyway, we'll see. In the meantime she's sent you a sedative draught. Mr Suckbitch has had a good look at it, and a taste, and he thinks it could help.'

It did. Rosalind sank far below her trance and her stupor into a deep sleep. When she awoke the light was at the same point of fading as it had been the day before when she was deciding to go down to the river, and the twenty-four hours which she had only partly lived through now came rushing at her, with all their implications. Terrified, she started to get out of bed. Mrs Bradbeer, on the watch next door, hurried in. Rosalind made wild gestures, asking for writing materials, and Mrs Bradbeer, who had them ready in the room, gave them to her. Rosalind sitting on the edge of the bed, wrote 'Alice' and frenziedly seized Mrs Bradbeer's hand.

'Get back into bed, Rosalind, and I'll tell you all about it. That's right. Alice is being well looked after. I saw Mrs Rolle in the village and told her what had happened, in confidence, because I don't think there's much point in spreading the news about just yet, do you? Mrs Rolle decided to go straight up to Sparkhayes to invite Alice to stay with them for a few days. Alice isn't ill, you know, but the change will help her.'

Less wildly, but still imploringly, Rosalind clutched Mrs Bradbeer's hand again, as though begging her to say more.

'She's at the Rolles' now. Mr Suckbitch went up to see her this afternoon and they had a long talk. Your letter broke the news to her, you see, and Mr Suckbitch was able to give her the details after you'd written them down for us.'

Rosalind pointed in what she thought might be the direction of the Rolles' house and then at herself.

'You'd like Alice to come down and see you?'

Rosalind shook her head and looked anxiously at Mrs Bradbeer.

'Oh, I see. I'm sorry, I was slow. Did Alice send you a message?'

Rosalind nodded, holding her breath.

191

'Yes, she did. I was coming to that. She sent you her love.'

Rosalind burst into tears for the first time. She buried her head in the pillow, sobbing and wailing. Mrs Bradbeer, weeping herself, went quietly out of the room and shut the door.

The next morning Rosalind was sufficiently recovered to show genuine interest in Mrs Bradbeer's suggestions as to how she could speak again.

'Lord Burghley's cousin was in full cry – and that was saying something, I assure you – within a week,' she began encouragingly. 'You'll soon be getting your voice back in short phrases, in normal everyday circumstances, starting with yes and no probably, but you'll want more than that. Young William's doctor told him to practise some kind of public speaking to get full confidence and fluency again. "Try saying grace," he said. In a hall full of people that can be quite an ordeal, you know. "Set yourself some small piece," was the doctor's advice, "a few words that anybody could manage, say it and stop. Next time a slightly longer piece." Well, it worked. Young William started with *Benedictus benedicat*, and his voice began to shake by the last syllable, but he ended up with something the length of a psalm, and not a tremor from beginning to end. You know some graces, don't you? Tell Mr Suckbitch how far you're going to get, half the first line perhaps, and he'll finish it for you. Mr Suckbitch and I aren't exactly a hallful of people but we'll look as numerous as we can. Now would you like to try this method?'

Rosalind started to nod but said 'Yes' instead. Mrs Bradbeer clapped her hands and went merrily off to brief Mr Suckbitch about the part he was to play, remarking that novelty was good for everybody.

Rosalind mentally rehearsed the grace she had said the Christmas before. At first she thought the opening line 'O Lord which giv'st thy creatures for our food' was rather difficult to say in any case, and wondered if she should choose Alice's grace instead: 'O Lord our God we yield thee praise' was undeniably easier. But as her spirits rose she decided it would be more natural to use the words which were hers by custom. She wrote out a fair copy of the verse for Mr Suckbitch's benefit, marking the places she hoped to get to at successive mealtimes.

In the event she beat Lord Burghley's cousin by a day. She now felt ready for the talk with Mr Suckbitch that she knew she must have as soon as she gained sufficient confidence. She was astonished how strong she seemed, how capable of discussing painful subjects without breaking down. Her grief was as keen as ever but her guilt was losing its edge, and her intellectual curiosity found enough material in what had happened effectively to stop her brooding and to make her long above everything to hear the truth.

Her manner of asking Mr Suckbitch if she could speak to him and the fact that she asked at all, seeing they met constantly now that she was downstairs again, showed him what was coming, and he welcomed it for both their sakes. He escorted her to a big chair, piled with cushions, in front of the fire in the beautiful parlour, and poured her a glass of malmsey, and waited.

'Mr Suckbitch, Xavier was a spy, wasn't he?'

'Yes. How did you find out?'

'The first day I was ill I couldn't think clearly at all, but later I could, and I began to work it out. When I was down by the river that night and I called to Xavier, he shouted "Please?" That isn't English, not real English. I knew you wouldn't have taught him to say it, and if he'd been imitating anybody at Sparkhayes he'd have said "What?" or "Eh?" or "Yes?" or "Hello". So I thought he must have been taught English by somebody in Spain who was sort of translating from what they would have said themselves. Yet he was supposed not to have known English before.'

'Very clever, Rosalind. Anything else?'

'Yes, when I started to look back. Those two short sentences in the betrothal ceremony, he took half an hour to learn them. Yet he was intelligent. It was somebody acting and not getting it right. I thought it was odd at the time, but I didn't draw any conclusions.'

'I imagined you were going to ply me with questions,' said Mr Suckbitch. 'I was wrong.'

'Oh, no, you weren't. I *am* going to ply. Was it Xavier who tried to light the bonfire on Accession Day?'

'In all probability.'

'Was it Xavier who was talking to Mother on the bridge the day before she died?'

'Quite definitely yes. Obed recognized him. He told me the next morning when he fetched me to interpret. A great many things fell into place then. I'd been wondering who the man on the bridge could have been.'

'How did you know about him? I thought it was only our household who knew.'

'You told me. Do you remember? You were asking me about the cause of your mother's death and I offered to consult Dr Woolton about it. I naturally enquired if I had all the relevant facts to tell him and you said, without meaning to, I got the impression, that she'd been down by the river the evening before talking to a strange man. It struck me as being relevant to quite another matter so I made a note of it.'

'A real note not a mental note. I remember now. I thought you were putting something like "Ask Dr W. about J.M.". But, Mr Suckbitch, you're not telling me that *Mother* was a spy?'

'Oh, no, but Xavier was certainly trying to get information out of her. She was a good choice, living well out of the village, and being a lively intelligent woman who innocently enjoyed showing off and would easily get carried away into saying more than she meant.'

'But what did she know that would be useful to him?'

'Quite a lot: about the militia, the bonfire, even Toby Rolle's cannon; he'd been talking about it even before she died and I imagine she thought it a good joke. She knew all the gossip about the fortifications at Sidmouth and Exmouth; she probably thought they were a good joke, too. And she would have been shrewd about the likelihood or otherwise of local people supporting the invasion, shrewder than Sir Walter Raleigh. The Spaniards needed to know that kind of thing.'

'But how on earth did Xavier get her to meet him there in the first place?'

'We shall never know of course. He would have had a convincing cover story: a Dutch businessman working from Exeter or something like that. Most of our own spies were Dutch businessmen. And I think he must have played on her dissatisfactions and her aspirations. He represented a wider and more exotic world.'

'That's very likely. I think Mother went straight from aspiring to be a yeoman's wife to feeling trapped as one.'

'Without any transitional period of satisfaction?'

'Yes.'

'I can't comment, Rosalind. You may be right.'

'When Mother died – which I suppose Xavier must have heard about. . . .'

'He would have watched the funeral procession going down the valley.'

'And noticed she was the only one he couldn't see.'

'Yes.'

'Why didn't he get in touch with somebody else?'

'He tried. With you, for one. Remember the footsteps down by the river that day.'

'I was drunk. I thought I'd imagined them. And Obed went to look.'

'Yes, and he saw footprints where the man – I think we can call him Xavier – had been standing in wait. And there were a great many odd things happening at that time. Lights in strange places. Dogs barking and cats spitting for no apparent reason.'

'If Obed hadn't recognized Xavier, would you still have been suspicious?'

'Yes, he made a bad mistake in saying that he came from the *San Salvador*. At least, that was credible in itself and he'd got himself up beautifully to look the part. But he shouldn't then have said that he came from Toledo. The *San Salvador*, as we knew from our spy in Corunna, was part of the squadron provided by Guipuzcoa and that's in the far north.'

'What made him say Toledo? He didn't have to.'

'Over-confidence. He probably thought it was the only town an ignorant Englishman had heard of. Toledo blades, you know.'

'Two questions more, if I may, Mr Suckbitch.'

'Of course.'

'How would you describe yourself in all this? A spycatcher, or is there a more polite word?'

'A dilettante,' said Mr Suckbitch mournfully, 'and that's an even less polite word. Xavier may not have been the most efficient spy in the world but he was a professional. All I did was, in an amateur way, to collect what information I could and pass it on to Sir Francis Walsingham, and go up to London to see him if anything unusual happened. He then took the decisions.'

'He told you to keep Xavier in the valley?'

'Yes, it was an order but people don't have to obey orders mindlessly. I agreed with it. So you mustn't say, Rosalind' – Mr Suckbitch suddenly sounded peevish – 'that you killed Xavier. I did, if anybody did.'

'That's my last question. Who did? In the accepted sense of the word killing, I mean, not in the way you and I are using it.'

'I don't know. It could have been Walsingham's men, for obvious reasons. It could have been his fellow countrymen, for reasons that we can only guess at: colleagues who didn't trust him or perhaps had detected him in some treachery, or participants in some long-standing family feud. Or just possibly a couple of local Englishmen who don't like the Spaniards as much as Mr Hall would want them to.'

'There is one more question after all. Where is he?'

'In heaven,' said Mr Suckbitch the agnostic firmly. 'He was a brave man. But I know what you mean. There's been a thorough search, and the answer, I think is: buried in a peaceful field, or, much more likely, taken to a deeper part of the river and sent quietly out to sea. You're pale, my love.'

'Yes, I'm feeling pale, and I'm starting to shake.'

196

'You stay here by this good fire' – he hurled on several logs – 'and drink another glass of malmsey' – he handed her one – 'and think it all over. I have to walk down and see Noah Hall. When I get back, we'll have supper and a game of cards with Mrs Bradbeer.'

15

ALICE and Rosalind went back to Sparkhayes for Christmas.
They felt it to be their duty, and they both realized they would
have to come out of hiding sooner or later and that the longer
they left it the harder it would be. So on the afternoon of
Christmas Eve, Farmer Mutter came round to collect them,
first Rosalind, then Alice, and they drove back to the farm,
as in the days of childhood, which seemed so long ago now,
when their father had driven them home from Rawridge.

Any awkwardness the sisters may have felt in meeting again
was mitigated by the weather. It was a bitter day and their hosts
had muffled them up so well against the flurries of snow which
swirled round the open cart that the only communication they
could have was by means of their eyes – Alice did in fact wink –
or by shouting through woolly scarves which they did not
attempt.

They had left Sparkhayes as girls and returned to it as women.
The house where they had spent the whole of their lives now
seemed to them a baiting-place on the road where, as conten-
tedly as possible, they waited for the next move, in more subdued spirits but in better tempers than when it had stood for
a perpetual present as well as for the past. Their father found
them at the same time more responsive and more self-contained.
He never spoke to them of what had happened and they had
no wish to confide in him, knowing how utterly useless it would
be. Neither did they confide in each other; it was not till years
later, when many different, and day-to-day things had inter-
vened, that they spoke of Xavier. In the meanwhile, they
independently kept their common secret, and conversed, though

more supportively, in the bickering language of their girl-hood.

The most that could be said for Christmas Day was that it passed quietly, but to the sisters in their present state of mind this would have been high praise. On the Feast of Stephen they did not dismantle the trestle table in the hall as soon as dinner was over but sat down at it together to write letters to their hosts. They expressed themselves with warmth and gratitude, secure in the knowledge that they could see their friends again at any time they liked, and in a more cheerful guise than that of refugees. There was none of the bitterness of enforced absence in this very temporary parting. As they wrote they kept glancing at the fire, in front of which Alice had sat hand in hand with Xavier, and Rosalind had lain ill on the night of his death.

'You look older, Rozzy,' said Alice, as she raised her eyes, searching for the best way to begin her next paragraph.

'I daresay. I'm taking over from old Joan. Her place in the chimney corner hasn't been filled yet.'

'I don't mean old in years. I mean the sort of person Aunt Martha couldn't send on errands.'

'Well, now, that's true. We've been home for forty-eight hours and she hasn't.'

'I feel old in that sort of way, too.'

'You look lovely, Alice, don't misunderstand me, but you do look a bit sort of drawn.'

'Well, as long as I don't look a bit sort of hanged and quartered.'

'That's what made Lord Burghley's relative lose his voice.'

'I didn't know the Burghleys had a traitor in the family, but I'm not surprised it made him lose his voice.'

'Don't be daft, Alice. I mean he happened to see an execution.'

'Serve him right then, for snooping.'

'Oh shut up, and let me get on with my letter.'

January was a healing time for both of them. The valley was now in the full grip of winter, but the violence of the weather in the fields and lanes brought its own form of comfort, and they went about their work indoors, kept warm by the huge fire, the thick walls and the heavy thatch, with something like a will, feeling that in spite of everything they were taking their place in the yearly cycle of life.

February was milder. The river thawed, and all the signs pointed to an early spring. One night Rosalind was awakened by Alice's moving restlessly about in bed. This was unexpected; Rosalind used to say her sister was the original log that people were supposed to sleep like, and Alice always denied having dreams.

'What's the matter, Alice?'

'I've got such a pain.'

'Where?'

'I don't know how to describe it. It's not my stomach, it's very low down, sort of where my legs start. Groin, would it be, only it's both sides.'

'What kind of a pain?'

'Clutching, as though a lobster kept walking downwards from my hips, grasping as he went. Ow. *Ow.*' Alice rolled over.

'Shall I go and get you a hot drink? Or I could fill up the warming pan – the fire'll still be on, it must be quite early – and warm up your side of the bed.'

'No, it's all right, thanks. It's dying down a bit now. I'll try to go to sleep.'

What must have been some hours later she woke her sister again.

'Rozzy, I'm bleeding.'

'Shall I get your things?'

'No, I've had them on all day. It's something else, it must be.' She thrashed about. Rosalind held her hand.

'Rozzy, something's coming out.'

Rosalind threw back the clothes and ran round to Alice's side of the bed.

'Alice, let me help you up, on to the chamber pot.' She practically lifted her sister out, pulling off one of the blankets and covering her with it. Alice sat there beside the bed, groaning, her head against the mattress, while trickling sounds, of which they now both realized the meaning, led at last to a definitive

200

splashing thud. Alice shook violently, while Rosalind held her arm round her shoulders. After a while Alice crawled back into bed.

'Alice, I'd better take this down to the privy. It'll soon be dawn.'

'Yes. Thank you.'

Rosalind wrapped herself up in the blanket, arranged a cloth over the pot and went out of the bedroom. Farmer Mutter next door stirred and grunted.

'It's all right, Father. Alice has been sick. I'm just going down to the privy.'

'Is the maid better now, then?'

'Oh, yes, perfectly all right. It must have been something she ate. Sorry to wake you up.'

Only too glad to find someone else in command, her father settled back to sleep again.

Rosalind started cautiously on her difficult journey. 'Oh, oh' creaked the floorboards as they always did when anybody first set foot on them, going on to make their familiar strident but conversational lamentations as she moved to the top of the stairs. Still the house slept undisturbed, and Rosalind felt her way down the spiral staircase, assured by the glimmer from the little window at the turn that dawn was indeed breaking. Across the passage and through the hall she went, more confidently now. The flagstones threw up a spiteful chill but at least they did not creak. The backdoor latch did, but as she stepped outside and looked up at the house it was still in darkness. She was safe enough now.

As she paused in the back courtyard, the farm, though clear in outline and in many details, looked completely isolated, an entity all by itself in the middle of unknown country. It usually seemed an integral part of the valley but now, enclosed in an even, motionless grey mist and the remains of night, it appeared to be the only place on earth, dependent on nothing else. It was a mild night for February. The banks of great trees along the top of the back field looked out of season in being so entirely bare.

She left the cobbles for the cold wet grass of the field, walking carefully over the lumpy ground towards the stream which served the privy. She could not yet hear the running water, and there was absolute silence as far as man and beast were concerned. Only the birds were noisy. A cock crowed endlessly, a wood pigeon cooed, and all the owls on the farm hooted at each other, one of them, the nearest, giving a weird two-fold yelp before going into its more familiar wail. It sounded as though they were desperate to catch all they could before the light came to interrupt them.

As Rosalind approached the privy, half a dozen rats scattered with a swish through the grass. Always glad to see them leave, she was particularly glad on this occasion. She had put her hand out to the privy door before she realized it was unnecessary to go inside. The stream was all she needed. She went to where it ran away strongly beyond the privy, down a steep piece of field to the east, and bending low to avoid splashing her nightdress, tipped the contents of the pot into the water.

The light that even in these few minutes had been brightening behind the mist now gleamed on the red water, which began to clear almost immediately as more water bore down on it and carried it away. Three times Rosalind rinsed out the pot in a little pool among the stones and each time the water she tipped out was fainter and fainter pink till it ran quite colourless and the stream had carried every trace down to the Otter and out to sea.

Alice stayed in bed for two days while Rosalind, downstairs, made remarks about bilious attacks and surfeits. She took up food which Alice ate steadily as if with a firm intention to get well as soon as possible. Each time she thanked her sister politely, answered that she was feeling much better and said nothing more at all. On the evening of the second day, Rosalind, on her way to the top of the staircase carrying an empty plate, encountered Nicholas.

'Alice'll have to go to hospital,' he said. 'She can't be looked after here. She'll have to go to hospital.'

Resisting the impulse to strangle Nicholas and throw him

down the stairs, Rosalind sought out the originator of the speech.

'There'll be no need for Alice to go to hospital, thank you, Aunt Martha. I can look after her very well, as I, and only I, have been doing for the last few days. In any case, she's getting up tomorrow.'

Aunt Martha put up no fight. 'You maids, I don't know what you gets up to,' she said, but mechanically. It was clear she had no suspicions. Alice did get up the next day. She thanked her sister once more, and most affectionately, for all her care, and said not a word more about the incident.

Spring came early to the Otter valley and more radiantly than the girls could ever remember it. Released from winter before they had dared to hope for release, and with no threat of another Armada to make them dread the lengthening days, the inhabitants whistled and sang and wrestled and courted. Neighbours who had not been seen for weeks appeared in the landscape. Rosalind glimpsed three men on horseback but said nothing to her sister.

Obed came up from his cottage one morning carrying a bunch of daffodils. The Sparkhayes daffodils were out, but they were small and brown-edged and by no means as fine as these. Obed handed the bunch to Alice.

'Why, Obed, how lovely. Where did they come from?'

'Dunno,' relied Obed expressionlessly. 'Some chap left them. Yellow-haired chap.'

Alice went pink and looked extremely pleased.

'Well, Obed,' she said more archly than Rosalind had ever heard, or imagined, her speaking, 'if you see the yellow-haired chap around anywhere, please tell him how much I liked them.'

The message obviously got through. Next day Dick Pulman entered the yard, dressed in his working clothes but with his yellow hair curled on his shoulders and his moustache cut in what the Honiton barber called the penthouse style. Alice strolled out to meet him. After talking for a while in the court-yard they walked off down the lane that led to Moon's Ottery, and the village took up the story as though it had never been interrupted.

Alice and Rosalind were now on the easiest of terms.

'Alice, I'm not altogether teasing, but do you think the Pulman brothers *will* declare an impediment at your wedding?'

'No, love, of course not. They don't want Dick, or at least they may, for all I know, but they'd have faced that years ago.'

'Oh, Alice, isn't it funny how different, how *opposite*, things turn out to be. I used to think if the brothers didn't object it was because they didn't want the woman. I felt truly sorry for old Miss Pinn, being rejected, but it was really that hobgoblin from Rawridge they didn't fancy. Whatever was his name?'

Rosalind went happily down to Moons the evening after Dick's visit, ostensibly to tell Mr Suckbitch and Mrs Bradbeer about this new development, just in case they had not heard of it, which was most unlikely; not that any motive was really necessary, she saw them so frequently. It was a strange walk, heady with all the smells and light and exhilaration of spring. Everybody was out of doors and there seemed to be a pleasant understanding among them all that they should wave to her; encouragingly, it struck her. She saw them all the way along: from afar, the Pulman brothers riding out; in the top lane, Mr and Mrs Rolle exhorting Turk to some course of action which he was disinclined to take; outside the tavern, Obed drinking with Zachary and Joseph; in the distance, Mrs Clapp leaning over her garden wall; in the far distance, Mr Hall busy in his glebe; and they all waved. As she turned into the Moons lane, she felt it had been quite a Progress.

She was halfway up the hill to Moons when Mrs Bradbeer came round the corner stepping briskly. Rosalind ran up to her affectionately. Before either of them had time to mention Alice and Dick, however, Mrs Bradbeer, with a kiss and a hug, said that she was in a hurry but that Mr Suckbitch was at home, and went purposefully on down the hill. Rosalind waited in case she looked round and in fact as Mrs Bradbeer came to the next bend she turned to wave. Moreover, she called something which she seemed to need to be at a distance to say: 'Now don't you be giving me the sack, Rosalind Mutter.' With the cheer-fullest of faces, she continued on her way.

Rosalind walked slowly on. She knew now why she was going to Moons and why she had fancied that everybody was waving encouragingly. It would not be as simple as that, however. Mr Suckbitch was at the table in the parlour, with pen and ink in front of him, looking rather pleased at something he had just written. He got up to greet her and with a resolute air handed her a piece of paper.

Henry + Rosalind = perfect happiness.

Rosalind read the message and stood holding the paper in silence. Then she stepped to the table, took up the pen and wrote:

Especially minus Xavier.

She feared that the quip was heartless and she realized that minus was not a word; she had only used it because the sign might look like a dash, which would make no sense. The immediately important thing was, however, that Mr Suckbitch should know that she had loved Xavier.

The pen had spluttered with her vehemence, sending some drops of ink on to the polished wood. Mr Suckbitch, who would normally have spent ten minutes fussily wiping them up, took no notice at all. He read what Rosalind had written and took her in his arms. She laid her head on his shoulder. Forgetting the language of Dr John Dee, 'As long as life lasts,' he said.

'My dear Rozzy,' said Alice next morning, looking out of the hall window as they were preparing breakfast, 'you seem to be able to get people out of doors as early as the Armada.'

Rosalind, blushing with happiness, wondered at the same time how her sister could mention the Armada like that and whether it meant that she thought of Xavier or that she did not. She concluded that Alice did, and put her arm round her sister.

'Alice, let's have a double wedding.'

'Certainly not. I want you to do the food for mine.'

Mr Suckbitch came into the hall, having disentangled himself respectfully from Praise-the-Lord's stagy welcome. (Praise-the-Lord, by the common desire of those he left and those he went to, was going to accompany Rosalind to Moons.)

'Rosalind, can you come down to the river with me?'

'Now?'

'Yes.'

'But, Mr Suckbitch – Henry – I'm laying the breakfast.'

'You run along, love,' said Alice. 'You could get away with murder today. Make the most of it. I'll finish the porridge.'

So Mr Suckbitch and Rosalind walked down the hill together, for the first time. The mist had gathered in its usual long line over the river and the sun was beating hard into its white brilliance.

'I've never been down to the river at this time of day before,' said Rosalind.

'I thought not. That's why I particularly wanted you to.'

'I've always been getting breakfast.'

In fact Rosalind had not been down to the bridge at any time since the night of Xavier's death. Now as they approached the white wall she took Mr Suckbitch's arm and they stepped into the mist together. But, strangely, they were not in the mist at all. They walked towards the noisy water and everything immediately around them was plain and clear: the stones on the road, the bark on the trees. As they moved they seemed to carry the clear air with them.

Trying to work out what was happening, Rosalind released Mr Suckbitch's arm, ran over the bridge and looked back. The early sun struck warm on the nape of her neck but the tip of her nose felt cold as she faced the shrouded valley. Sparkhayes was no more than a white glow, and its trees were less solid than shadows. The corner of the field nearest to her was covered with droplets so distinct she could have counted them, yet a little further away the mist crept about like smoke, hiding the grass. Mr Suckbitch, who had stopped at the other side of the bridge to watch her, was hazy and huge. She hurried back and found him in normal daylight again.

'The mist,' she said. 'It's everywhere we aren't.'

He nodded. 'It's a trick of the sun,' he said. They stood looking down the river from their patch of clarity into the hidden distance. Rosalind thought of her mother, of Xavier and of Xavier's child, who had gone down the valley towards the sea, along the path that everybody else had taken, or would take.